Arlene

MY
HAND
MITTEN

Enjoy Life! ☺

A RARE BIRD BOOK
LOS ANGELES, CALIF.

MY
HAND
MITTEN

A NOVEL BY AUSTIN THACKER

THIS IS A GENUINE RARE BIRD BOOK

A Rare Bird Book | Rare Bird Books
453 South Spring Street, Suite 302
Los Angeles, CA 90013
rarebirdbooks.com

FIRST TRADE PAPERBACK ORIGINAL EDITION

Set in Minion Pro
Printed in the United States

10 9 8 7 6 5 4 3 2 1

Publisher's Cataloging-in-Publication data available upon request.

*F*OR MY FATHER, WHO *told me that I was only in a valley, and over the mountain was a town full of safety and health; that one day I would look back at my time in the valley of death, and it would only stand as a moment in my life. His wisdom and reassurance is one of the reasons why I'm alive, he is my hero, he is my rock.*

For my mother, who carried a sea of love, endless grasslands of pain, and mounds of strength on her shoulders while my life hung on the weight of dental floss and the will of God. I don't know what I would do without her.

For Lylah Lee Paton. I watched your funeral video another time and can hardly keep it together, even after so many years. We fought the same battle at the same time, yet I would have gladly taken your place. Although I know deep inside that once you left you never stopped smiling, and therefore you were victorious. Jesus said "Daughter, run to me," and you ran. Then you flew. (August 15, 2010–August 26, 2014) Choroid Plexus Carcinoma.

For Sebastian Meyer. Hey, man, I am sorry that I didn't visit as much, but I couldn't bear the thought of losing another friend. I prayed until I fell asleep on the floor, my tears drying on my face, hoping that God would agree with my demands. Yet God works in mysterious ways and wanted you home. Save a spot for me, as well as a Wii controller and we will play

Super Smash Bros Brawl once again. This time though, not one of us will be in pain. (January 20, 1996–June 7, 2016) Grey Cell Lymphoma.

For the nurses, Dr. Kopp. and Dr. Katsanis, who all saved my life. I will always be grateful, and my debt will never be paid.

For Savana Sasser, who has stuck by my side through middle school, cancer, high school, and now the beginning of adulthood. You are my best friend.

For my PTSD. You are like a rattlesnake on my doorstep, once I step into the fresh air you attack, sinking your fangs into my pride, and my hope for a better tomorrow. Yes, the pain from you drove me to this laptop, and your pain drove the thoughts that created the tragedies for my novel. Yet everyday I will step outside and face your pain, everyday I will bear your venom and use its wisdom to sculpt a better tomorrow. Yes, you make me feel petrified, you make high school all the more difficult to relate with others, but one day I will grow an immunity to your poison, and when you strike, my smile will not fade, and my wisdom will continue to prosper.

For God, who has given me more time and saved my life.

POST-TRAUMATIC STRESS DISORDER

NOUN

Medicine

A condition of persistent mental and emotional stress occurring as a result of injury or severe psychological shock, typically involving disturbance of sleep and constant vivid recall of the experience, with dulled responses to others and to the outside world.

—*Oxford English Dictionary*

The Rage

July 30, 2017

I T'S TIME. GATHER UP, children, around the tree, come on! Hurry and rest around the bark, I want to tell you a story. It's a very upsetting tragedy in a small town that deals with a man, a woman, and their unrecognized love that is on its worldly end. Listen children, carefully. To every whisper and detail, because this story has an end, but hinted throughout from the irony of life and shown through a pattern of worldly chaos, through a life of constant defeat and a single victory.

It began with the rain, slowly, willingly falling from the dark clouds above, making the scorched dirt into a soupy heap of muck, while the cacti stood like monuments to the sky. Thunder rumbled with rage, building up, then slowly subsiding, while the cold-blooded creatures of the Sonora Desert were resting and avoiding (but at the same time cherishing) the chilling winds from this steady storm. The mountains blackened the horizon, only periodically lit from the neon-blue streaks of lightning coming from the gray sky, incubated perfectly with friction, pressure, and most of all, heat. This is nature's natural rage, rage toward pollution, rage toward global warming, rage toward humanity. Besides the thunder, there was no sound but the tapping of the rain onto the concrete roads in a well-timed pace, while it drizzled down with an absolute sense of detest toward itself. Everything was colorless without the rage: the animals, the buildings, and the desert filled with its low, prickly cacti, all casting even darker silhouettes than night can offer. Except for one pair of police headlights, with an engine noise growling steadily, in a way harmonizing with the rain from the car's idleness and vibrations.

The dark outline behind the driver's seat window stared lazily at the rhythm of the raindrops tapping on the front windows, *tap... tap...tap*. In his free time, he lifted weights, never breaking his record, never growing stronger than he already was, as every day he lifted the same light weights. Old age slows down the growth of muscle, but Mark Wegman never thought he was old. He had brown hair and five o'clock shadow flooded with individual grays, a forehead with deeply imprinted wrinkles, as well as well-defined hands and a body full of many forgotten scars, but he still saw himself as twenty-three—as the heroic, muscular magician, marine, lover, father, and motivator for all. Those bright green eyes were the same, this was true; those young, passionate eyes had always been the same.

However, there was one major difference between then and now that separated him from being the man he was before. A difference that he had been struggling with every day for the past twenty years and, in one way or another, would struggle with for the rest of his life. It was every individual struggle, every disaster that had taken hold of him and his own family. Each one, carrying its own level of strength, its own weight of guilt toward his inability to control, weighing on one side of a scale, with the other side being sanity, tolerance, acceptance. These were his demons: they were a legion, roaming freely in Mark with contentment, satisfaction, and comfort. Each one, very glad to be there as much as the other, as if Mark's mind were a private, gated community with notoriety in its higher status. But there was one demon that was significantly larger, more ruthless and active, making the others seem petty, almost meaningless. This demon was the reason why Mark was so unstable, why he stared at the rain the way he did.

This demon was the memory of her in their youth. Her rosy cheeks, lovely brown hair, and chocolate-colored eyes.

She's like an angel from heaven, he'd always thought. Now Mark looked at a chipped pine-green door and longed to see Mary standing in health, smiling with intent to hug, paint, cook, and cry tears he never could. But behind the door lay a sick woman, who could only cry, couldn't cook or draw, but (as he knew with certainty) needed his love.

Her immune system made visitations risky, though. Only a lone nurse could enter and only to adjust the singular air-conditioning unit on the windowsill and to change her IV medications hanging on that solid white pole. Mark could hear her whistles on the other side of the door (but could never distinguish the difference between her and the air-conditioning unit, as they both exhaled with such effort). He then decided that he had a choice: to see her one last time and both die from this degenerating airborne illness, or to wait for the single nurse to strike eureka and give them the freedom to spend whatever their youth had left to offer. For now, though, he could only visit her through frantic panic as the memories flushed through his eyes, while he moaned and cried on the floor as the dwelling thoughts continued to torment him, as the scale of sanity began to lean more toward chaos.

Then, while he continued to gaze through the rain in his idling police car, almost out of nowhere, Mark Wegman began to smirk. It was a devilish smirk that sparkled through the muscles from his aged face, which soon morphed into a wild grin, then a hysterical fit of laughter, uncontrollable and frightening. He thought of stopping— in fact, Mark wanted to stop—but like a cat who has been drawn by curiosity, he had no power. Tears rolled down as his deep laugh continued, as he pounded his hand on the driver's window and stomped his foot like a mad dog. Then, as swiftly as it began, it ended, all the insanity. The unwavering urge to laugh off his present madness ended. He then continued to stare nowhere in particular, just at the raindrops, streaks of wet residue left on his face—he didn't bother to acknowledge it. The scale, once so balanced, now stood crooked as his sanity slipped from sight, and madness now powered his ATP, exiting the mitochondria of his cells, powered by every breath he took, then released through every step taken. His hatred seeped through his pores; his despair leaked through his eyes. Mark was no longer a ticking time bomb but more like a mine in the jungle of Vietnam—a little weight on his shoulders and everything would fall apart. The world would know his name.

The silence was interrupted when his phone began to vibrate violently. Mark reached deep and picked it out, always hoping it was Mary, her wonderful voice shining like it did once before. His phone was an old Motorola Microtac 9800X from 1989, nicked and tattered in so many places, as a twenty-five-year-old phone should be. He found comfort in its consistent dark gray color, the single antenna, and the simplicity. Mark saw who it was and quickly opened it, like a child reaching for a twenty-five-cent gumball.

"Hey Mark, I was wondering if you and your wife would enjoy some Mama's Pizza! I brought a family size into the station and a medium for you and Mary! The pizza is fantastic, and she might eat a little once she smells the delectable pepperoni! The healing powers of pizza are always surprising!" Mark smiled again and responded.

"Mary and I would love that."

"Well look out your window, I'm right here. Thought I'd drop by so your night isn't such a drag."

Mark quickly turned his head and saw Tom knocking on his window. His dark skin, jet-black hair trimmed short, and skinny composition were a warm sight to Mark, like the unrecognizable scent of childhood or a reunion back to your hometown after decades of absence. The police officer remembered continuous nights of them together at the marine station, drinking soda and eating spaghetti with Mary. Mark loved Tom like a son.

"It's a slow night," Mark later stated while glancing at the raindrops, Tom sitting by his side with a feather-light smile.

"That's great! This means no crime!"

"No, there's always someone lurking. Someone we can't trust—I can feel it tonight. I can feel the need for justice and authority." Mark's voice became dark like the air.

"Mark," said Tom. "Tonight's a good night, with good intentions. Even when times are rough, you can trust that God is with you." Tom turned on the radio, and a country song about the western frontier was on.

"You're right Tom," Mark happily stated, although he was slightly bitter toward God's name.

The police radio rang and Mark picked it up. Tom was already gone. In fact, Tom disappeared long before. Mark imagined Tom setting up the medium pizza with pepperoni at his house, maybe giving the nurse two slices, one for her and one for Mary. The nurse might shake her head and demand that it simply does not fit in Mary's liquid-based diet, but Mark trusted that Tom could get it past the nurse. There was still a long night ahead for Mark.

"Mark," the old, portable Bearcat BC200XLT blurted out through its ancient speakers. "We have a call on a suspicious character driving around in a yellow Toyota Camry at the neighborhood on Sixth Avenue and Elm Street."

Mark swiped up his radio with quickness and responded, "I'm on North Sixth Avenue and Speedway, I can check it out." He set the Bearcat down, revved the police car in cocky, explosive joy, and sped down the road with exhilaration.

The town was silent; water gathered in multiple corners of the cracked street, and rain poured from the sky. No one was out because of the harsh storm, so this poorly cared-for town was eerie, an incubator for unlawful acts, or so Mark desired. Action, adrenaline, a chase against time, chancing his cards with death. A drunk homeless man like in *Grand Theft Auto* would have been like a flakey almond and butter-coated bear claw to Mark. Or even better, if there were also a child in the back seat, hysterically crying, wetting their trousers, and gasping for air. Mark would then get shot, and in his final breath of consciousness, he would shoot the bastard right in the creases of his forehead for everything that stood for justice. This was what he dreamed about. Yes, he had a gun. He had snuck it into his car without anyone's prior knowledge that morning, since he was only a community resource officer. *This yellow Toyota Camry, what do you have to promise?* Mark thought. A raffle, with promise for something more than teenagers past curfew, neighbors bothered by loud music, and sometimes even periodic prank calls. Yet as Mark dreamed on his way toward every case, he deeply and darkly craved.

There was another goal, though. Another craving, another haunting desire on his way to any call. *Aaron,* Mark thought, *I'm going to prove you wrong.*

The car spun down toward the intersection of North Sixth Avenue and Speedway, with an unnecessary siren echoing through the city. The drive wasn't long, and when he reached his destination, he swerved onto the slightly elevated road. There was clear water running down the street. Mark passed the sign reading East Elm Street, only visible with those shimmering headlights. "Toyota Camry, yellow," Mark whispered under his breath. "Toyota Camry, yellow…Toyota Camry, yellow…Toyota Camry, yellow…" Then he found the suspicious car.

Mark slowed abruptly.

Why prove Aaron wrong? Aaron controlled Mark's calls; he controlled his contribution; that's why they always called him directly through the Bearcat, called him by name. Mark wasn't dumb. He knew Aaron was the one who enforced it. Aaron knew how much stress was on Mark's shoulders, but Wegman had cravings—he desired something more.

Mark's lights warned the other driver, but the siren helped him understand. The Camry was being signaled, and the driver finally caught on. The yellow Toyota Camry pulled off to the side of the residential road.

Mark then waited as he recorded the license plate through the Bearcat back to the station, but this didn't take more than fifteen seconds at most; he also waited for something more. Maybe a chase would begin, maybe the driver would take his chances on the road instead of the law. Mark dreamed, but nothing. Then soon he began to feel uneasy, a little frightened himself, but Mark didn't understand why. After about five minutes, nothing. He smirked and decided it was time to end the charade. The officer reached for the door and an old-school ticket book, then stepped out into the damp atmosphere. He was killing time like the car ride, creeping his way over through a stroll between the gap from his window and the Toyota trying to build tension. A slow, prideful, and empowering walk many police officers practice, but his was especially slow, one soft step after the next, knowing that after the arrest, there'd be nothing to do for the rest of the night. That's how Aaron worked; Mark hated Aaron. He studied the car, the old yellow Toyota Camry with the paint chipped off every corner. Mark took note of everything.

"Probably bought at a yard sale," he grunted while chuckling as light as a feather and feeling his well-aged hand over the Camry. Chipping off the paint, expanding the Malaria-colored chipped corners, a color between faint yellow and camo green, until he finally made it to the driver's window. Mark then knocked on the Camry, and ever so slowly, the driver of the vehicle manually cranked the creaky window down.

"License and regist–"

"Here you go, officer," the young boy squeaked and passed over the car's information. He then turned back to the Camry's ancient squealing vents and attempted to stay warm.

1 6   A U S T I N   T H A C K E R

Mark glared at the boy and smiled. *I'll have fun reading your rights while I push your face in the mud*, he thought. The police officer then began to look at the paperwork given to him, getting drenched in the rain. Mark couldn't care less. He first studied the registration, then the license, searching for what he usually found in his runs: children past curfew. On it was a picture of the same boy with short, thin brown hair, more color and weight than he presently wore, as well as his same glowing blue eyes, much fainter in his current appearance. The boy also smiled brightly in the photo; you could see the excitement on his face. Mark found it to be tacky.

"Mr. Tyler…Castillo." Mark paused for a few seconds to glare at the boy. "You're sixteen. Is this correct?"

"That is correct."

"And you are driving this late at night, is that right?"

"Yes," Tyler Castillo said with guiltless acceptance. Mark raised his eyebrows, but with more anger than shock.

"And why is that?"

"Because I was born sixteen years ago."

"That's not what I asked. Why are you out this late at night? You do realize that curfew is at ten."

"Well, if I understand correctly, it's nine forty-five. I haven't broken curfew, officer. May I please go? I have an emergency." Tyler added his usual know-it-all stresses, emphasizing and extending the two L's in "well."

"Oh? I didn't know I was talking to a wise mouth. Please go on, please tell me about this…emergency," Mark said with a dangerous spark in his voice and a sly smile. The boy at first didn't know what to say, blown away by this immediate change in emotion but not as afraid of Mark as a sixteen-year-old should be, not even close. Tyler was afraid, though, but not of the police officer before him—he was afraid of something else. Mark saw this and felt incompetent, a little uneasy.

"I-I believe you're stepping out of your boundaries, officer. I don't have to give you that information." The boy shivered.

"Is that so?" Mark said with his smile, unchanged.

Another very brief silence occurred while Mark glared, hoping to frighten him, to make him believe that Mark was contemplating something, and a good ol' stare at Tyler would be the deciding factor for this unknown choice he would make. Mark was making no decisions, but he was staring at Tyler for another reason. Mark was searching for an accusation, something illegal.

Mark Wegman did notice features he hadn't seen before, like the hoodie over his head, the car heater whistling faster than needed—*ignore the similarities, ignore the whistles*—his yellow teeth and a small red spot on the back of Tyler's hand from a needle prick. Mark guessed they were all drug related. Tyler had to weigh less than a hundred pounds, his clothes baggy and worn but not too large. Tyler shrank. He was pale and sick. His lips had no hint of red. They were as pale as his old Nokia. How could he be driving in his condition? He even talked with a little flare in his voice. Was he on drugs? He must have been. There is no way a boy like this could even function right now. Then Mark saw it. It was a prescribed bottle of morphine, and it seemed empty. *He's a junkie,* Mark thought. *Popping these pills and waiting for the next high. Shivering and shaking like a junkie would, slowly losing control as he drifts farther away from his last hookup. Oh yes, he's a junkie, and he's all mine.* Mark's scheming grin widened beyond belief, and he could barely keep in squeals of excitement.

"Wait here," Mark told Tyler as he almost sprinted between the gap from one car to the next, the blue-and-red lights occupying the black, damp atmosphere.

"Please officer, I have to go," Tyler yelped.

"If you can't tell me, then it must not be that important, and if you drive off I'll take you in for resisting arrest," Mark yelled over his shoulder, not even attempting to hide his joy—thrill that Tyler mistook for insanity. He thought of driving away out of desperation but didn't.

"You can't do this, you don't have a reason for pulling me over," Tyler yelled out the window in one final attempt.

"Oh but I do, my own personal junkie," Mark uttered to himself while opening his car door and speaking into his old Bearcat . "This is Officer Wegman one-four-five-one, and I'm at the crossroads of—" he shined a flashlight at the street sign. "North Sixth Avenue and Elm Street. I have a sixteen-year-old boy, his name is Tyler Castillo, and Tyler has an empty bottle of morphine. He has rotten teeth and is severely skinny, I'm guessing around ninety pounds. He also has numerous needle pricks around his arms and body, which I assume were from other drugs besides Morphine." Mark wouldn't know until the next day that he was correct, Tyler did have more than one needle prick, although at the time he was gambling with this claim, lying for the sake of the chase. "The kid is oblivious that I know and seems to me was on his way to refill the morphine bottle, possibly other drugs. The way he acts and moves, he's a junkie for sure. With your permission I would like to let him go, then proceed to follow the boy, to see if he would lead me to his prescriber, and possibly the dealer. I would not interfere if he does lead me, and if he does I'll give you my location and will not interfere. " There was a short stutter of silence as Mark waited to see if they would believe his second lie, because Mark would get involved, he would interfere the second a grain of sand was out of place. He would not call the office for backup, he would handle the entire situation solo, and later he would tell them that he was caught at gunpoint and had to act fast before they blew his brains out from temple to temple.

"Mark, this is Aaron Hudson down at the station, are you sure your assumptions are correct? And you will not act at all if the situation escalates, you swear on your life."

"With all due respect, Aaron, I wouldn't have brought it up if I didn't think so," Mark said grinning. There was a very long silence and arguing in the background. Mark could hear a few mumbles. "It's been a local case for years... He's not authorized... The danger... This might be our only choice... I'll control it... Don't talk back to me." Then there were only whispers and the steady raindrops on the window as Mark waited, his stretched-out foot getting drenched from the rain while the rest of his body rested in the car. He was shaking with excitement, anticipation, wanting to have one foot out once he received his approval. Then Aaron spoke with a harsh tone, yet quiet voice.

"You have my permission, Mark, but if you're in danger, if anything happens, call us and get out of dodge. Do not get involved at all. I don't want you to leave your vehicle. If this child doesn't lead you anywhere, stop following. If he does, and there's even slight suspicion, call us and stop following." Mark's eyes lit up more than they ever had, his skin glowed with so much color, and his mind was racing with possibilities. Aaron sighed through the Bearcat, his voice full of grief, full of regret, and continued. "You can't do this alone, Mark. You are loved too much and you know it." A bright light lit up Mark and Tyler's cars, along with the houses and the street for a split second. The rain stopped. Thunder followed and crackled in the background. Silence, then the rain began again. Mark flinched, but Tyler didn't; he didn't notice the flash of light, and neither did Aaron at the station about six miles back.

Mark's hands were now clammy, and the color that was present seconds before disappeared. His mood shifted so drastically, as quick as the lightning striking the absent desert. Mark was now utterly frightened, a whole new person. "I know, I will... Thank you," Mark whispered as if he were disclosing a secret, and with the same whisper he spoke again to himself, not knowing that he was shaking, and shaking only from the power of the word "love."

"I promise, My Hand Mitten, you'll be okay. I'll be damned if you are not. I'll push forward for the both of us." Silence, the rain in the background, slightly more aggressive, but like the shaking of his own hand, he did not take notice. Silence; then a broad smile appeared, each individual off-white tooth sprouting behind his lips. *This is my chance to prove everyone wrong. No more smiles, no more pity, no more downcast looks at my strength to handle the shit of this world.* While holding Tyler's license and registration, he left his car and walked the distance again, this time with height and confidence back to the rusty Toyota and the weak, tired Tyler Castillo, the color of pale moss lightly painted on his skin.

"Here you go, Mr. Castillo. Thank you for your patience and cooperation," said Mark, while handing him his papers.

"Thank you, now please excuse me but I have to— "

"Yes, yes I know, your...*emergency,*" he chuckled, grinning wildly. "Have a good evening." Mark began to walk back to his car. *I'm ready to get this bastard, this brat that thinks he owns the world. No, not a brat, a snarky little Mexican immigrant, that has no parental guidance. Get him deported back to the country he came from. A dirty, poor—*

"Why are you upset?" Tyler yelled out of the window while shaking, cutting off Mark's thoughts.

"What?"

"Exactly what I said."

"I'm not upset," Mark snarled. "Don't accuse me of random— "

"Then why do you cry?"

"I NEVER CRIED!" Mark shouted while thunder struck behind in the nearby hills. He thought about earlier that night and lightly grazed his cheek in wonder, again not knowing he was shaking, but it was even worse than before.

"You didn't have to," Tyler muttered, bile rising in his throat.

The time it took to march between their car windows was enough for Mark's pride to spring him back into a devious grin, fighting and overpowering these thoughts that were also rising like bile in his throat. Mary was going to be okay, and he was about to get a promotion because of this arrest, he knew for certain. Maybe he'd even be on the news. Mark's actions bringing to justice these rough edges of town. He'd heard Aaron speak to another police officer behind those glass doors. Drug crimes were on the rise. If he was able to catch the entire gang, no doubt Mark would also have his own glass office with white shades, and the more he thought about this idea, the more excited he became. *Respect*, he thought. *Respect.*

"You speak lies, you don't know my past, and you don't know me!" Mark yelled at Tyler without a glimpse back as he opened his door. "And trust me, you wouldn't want to know me *or* my demons. They're too much for someone like you to handle." He stepped into his car and closed the door, with Legion laughing and howling in his body. The rain continued to drip at an even pace, and Tyler started his engine.

"Pray to God. He will listen." Tyler drove off and lightly sprayed the air with a mist of rain. Mark didn't respond, didn't move, and the wind began to calm down. Silent, steady tears began to roll down his face a second time. He thought of Mary. His mind was spiraling out of control. Another word, another word that stung him, maybe even stronger than "Love" was "God."

"God? What has God done for you?" Mark revved up his engine. "Besides give you grief and throw you into this miserable, broken world!" The rain continued to increase in speed, the air current picked up once more, and Mark drove off. He began to follow Tyler with insanity, with eyes like the devil. In a way, Tyler was running from the devil.

Now, children, Mark wasn't always like this. Please don't mistake his anger for hatred. He was a very nice and gentle man, and a romantic. Mark played his emotions close to the vest. If you walked into the downtown police station during the years he was in his prime and asked anyone what Mark was like, they'd tell you he was gentle or kindhearted. But he could also be very aggressive, secretive, and sometimes unresponsive and distracted. They'd say Aaron was hard on him, always busting him and keeping him in line. Mark had a great gift when it came to forcing people to justice, but Aaron always disapproved of his methods. Some thought he was bitter from their childhood, because Mark's was normal, with a group of friends and parents who loved him. The type of parents that Aaron never had, parents that even fortunate children with allowances, bicycles for Christmas, and understandable punishments sometimes felt cheated by when stealing a glance at Mark's perfect family. His father, Henry Wegman, was not highly educated and was always searching for work, but after long workdays, he never went with his construction friends to the bar for a quick beer. He went home without a second to spare, to kiss his wife and play with his child. Play, it seemed that he always played with Mark, tossing a tattered and torn baseball around, which was so old that the baseball seemed to be a family member all on its own. Therefore, when Mark saw that ball resting in his father's hands, an old excitement would rise up in him, and he would know exactly what was going to happen next. They would also play Cowboys and Indians. His father would take out a large hawk feather he'd found after the monsoon season and a straw cowboy hat from a thrift shop for fifteen cents. Then they would run around like dogs with their tails on fire, and Mark would scream with laughter when Henry picked him up and hung him upside down from his legs. "I gotchu!" Henry would say with the hawk feather tucked behind his ear. "Is time for da boiler!" He would then place Mark in a huge, rusty pot that his father also scavenged and stirred him with a large stick while Mark uncontrollably laughed.

Henry was in good shape because of his young body but was worked ragged day and night in a struggle to support his family. He was as tall as Mark, six foot seven and broad, a freak in the world but a prophet in construction. The town of Tucson was steadily growing in the death of the seventies and the dawn of the eighties, expanding closer and closer to hundred-year-old ranches outside of the town, but no fantastic, new industry swept the desolate Sonoran Desert and called for such projects. There was only a rise in national population and rich, retired individuals who could afford to escape the northern winters. Suburbs were slowly being built into towns of recent formation like Oro Valley and new additions to more dated, dissolved parts of ranches like Vail. But management always found a sort of fondness for Henry, not only because of how much he could lift, drag, pull, and tear down. Henry also worked in construction for so long that he picked up a good understanding of Spanish, since many of the workers he spoke to were from Mexico. Henry was also a man of huge faith and understanding, like a cool breeze through their long-sleeve yellow vests. Henry was a comfort for everyone. Therefore, management always recognized him as the official translator, recruiting officer, and the voice of his working community. When the employed had an issue with management, they heard the complaint from Henry, with his poor articulation yet sharp mind and controlled thoughts. Henry was not good-looking, with crooked teeth, extended ears, and a bit of a lazy eye, but his certainty and understanding made everyone seem to understand why he was in charge. Henry was a leader, although underpaid and overworked.

Mark's mother was also a workaholic who worked a full-time job during the night at an old waffle house but also took care of their house in the mornings and evenings. She still didn't work as much as Henry, but it was close. Her hours were usually from eleven to five in the morning, which was when Mark and Henry normally woke up to cook breakfast, expecting her home. They would make two plates of oatmeal, and on the weekends an egg or two (sometimes even bacon), along with a single dinner plate for Isabell. She was kind, shrewd, and calculated, witnessing the world in a very different way than Henry, who could find beauty in Genghis Khan if he tried. Isabell lived in the world with a hint of bitterness hanging on her lip like a ring but still cherished her family with great appreciation. For about thirty minutes, Mark would watch his parents laugh and eat merrily, his mother tired and worn, his father energized and rested. Then Henry would leave from six in the morning to six at night. Isabell and Mark would spend about an hour cleaning the house before Isabell gave him a list of chores to do while she slept. Mark would rush through those tasks so too much of the daytime was never wasted, and then he would leave with a smile on his round cheeks, knowing that what he accomplished would better his family and please his parents.

During a school day he would normally have a single task to do in the morning and another when he got home, his father still working and his mother still fast asleep. However, it was the weekend, so he was free from the chains of responsibility for the rest of the day.

Whenever Mark's father was off, he spent all his time showing Mark how to hunt, fish, sand, and build dressers and nightstands, an entire day of bonding time, sometimes driving away for the evening to embark on an adventure. When his mother had the night off, they would watch television together, shows like M*A*S*H or The Six Million Dollar Man, in which his mother loved to point out the flaws between the plot and reality. She would roll her eyes with a little smile under her nose, and Mark would cuddle under her arm, hypnotized by the bionic human and his own creativity. Mark loved his parents more than the world, believing, as every child did, that they were perfect. He was sure of it and wanted to be nothing less than perfect like them, until his father told him otherwise. "You ain't goin' through life wit' no callus on your hands," his father once said with his soft voice. "And I ain't raising no jelly bean. I'm raising a man. So far I see yo' are. Yo' start no fights, yo' keep from them, and stay nice until they in yo' face, tooth peck close to yo' nose, and yo' smell they butt breath." Mark laughed as Henry got very close and wiggled his nose at Mark. "I erm proud, son, and you'll do better than your ol' man."

Mark heard and obeyed every word: do better than his old man. He knew he must be better than perfect, the noblest man in the world. Therefore, no kid on the block ever pushed him around, as Mark couldn't be baited into fighting. The class bullies laid off once Mark laughed and stretched out his hand to shake when they tried to pick a fight. Soon, everyone seemed to adore Mark. He was such a trustworthy, honest boy.

Mark's charm worked for him, although Aaron had trouble making friends, had trouble talking to others. "Hey, you're funny. My name's Mark, do you want to play Cowboys and Indians?" Mark enthusiastically asked one warm spring Saturday on the road of Mark's cul-de-sac. Aaron lived two miles away. He walked the sidewalks and streets to find someone to fight with, like his father did to him. Aaron's parents were never home and never seemed to care where he was or what he was doing, and even at the age of seven he carried the feeling that they would rather have him dead. In fact, you could say the family situations of Mark and Aaron were completely opposite. Aaron and the bruises he hid with long sleeves in the summer, the belt that always swung from left to right on his door when it slammed. Just like the traditional baseball with Mark's father, there was the traditional belt for Aaron. When his dad held it, his hairy knuckles wrapped around the leather and sometimes a beer in the other, he knew what would happen next; he knew what was going to happen to both him and his emotionless mother. Then there was Mark with his packed lunches from his loving mother after she came home from work and a note of encouragement that was always in there. Usually a small phrase like "God loves you" or "You're our guardian angel," but no matter what it said, Mark always blushed and hid his face from childhood shyness. There was also his father, who would give up the world for his family, who carried with him such a confident and loving aroma that others seemed to trust almost instantaneously. Aaron looked at Mark with a little amazement. Mark was in the other second-grade class but popular beyond belief. Aaron knew who he was, although he never spoke to him until now.

"What makes you so sure I want to play with someone as gross as you? You ugly turd!" Angry Aaron bellowed with a single stride backward, afraid of Mark and this random kindness.

"Because we're going to be best friends!" Mark quickly responded while his red cheeks puffed out. Aaron stopped, out of his comfort zone and stupefied—no one *ever* dared to communicate with "Angry Aaron." Especially like this. He attempted to be open and played with the others, but at pickup time, Aaron watched children leave, watched their mothers kiss them on their cheeks, and their children disrespectfully wiping it off while complaining to not embarrass them, affection he longed for. Aaron accepted and embraced the name "Angry Aaron." It made him more than the boy to be pitied for walking home alone.

"Well…as long as I'm the cowboy!" Aaron commanded gladly while reaching out for a handshake.

"Sounds like a plan!" Mark merrily announced while shaking his hand. Aaron saw something in Mark that day, and from then on he never walked home alone again.

They began to accompany each other in make-believe adventures. Mark and Aaron would sometimes walk into the desert and find their way back in the morning. They would play golf in the streets, shoot cans with a poor and beaten BB gun, steal pomegranates from a neighbor's yard. It was the life of the latchkey kid, nearing the end of disco music, Vietnam, Ronald Reagan, and the beginning of MTV. They grew callouses on their hands, like Mark's dad wanted, and on their feet from climbing trees and old sheds. There was dirt in their socks and hair after every adventure. Mark taught Aaron about his father's rules for fighting and how to play baseball, while Aaron taught

Mark how to duck from punches and his thoughts on how to throw one. They would laugh so much from each other's jokes, impressions of Donald Duck and Clint Eastwood with their candy cigarettes pinched to aim toward the sky from their closed lips, puffing like sailors and arguing who would be the good, the bad, or the ugly.

"Mark...Mark...Mark!" seven-year-old Aaron impatiently said as they walked out of a dusty and old 7-Eleven and cautiously paused at the road. Aaron continued to tap his shoulder out of the urge to speak. They were heading to a shady spot under a secluded bridge, as the first days of their summer were proving to be just as dry and scorched as planned. "Mark!" Aaron said again, this time even louder, "you're sooooo ugly, Medusa...Medusa would turn to stone if you looked at her."

"Really?" Mark questioned in partial amusement as he watched a few isolated cars pass by.

"Yeah! You'd be the Ugly Mark. I swear it! I swear it on my... Mark, wait up!"

Mark was already walking across the street, confident in his stride while opening the pack of Bazooka Bubble Gum he'd bought for fifteen cents. The cashier was friendly enough, mostly absorbed in the novel he was reading to care any more than he did, but he cared enough to realize how young they were. Mark was older than Aaron by nine months, eight years old and already taller than four and a half feet, but still young.

"They must live close by," the middle-aged man said for his own comfort, while scratching his receding hairline and opening his book once again. But the fact was, they had traveled a few miles south to reach the corner store in town.

Aaron began to jog toward Mark in a hurry as his need for attention was still not fed. He continued to stare toward Mark as— in the middle of the street—he turned around and smiled back.

Aaron later told the police that Mark stood in the road, smiling back for almost five seconds, but the moment was only about two.

"Would that make you the bad then?" The words came through more like a comment than a question, but as always there was no fire in his words, Mark seemed to be pleased. "Then who's the—"

A finely polished 1968 Toyota Corolla came from the left and smashed into Mark's ribs, crashing his face into the hood and creating a crunching sound of bones and teeth crumbling from the impact. He flew back about three yards, landing on his back without a sense of day in him. The 7-Eleven cashier dropped his book onto the ground with his mouth wide open, showing some recent silver fillings in his molars. The car halted with tremendous force, yet lagged and smashed into Mark with an impact of about thirty-five miles per hour. The cashier heard the high-pitched screech of the tires on the concrete and saw the body crash onto the ground. He ran to a payphone and was the first to call 911. Bubble gum and blood were scattered around the road, and Aaron acted as if he were just frozen by Medusa, mouth as wide as the cashiers and frozen in the middle of the street.

The driver jumped out of his vehicle with a cigarette in his hand, ran to a payphone, and called AAA, then 911. He was the second person and last person to call the police. The middle-aged man checked his car before he helped Mark, feeling the dented hood with care and gentleness. He was shaking from despair and anger. *What the hell was that boy doing in the road?* The man thought with burning rage, then ran to the boy with a phony face of distress, accompanied by the corner store clerk who turned Mark on his side as he began to cough, cry, and wheeze from the shock. The man was silent, though— Cleveland Jones, two-time DUI felon, had been trying to light a cigarette before hammering on the breaks.

"You got a light?" Cleveland asked the clerk.

"No, sorry man," the clerk responded without a glance up, taking off his shirt to substitute as a pillow for Mark's head. Aaron was frozen until a police officer asked him if the boy was his friend, and where they lived. All that came out of Aaron's mouth was barf, all over Jones's Corolla.

The doctor told Mark's parents that because of his extra foot in height, he was not pulled under. They were all very grateful, even after three broken ribs, a shattered wrist, twenty-one stitches, and his broken baby teeth. Mark lived, and his mother told him that it was because of God. God had a purpose for him, and he was going to achieve great things. Mark listened to every word as if it were law.

Years later, Mark found out that his father and mother both picked up other jobs in order to pay for his expensive medical bills, since they were at fault for allowing their child to wander so far from their home. They felt awful, watching him try to peel a banana with his hand and teeth, having trouble standing from his crushed ribs, and waddling around in pain. Therefore, Mark's parents bought him a birthday present that was far more impactful than any present he had ever been given. When he ripped the newspaper off that Ringling Bros. magic kit, his eyes and cheeks lit up with color, then he screamed with joy and laughter, wiggling his body, his sling, his titanic bandage over his ribs and on his forehead, like he were about to launch into the stratosphere. From card tricks to little plastic bunnies popping out of hats, Mark loved it. It became Aaron and Mark's obsession, the compelling force that bonded their friendship, what made them unique to each other, different than the other classmates in school.

"If only I could poof away Amy," Aaron said angrily while blushing.

"She must have done something horrible," said Mark. "You can't even talk to her without turning red!"

Aaron looked down very shamefully and spoke with a tiny voice. "Ye–Yeah that's why."

You're Asking Too Much

THE WIND RUSHED THROUGH the cacti, hissing as the rain spiraled down, drumming an upsetting offbeat melody. Even though Mark's anger was raging, he never lost his desire to become entirely invisible. With his headlights off, Mark began to follow the old yellow Toyota Camry with a wild grin on his face. Tyler was the first who rolled out from the scene on Sixth Avenue and Elm Street, heading east on Elm toward the endless darkness, as Mark went north on Sixth, turning right on a parallel street to Elm, called Lester. He then turned off his lights, turned off Lester onto Fifth Street, and left on Elm, following gullible Tyler, sharing the same endless darkness and the Toyota's headlights. The Camry was speeding through those older buildings from the seventies and eighties, past some houses that Henry even helped build, but all Mark could think about was the rush he felt, the excitement and all the endorphins that made him almost weep with joy. It was a secretive, dangerous chase, death sneaking behind Mark as Mark snuck behind Tyler. He felt death's presence and sensed comfort, comfort to be as close to death as his wife was now. As they passed Fourth Avenue and hit about fifty-five miles per hour, Mark began to yell with exhilaration.

"You want to preach to me, preacher boy? You want to tell me about God and his righteousness while you speed down Elm Street to pop pills and inject heroine?" They passed Third Street and both rolled the stop sign. Mark burst with laughter, and some snot ran down his lips before he aggressively wiped it off. "Is the morphine *that* necessary? That worthy to step between you and your holy land?" They passed Second Street at around sixty, and Tyler passed out on the wheel, slowing abruptly. "You're sick, you sicken me! You—" Mark gasped for air and slammed on the breaks, which slid from the pouring rain and pounded into the bumper of the Camry, sliding both down the road with a whiff of symmetrical speed. They both slid together like a child falling off a sled into icy slush, board following closely behind. They slid so far that the two cars, the two drivers, reached First Avenue, a lonely number. Tyler's totaled Camry hit the street sign as the thunder rumbled, then slowly died off as the time went by.

Mark barfed and lost consciousness, the vertical, cold rain wetting his cut cheek. He began to dream of the past again. It was easy to dream of the past.

They were on a bridge, an old bridge next to the city. It had been years since he was hit by that car, all that remained were scars worked in deep and a memory ignored by many years of laughter, many years of their playful magic. Mark grew more than a foot during that time, the tallest seventh grader in their school at a height of five foot nine, beginning to broaden even at his youthful age. Aaron was nothing like this; his height was average, although very slim. The sun was setting, the day was dying. Mark was thirteen and Aaron was twelve in the fall of 1981. Aaron marched toward Mark in rage, which was too common to be a surprise. Aaron's long hair, his KISS shirt under a thin white sweater, rolled closer while Mark watched him stomp over. He remembered his face, the young wrinkles from Aaron's angered expression. His glaring eyes, the bruise on his left wrist, and the black eye that his mother helped him hide with her foundation. He knew Aaron would always be angry when his old man got a hand on him, and he tended never to mind the anger pushed his way. In fact, Mark enjoyed it, knowing that after Aaron felt better after his outrages, he felt more control in his life;

it was a way for him to vent. A time for Aaron to speak when he needed to, and Mark could respect that; he could lend an ear and listen. But that day on the bridge stood out more than the other occurrences—it stood out like a ladybug in the grass.

◆◆◆

"You're sick, you sicken me!" Aaron yelled.

"Really? Why is that?" Mark questioned with a little laugh.

"Because you hang out with... With HER! I mean, to hell with her. We're a fricken' team, Mark. I mean, am I not good enough? I know I'm not beautiful, but at least I don't—"

"Save it, you nut. She's just my friend."

"No, no, don't say that. I see the way you look at her, a look I've only seen in movies, she's a game changer," Aaron aggressively stated with an overinflated grin, a face that said, *I caught you, now it's time to fess up.*

"Don't change the path we started! She flirts with everyone. You're no better than anyone and it'll end just as soon as it began. I'll have to stop this madness that *you* decided to get us into. I have the power to stop this!" Aaron yelled with fiery anger. As always, Mark smiled with the same gentleness and glowing face, the same gentle voice.

"I'm not going to marry the girl, calm down." There was a silence, and they burst into laughter. Aaron tried to fight it, like an infant fighting his pasty dinner, but soon he couldn't help but crease up with snorts and crackles.

"I guess not. You're right, man, I was overreacting. Sorry about that," Aaron stated in a tiny voice.

"No problem. We have a plan, but life is too mad to plan. I'm going to play it by ear." Mark turned around to look over the bridge and pulled out a block of Bazooka Bubble Gum. Aaron pulled out a very worn deck of cards he'd bought on a family vacation to Las Vegas years ago and began shuffling with his thin hands, bending and shooting them from one hand to the other, with ease and comfort. He loved that specific deck; it sat on his nightstand while he slept and his right pocket while he walked. He felt control from them. It made him feel secure.

Mark and I in Las Vegas, he would always think with a smile while nodding off into sleep. *Living in Caesars Palace, please God, please!*

"Hey, by the way, are you coming to my house tomorrow to rehearse that magic trick?" Aaron casually asked.

"I'd never miss it for the world!" Mark stated happily. Though he didn't know how to tell Aaron that this girl was also invited, the woman whom Aaron had decided to choose this specific day to rant about.

It had surprised Mark; the topic was so out of the blue, he didn't even know Aaron knew he was seeing her. Their relationship was such a deep secret between the two, and he was going to introduce her to Aaron during that specific rehearsal. All Mark knew was that he couldn't stop thinking about her, even as he watched the sun set into the mountains, he could not help but giggle from the butterflies in his stomach. He was already daydreaming about marriage, their children, and how wonderful it would be to spend their life together snuggling and talking about their dreams like their last date. That word, *date,* tickled his tongue every time he said it. He never felt this toward any girl, but there was no way Aaron would ever allow such a feeling after what was said.

Rats, Mark thought to himself. He then closed his eyes, counted down from three, squeezed his eyes even harder, and spoke.

"I even invited a stunt girl, she's really good and is willing to do whatever we want her to do. You need to give her a chance Aaron, she won't be that bad."

Aaron turned on a dime when Mark spoke of a "stunt girl" and froze in complete shock. His mouth open, skinny hands stretched out to his sides in an expression of nauseating disgust. A thought whipped through his two ears. (Angry, Lonely Aaron.)

And he grew with anger.

"No, you tick-infested, hairy Incredible Hulk, I will not tolerate this garbage. You need to show her the door and properly kick her out."

(Angry... Lonely... Aaron.)

Mark would have rolled his eyes and laughed, but he needed Aaron's approval. Mark could do anything he wanted, but he couldn't tolerate what he knew Aaron would do. Aaron, the trash talker in their school with a terrible reputation for starting the most random fights out of completely nothing. He once threw a muffin at a young fourth-grade girl in the cafeteria. He later told Mark that she rolled her eyes at him and mouthed the word "ugly." Young Julia Stratton, who still cannot walk around school in their line without holding her teacher's hand, and is the principle's daughter, had done no such thing. Mark turned around and spoke hastily.

"Well, I was wondering if she—"

"Dammit Mark!" Aaron stomped away from the bridge, but Mark followed. He was slightly angry about Aaron's language but kept the feelings to himself.

"No, you don't understand. I taught her some tricks, she's good! And we need a beautiful girl to perform tricks on, right? Everyone in Vegas has one. She is also so sweet and entertaining. She could make a crowd cheer from just her appearance, I swear, she's also—"

Aaron turned around. "But not like this. I'm not third wheeling for my entire adult life, it's supposed to just be us. Not The Amazing Aaron, Mark, *and* Mary, just us. No squat, because if you do this, then one day you'll leave and never look back, while I sit alone and keep buying Slim Jims, looking out for only me, caring for only me, and laughing with only me. Then I would never leave this dusty, crummy state! I would lose my chance for change while you two run around acting like the frickin' Brady Bunch."

They both went quiet; Mark didn't respond. Aaron knew he was angry and knew the reason why. Mark's eyes were sober, with not even the slightest curve of joy on his face, something so normal that it was terrifying to see him without. Aaron was at a loss for words, searching to say anything at all to break such an awkward connection. He knew all Mark cared about was the girl, Mary. He knew that Mark was serious, that they were serious, and that nothing was going to stop them from seeing each other again.

"Besides, we need a smoking hot girl, not a beautiful one," Aaron quietly stated in embarrassment. Then Mark smiled, shattering the frightening tension off Aaron's shoulders. He received the approval he'd longed for.

"Yeah, well, she's still coming tomorrow." Mark looked at a cheap supermarket watch he'd been given as a gift from Henry and flinched. "Oh, tie my pants on a fishing pole. I have to go," Mark said in a terrible Southern hillbilly accent while giving Aaron a wink. "When we meet up, be on your best behavior, or you'll regret it." He began to run, and Aaron stared at him while slowly disappearing.

"Now you're asking too much," Aaron whispered, kicking the dry dirt and watching the sun fall behind those mountains. He'd made a decision the night before and didn't dare tell Mark. Aaron decided that the next time his father hit either him or his mother, he was going to fight back, a thought that ran goose bumps up his spine and frightened him beyond compare. Aaron was going to revolt because, after all, it was the age for children to rebel.

◆◆◆

MARK'S DREAM WAS SHORT-LIVED and faded away into nothing but a voice, a blurry voice that began faintly but grew stronger and stronger until the face of a blonde nurse emerged, rushing him into the ambulance and yelling at the driver.

"Go faster! He's bleeding out from his head. If we don't get blood soon, we'll lose him!"

Mark woke up and nearly sprang out of his bed, icy sweat dripping down his forehead. Mark's usually strong voice was replaced with a raspy, misty murmur, and then pain surged through his head and spine. Mark, still half asleep, quickly checked his head and found no huge gashes on his crown, except an old scar.

"Wha—Where am I?" Mark quickly yelled in a weak and awakened voice.

"Whoa, Mark, calm down!" Aaron woke up from his light doze and sprang from an old hospital chair in the sun with great speed, gently pushing Mark back toward the blankets. He was lean and quick, just like in his youth, with very dense bags under his eyes and a flimsy smile. Tom was in the light from the window of the small pine-green room as well, more bulky and small, but he never moved; he just watched with a smile.

"Don't move around. You don't want to create any more problems with your neck. You already look terrible! You're lucky nothing even remotely serious happened to you," Aaron chuckled lightly.

"Where am I?" Mark asked with a shiver of his stiffened body.

Aaron hesitated with instantaneous fear and recovered very poorly, Mark could tell.

"Y-You got into a car accident last night. I called your cell... umm...multiple times, and it wasn't like you to, you know, not pick up..." Aaron began playing with his fingers like a child. "But before I could track your phone, we got a call that there were EMTs assisting you out of your automobile. Though they didn't have to go far, since your car was right next to the hospital. All the ambulance had to do was drive a block or two down Elm Street and back to the hospital, a quarter-mile round trip. Others from our squad were here earlier to see how you were doing, but…but the doctor kicked them out and—"

"What day is it?" Mark yelped while springing up and noticing the pain his back carried. But Mark, with a quick tear that fell across his rough and pale face, sucked in the pain.

Aaron was shocked from the way Mark brushed the entire accident to the side, as if he'd just told him to think about his breakfast from the day before yesterday; it was irrelevant.

"Well, it's Sunday."

"My Hand Mitten—"

Aaron easily interrupted, "Is fine, her nurse checked on her last night and got everything she needed." Aaron patted him on the leg and gave off a very friendly smile, with a little more ease.

"And this morning? What about this morning?" Mark yelled. He didn't smile or breathe (and probably wouldn't until Aaron spoke) while thinking about the possible pains she would be feeling if not given her medications.

"It's—" Aaron checked his poor and used leather-band watch. "Five thirty, buddy, the sun just came up no more than half an hour ago, give me a break. But y-yes…she did."

"Dammit!" Mark yelled out of his usual anger.

Tom, in the light, frowned. "Mark, language, please!"

"Now you're asking too much," Aaron said immediately after Tom spoke; then he laughed and shook his head. It had become a habit, something Aaron always said without a single thought tied to it. It was as if Aaron had taken a step forward or swatted a fly from his eye—the words were natural. But Mark felt frightened, and his mouth dropped as he thought about his dream before.

"What did you say?"

"I said you ask for too much."

Mark looked down at the thin white blankets, pet them with his right arm connected to the IV he hadn't yet noticed, and calmed down from the thought of their beautiful past.

"Now isn't that so..." Mark paused and looked up at Aaron. "How was she?" He stared at Aaron with desperation for an answer of hope. Aaron smiled lightly and began to tear up from the question. He was always upset when Mark asked.

"She's good... She's real good," Aaron said emotionally.

Mark nodded, and led his eyes toward the bed blankets, then continued petting again, flattening out the creases. Other things invaded his mind, and Mark forgot about everything with the young druggie and the car chase toward the smugglers. *Does she mention me?* he thought. *Does she miss me? Has she painted? Is her hair the same? Impossible. She's still there, next to the air-conditioning unit, sick and in need of my me and my warmth.* Mark stayed silent, and Aaron frowned because he knew what Mark was thinking, what he *always* thought about, and then began to fiddle with his fingers once more.

"Don't take it personal, Aaron," said Tom. "Mark needs his time to think."

Mark's pondering of the past grew, and he became unresponsive. He fell back on the pillow and stared blankly at the ceiling.

He now thought of the dream, their history of arguing. There was so much. He first thought of them on the bridge during their argument about the stunt girl. How cute that reality would have been; then he thought of how Aaron never enjoyed Mary's company. Mary, her brunette hair, rosy cheeks, and beautiful smile, but Aaron was always so mean to her.

He began to venture through the past now, so overwhelmingly deep that those thoughts sent him into a thick, conscious dream. He knew that those daydreams wouldn't help him now, but what other way could he enjoy the simplicity of the past? How else could he marvel over the beauty of their friendship? The year was 1985, around the end of winter, when pollen and a few patches of grass and weeds began to run free across the desert floor. Mark was seventeen, and Aaron was sixteen.

◆◆◆

"SHE'S GOOD, SHE'S REAL good," Mark muttered with sarcasm. "Oh yeah she's fine, especially when you yelled her out of the house!" he said, exploding with anger and wiping the sweat off his forehead in a jolt.

"It's not my fault she can't take a joke, and this wouldn't have happened if YOU haven't started dating her!" Aaron yelled. He had a thin face freckled with zits and a dark purple bruise on his right cheek. Mark stepped closer—he was half a foot taller at an even six feet, despite Aaron's skinny appearance.

"Don't you *dare* bring this on me! It's been years, and you still can't accept her. This is on you." He walked away and then turned back. "I can't believe you yelled her out. Have you forgotten that it's only been a week? And may I remind you, you didn't attend!" Mark paced in a little circle, then turned back again. "You couldn't hold it in? You couldn't just stop and think how she felt to just lose her mother?"

"I didn't know the chick, and this has nothing to do with—"

"But you knew her! You knew Mary, and that's all that mattered." Mark stared angrily while pointing at Aaron, who shoved himself toward Mark, with their noses the width of a toothpick apart. Aaron almost threw a punch—the moment was right and ducks were all aligned, in some ways he waited for this moment, for Mark to finally snap. Mark's calm and kind nature was undeniably dazzling in its constant promise of stability. Aaron wanted to show Mark how he truly felt about Mary; in fact, with every outburst Aaron had, a part of him wanted Mark's reaction to be less unpredictable, more rash and outrageous. Aaron wanted a reaction the world would have given him for his appalling actions, and now Mark has finally offered a chance of reality. But Aaron backed up, turned around, and cast his attention to the ground. A pause in time occurred, one of those rare moments where nothing was said but everything was intended, and Mark finally knew.

"Why do you even stay friends with me if I'm a jerk-off to your girlfriend?" Aaron whispered and began to walk to the other side of his living room while rubbing his left forearm. "You'd be better off with just her."

Mark thought for a few seconds before speaking. He was disturbed by Aaron's less aggressive approach. He was confused. Except Mark's infrequent anger was still burning in his heart, defending Mary, and in the tears she'd cried over Aaron's disgusting personality.

"Honestly...I have no idea. Maybe there's some truth to that," Mark said viciously and stormed out. After Mark left, Aaron stood in grief, astonishment, staring at the ground and racing through his thoughts. *He's angry.* Aaron thought. *He blew up from my actions but doesn't even know how much he has pained me.* Aaron Hudson stood there, listening to the indoor fan and hearing the washing machine growl and shake. Then he whispered under his breath, in an unconscious reflex to the pain, a phrase repeated over and over again just like his famous "now you're asking too much" to convince himself the actions were not made up from his own insanity. "I loved her first." A tear from his right eye broke off and ran through those zit-filled cheeks, down the chin, past his skinny complexion, and toward the ground. That face soon fell into a spell of rage, and he stormed out of the house. Except what Aaron didn't see was Mark's large body, hiding behind the screen door from outside. His wonder made him devious and curious, knowing that Aaron had a secret. A secret he now knew, a secret that he may take to his deathbed.

◆◆◆

THE CURTAIN SWUNG OPEN and Mark broke out of his daydream. "Good morning, gentlemen. Sorry to interrupt, but I need to change Mr. Wegman's antibiotics," the young, blonde British nurse muttered. She was unamused, with too many drinks the night before and a dull headache. Aaron sprang up, pulled to this attractive woman. Once the nurse removed her face from the clipboard, she spotted Mark. His hypnotizing tan muscles, well-aged and attractive face. She couldn't stop staring. Who could blame her? Mark was very good-looking. She brightened for the man of her dreams, this man she'd read about in those many romantic novels late in her apartment. *It's him*, she thought. *It's Rodriguez, ready to save me from the orphanage fire and build me a house on the hill where we first met!*

"You mean my best friend?" Aaron began. "Yes, he's here. He was beginning to tell me about how grateful he was that *I* saved his life, but I was having trouble explaining to him how terrible of a condition he was in and how the amazing hospital staff saved his life, like you…nurse. You're a nurse, right? Anyways, may you please help me? Explain?"

She never looked at Aaron, too occupied and flustered from Mark and his (jawline, even five o'clock shadow, sparkling green eyes, broadness, popping chest) appearance, but Aaron's heart was beating too fast to notice anything but the side of her face. *That beautiful cheek*, Aaron thought.

"Umm, thank you, kind gent, but I'll let the doctor explain things."

Aaron melted over her accent and couldn't control his lips from blurting out whatever came to his mind while Nurse Jane Taylor edged over to Mark with flirtatious eyes. "Oh, you're fine, I'm just, just terrible at explaining instances. I can give you examples if that's what you'd like. We probably have lots in common." Aaron nervously giggled with his now clammy hands and blushing face.

"I'm sorry, sir, but I have another patient to tend to," she lied. "I just need to change Mr. Wegman's bag." The nurse finally turned to Aaron, and he saw those blue eyes, those elegant, blue eyes. He calmed down and began to think straight. *Come on, play it smooth, what to say, oh what to say?*

"Yeah, I have to use the bathroom, anyways," Aaron said after two unnatural snorts came out of his mouth from an awkward, hearty laugh. He then left for the bathroom on the other side of their floor, five rooms down to the right and past the front desk on the left. For him, she was too much to handle at once. In the bathroom, Aaron kicked the ground over and over again, rethinking what he'd done wrong and what he could have said instead.

"'I have to use the bathroom'?" Aaron said with a big kick. "'We probably have lots in common,' I said. I should have told her I was the chief of police, how much power I have, she could have been the one!" he said while tearful mortification emerged. Aaron then forced two more embarrassing blows toward the bathroom tile and the wall under the sink. "She's never going to talk to me again!"

Mark, back in the room, was trapped by the beautiful, flirtatious nurse and the embarrassment Aaron had left behind.

Tom leaned toward Mark's left ear and whispered, "Did you see Aaron? He needs more help than every sick person here."

Mark laughed, and then the nurse laughed, breaking the tension in the room. Then she saw Mark's bright smile and knew she had to have him.

"Your friend is really...something," she said, laughing again. Her bright blue eyes showed intent, but Mark never took count of her flirtatious signs.

"Aaron? He's a man full of mysteries."

"I'd like to consider myself a mystery," she said deviously. "For instance, if you could read my mind, you'd be very shy."

"Do you talk in your head as much as you talk right now?" Mark asked.

"Well, I…I guess so," the nurse said puzzled.

"Then I'm glad I can't," Mark's newly scratchy voice stated with great disinterest.

She was shocked by his answer. It stopped her heart. *I'm beautiful, have a cute accent, a cute nose, bright blue eyes, a sexy vocabulary, and a young body. What does anyone else have that I don't? He must mean something else!* she thought. Jane didn't notice his ring; Mark's simple yet severely tarnished silver wedding band had been taken off and placed in a plastic clear bag while in the emergency room by a young yet skinny intern, and then in the early morning another doctor, Dr. Kenny, had slipped the band back on Mark's left index finger before he awoke. When the new antibiotic was attached, and the machine set to pump the medication at a safe, steady pace, she turned to Mark, flipped her beautiful hair, and began to speak again.

One last try. I have to make it right, Jane thought while chewing on her thin nails.

"Now listen to me Mr. Wegman." The nurse let out an adorable giggle. "After this antibiotic, we will discharge you. But you cannot leave until you speak to Dr. Kenny." The nurse fluttered her eyes at Mark, but he never took notice, didn't care. He thought of the name Kenny—it rang in the vast desert of memories, but where? It was as if it were a face misted by time. Now the nurse, who was disturbed by the lack of attention, gave one last signal to win that amazing, beautiful man.

"Or you can stay until seven thirty, that's when I get off." She placed two hands on the bed and stared at the side of Mark's face, trying to be seductive in her basic blue scrubs.

Mark's eyes were loose, but loose from the search through his own thoughts. His reaction to Nurse Taylor's desperate attempt for a date (and maybe even a kiss or two) made it seem as if she were a ghost in a far-removed parallel universe. "No thank you, I need to get back to my wife."

There was a silence of shock and disappointment. Jane felt torn as her hand gently covered her widened mouth with surprise, grief, and embarrassment. She feet like Jessie Wright in *Passion for Fire, Book 3.* Where Perry Jones's memories spark back, and he leaves Jessie, his high school sweetheart, for his wife and children. Then he informs them that he works for the CIA as a sleeper agent, and the evil "Dr. Grits" had taken control of his memory, whisking his mind. But love had brought them back.

"Don't you have another patient?" Mark said with annoyance. Then he finally glanced over, and for a second they locked eyes. She finally saw them, those sparkling, rough, green eyes. Later she would say they seemed menacing, the eyes of a madman, but at that moment in time, Jane thought they looked more like dreamy emeralds, or freshly cut grass in a garden, and the rejection only made her burn with desire. But he was married, it was too late, the act was done. In the end, Jessie had Thanksgiving with everyone and she became an addition to their secret CIA circle, but that wasn't going to happen here.

Jane Taylor apologized as she quickly gathered her equipment, hiding her scarlet cheeks. "Yeah, I almost forgot, my, um, other patient. Cheerio, Mr. Wegman…Cheerio." She began to rush out of the room almost like a child. While Mark sat there thinking about the familiarity of the name Kenny, he drifted back to the thought of Aaron and their history once again, flowing from argument to argument with a smirk on his face, like a middle-aged Walmart employee remembering when he was a football star in high school. Then the events from the night before struck his attention. All at once they rushed back into his memory with deep clarity. The accident, the junkie, his uncontrollable hatred he had for the boy, and the tears he shed before it all. Mark had forgotten the accident so easily, even when Aaron had explained the event no more than twenty minutes ago. His mind drifted off because of the thought of Mary, his constant fear for her safety and preservation from the moment that would inevitably overtake her life. *What have I done?* he thought to himself. Mark remembered that *he* had collided with the ignorant and young owner of that yellow Toyota Camry while enflamed with his own self-agony. And with a simple observation of the event, he knew that the drug enthusiast's body had no cushion for ANY type of impact, especially at the speeds they were at. Was he alive? What happened to Tyler Castillo?

"Nurse," Mark's hoarse voice called. Jane sprang back like a dog hearing their owner's brakes screech in the driveway. She trotted over to stand on the side of his bed, twirling her hair and thinking about yet another supermarket novel called *Passion's Peak.*

"Yeessss?" she said, now understanding that she now had his full attention. The nurse saw those glistening eyes, a man well-aged yet complemented by it, with those gray hairs and faint wrinkles around his cheeks and forehead. She was ready for the confession. She was born ready. *How is he going to word it? Will it be romantic?* she asked herself. *I bet it'll be as smooth as a stone. Just like Donovan in* Love Me, Book 2. When Mark began to speak, the nurse cut off even her thoughts for a more defined sound of his voice.

"Last night, the car accident… What happened to the boy in the other car? The…the Toyota Camry," Mark asked, remembering now that the Camry was also a faint, chipped yellow.

"Who?" she asked with a dazed expression.

"They boy I ran into last night. The car accident?" Mark was dumbfounded from her ignorance, but at that moment he began to wonder if the conversation was worth his time or if it was too risky to discuss. He began to think of insurance, Tyler's medical bill, and the damage done to that horrid mucus-yellow Camry (Maker: Toyota. Model: Camry. Age: Old).

This boy's going to railroad me into the ground. He seemed desperate for money already. Then he'll live in Louis Armstrong's "What a Wonderful World" while overdosing on the money that should be for my wife, Mark thought. *If I'm lucky, I can convict him of his crimes, and the court will see me through as innocent, once the judge and their not-so-blind judgment see the child themselves.* He smiled with a thin grin from his own restful assurance.

The nurse took the smile as a flirtatious grin to her beautiful appearance. At this point, she was desperate. *Play it cool, girl, play it cool,* the nurse thought, almost exactly like Aaron's mental preparation. She gave him an expression that told him she was thinking hard, two fingers on her chin and duck lips, but the beautiful blonde already figured it out. After four years of nursing school and three more in practice, she wasn't in any way dumb.

"Oh, you mean the cancer patient? He's on the top floor, darling."

Nailed it! the nurse thought as she began to walk away, believing he was falling in deep love from her voice. She was correct that he did notice her voice, but instead, he cared more about the content than the presentation.

"Cancer patient?"

She turned around at Wegman's hoarse whisper. "Well yes, gent, he was on his way to the hospital anyways." She giggled, as if to say, *It's okay you ran him over—in fact, it was convenient.* But suddenly, Mark burned with anger, like a wildfire in the desert before the summer rains. Quick and hostile, with scorching alizarin crimson surrounding the area.

"Screw you."

The whisper made the room quiet.

"Excuse me?" Jane unthinkingly asked while stepping a few paces closer to the hallway. Mark's face was different, a newly arisen madness was upon it, something she at first couldn't believe.

"I said screw you!" He stood up in his bed and began to yell. "Get me out of this bed. Take me to the sixth floor." He began to walk off the lifted mattress, pain shooting from all directions of his body. She ran out of the room.

"Mark, get down. You're going to hurt yourself!" yelled Tom.

"Doctor, Doctor, come quick! The patient!" screamed the nurse, but before she could finish, Dr. Kenny rushed past.

"Mark, calm down. You're going to make matters worse." The doctor and Tom pushed him toward the bed while Mark ripped the IV out of his arm without hesitation.

"You are all insane. What have you done?!" he cried and pushed the doctor off. More nurses came to help, crowding the room.

"Nurse. Get some Ativan, now!" yelled Dr. Kenny. One nurse ran off with stealth and agility while Mark continued to yell and scream, pushing and shoving the hospital staff like rag dolls. Aaron finally came out of the hospital bathroom and began to search for that adorable nurse, blocking out the screaming and shrieks from Mark's room with fantasies similar to Jane's. He was finally ready—he'd had a long, nice conversation with himself in the mirror, only figuring out the present situation when he saw the gorgeous nurse frozen with fear. That was the day she quit her flirtatious personality. She came to the conclusion that her appearance made people go insane. Mark was living proof. Then Tom walked up from behind, exhausted beyond belief. His long black hair was gummed up, his plain white shirt was ripped on the collar—revealing a dirty shoulder—and he was missing a shoe that was under Mark's bed. He was even out of breath.

"Nice, nice job, Aaron, thanks for the help," Tom cried with deep sarcasm.

"I have it, Doctor." The floor nurse showed Kenny the needle above the hoard of nurses. Once he nodded, she removed the plastic covering on the tip and jabbed it into Mark's thick arm.

"You are all insane!" Mark yelled. "You are so naïve, how could you make such a terrible mistake?" His voice began to fade, and his reflexes dimmed down. "How could I make such a terrible mistake? How could I be so..." Mark tumbled back on his bed, and tears continued to roll off. "How could I be so...naïve?" All the nurses sighed in relief, and Kenny stared at the floor nurse with a serious look.

"How much did they give you?"

The nurse looked up while she continued to pant. "Four grams, Doctor..."

Kenny glanced at Mark. "He's going to sleep well," he said with a smile. "What was Mark angry about?"

"The car accident, sir," the frightened Nurse Jane quietly remarked from the back of the room. She was shaken and ashamed because of the urine in her scrubs, but Kenny left very gleefully. He walked to another room and yelled with triumph and gratefulness, throwing his fist in the air.

Irony

MARK QUIETLY SQUEEZED HIMSELF into a brightly lit, colorful children's waiting room and strolled inside. The room was quiet, with only a lone ceiling fan lightly buzzing and rattling around. He examined the empty room, desperately searching. He continued until he spotted Mary gently smiling. As Wegman began to quietly jog over, she stood up and did the same. When they got close, he dropped his bulky backpack and she jumped into his arms. They squeezed tight while Mark swung her in a complete circle and passionately kissed her forehead. They then sat down and quietly whispered.

"I'm sorry I was late, did I miss anything?" His right hand slid into hers, which quickly grasped it tight.

"No, I've just been sitting here like you usually do in a waiting room, I guess." Mary nervously laughed.

Mark smiled and quietly responded, "Don't worry, everything will be okay. They will check you in, tell you to lay off the prune juice, and kick you out. We'll be out in thirty with a lollipop and a sticker."

She giggled and gazed up. "You promise?"

Mark stared into her gorgeous brown eyes with a graceful smile.

"I promise."

Mark woke up sweating.

He was in a different room, a much smaller room, and attempted to move but was strapped to the bed by restraints. They were snug. Mark checked his feet. It was the same. The Ativan had worn off, but he wished it hadn't, so he panicked.

"Help, help! Where am I? Get me out! I need to go!"

A nurse peeked her head through the resolution-blue curtains and then quickly pulled herself back. Mark saw her and desperately yelled while panting, his voice much stronger than before, yet still weak, "Wait nurse! Help me, help me, get me out!" The nurse never came back, but instead Tom did.

"Be quiet, man, that doctor is beyond mad," Tom said while taking a chair next to the bed.

"But why tie me up?" Mark wailed. "Morons. I'm not a criminal, I did nothing wrong."

"Stop moving, you're going to hurt yourself again," Tom cried with irritation, yet at the same time with colossal care and love. But Mark continued to squirm in his thin white bed, wrapped by the fat yellow straps. Dr. Kenny finally confidently flew the curtain open and slowly shut it behind himself.

"Dr. Kenny, why am I here?" Mark said. Tom stood up from his chair and offered Kenny the seat willingly. The doctor patiently walked over to his bed and sat in the chair, not even glancing at Tom, who didn't mind and simply leaned on the wall. Mark felt lonelier since Tom was now farther away but ignored the feelings deep in his throat.

"You scared us all, Mark. Not one nurse would dare look at you now." Kenny chuckled. "My entire staff would have walked right through the front door if I didn't do what I did." Everything Kenny told him flew right through his head. Besides his buried feeling of loneliness, Mark was thinking of one thing and one thing only.

"Kenny, please get me out, I have to go."

Kenny patiently watched Mark, and slightly nodded. "Back to your wife? That's understandable." He pulled his stethoscope off his neck and slowly placed it on Mark's heart. He couldn't move. "I'm sorry, Doctor," said Tom. "He is obsessed with his wife." "It's funny, we never got one set of vitals while you've been conscious," Kenny said while again lightly chuckling. "Deep breath, please?" Mark did as he asked while glancing at Tom every other second to see what his expression showed, Tom smiled, and this positivity slightly radiated onto Mark. During the vitals test, Mark never spoke, and while Dr. Kenny and Tom continued to talk, Mark thought of Mary, Tyler, Aaron, and Kenny. Who was this man? And why was Dr. Kenny in such a good mood? Between conversations, all the doctor did was smile, but while he spoke, he seemed to force himself into a serious expression, to somehow hide his already noticeable joy.

"Mark, from the accident last night," Kenny strongly said, while wrapping his stethoscope around his neck, forcing the smile in his pocket and sitting down again. "You had minor head trauma and a pesky whiplash. It was no shorter than a miracle considering the wreckage. The accident should have left you in a much flimsier condition. We found both drivers knocked out cold, and at first came to the assumption that you lost consciousness because of the wreckage. But Mark, we later learned that you lost consciousness not because of the wreckage, but instead because of anxiety." Mark never responded. "Now, if you'd like, there are many counselors in our hospital, all willing to talk to you. And you can thank me later, but I got you an amazing counselor for no cost."

"No," Mark said sharply.

"Mark, you don't have a choice." Kenny never looked away from his eyes. "Do you even understand what has happened? We found you completely totaled, and the car you rear-ended was in an even more severe condition. We found the boy you hit in an unresponsive, comatose state, and we found you in an unconscious, strained sleep. We first believed that YOU intentionally slammed into the boy's car."

"I did not!"

"Let me finish!" Kenny stood up from his chair and Mark silenced. *Fighting wouldn't matter anyway,.* Mark thought, *It'll prove him right, that it's safer with me tied up. It probably is.* Kenny calmed down and sat in his chair. Tom stood in the corner, feeling the awkwardness from the fight and searched around for a way to escape the room.

"Hey guys," Tom awkwardly expressed, "I think It's about to snow, I have to let my cat in." Mark stared at Tom, wanting him to stay.

Kenny talked over Tom, and he felt offended. Kenny didn't care. "Now after we hooked you two up, got blood samples and vitals, we found out that he was severely dehydrated by a bacterial infection called C Diff."

"I didn't know." Mark's words never passed his ears. Kenny continued.

"Since you were on duty during the accident, the district almost fired you. But many men in your department vouched for you. They gave good feedback."

Mark never moved, Kenny paused to see if there would be a reaction, and when there wasn't, he moved on.

"But all we and your department ask for is that you talk to someone. A three-week session all on us, the hospital, all of it is set up. You come in every Monday and Friday." Mark wasn't amused by his talk. "And if you enjoy it, you can pay for more. But we made the first three weeks mandatory."

"And if I don't?" Mark glared up at Kenny; he shot the glare back. "You'll show."

"Why even do this for me? We don't even know each other," Mark said in a harsh tone. But Kenny took the statement differently. His face froze in shock.

"You don't remember me?"

Mark was puzzled.

"The hospital? Your wife?" yelled Kenny, not forcing his shocked face like the grave expressions before. But Mark thought hard—his wife, the petty war, the doctor's diagnosis, and painful reminisces of the unsettling dark pit from this short life—but he found no memory. "Dr. Kenny, it's not your business to interfere with my personal life. And don't talk about my wife, ever!" He glanced up again, forcing his eyes to meet the old and gray doctor. Kenny wasn't thrilled. It made him grieve painfully and burn with rage, but there was mostly despair and failure. Mark's eyes began to well up with tears. He thought of it all, because of that doctor's carelessness of words, forcing him to recount his entire past.

What an inconsiderate, careless doctor, he thought, *stupid, worthless man. Why do I remember so often? They sicken my mind and haunt me every second. I don't understand why I unconsciously torment myself with these devilish memories I call the past! He did this to me, how does he know me? He's making me feel like a fool, with his files given by the hospital, that's how he knows, that's how he knows! In reality, he's clueless. Clueless people are cruel.* Mark continued to cry, and his memory invaded his mind like a bacterial disease. One cell at a time, until the entire body was useless.

While he daydreamed, a nurse popped her head out of the curtain. "Doctor?" she asked quietly. "Is Mr. Wegman going to be discharged?"

Kenny slowly looked up, wiping away the water in his eyes to see the nurse, slightly shocked from his emotion. "I want a scan on him before we let him go. Now please, take a break."

Tom finally interrupted from the corner. "Yeah, I'll take a break, too."

Mark's breathing was getting louder as he began to silently yet violently cry. There were two sides to a coin, different sides to a mountain. In his past, there were moments when the sun seemed to kiss your skin, and spring's scents and sounds seemed to never end. But there were other moments when you never left your knees from prayer, and your spine never stopped its icy tingles. If you were pained enough from weak knees and tired eyes, those days would come back and haunt you again, more than the barbecues on the Fourth of July and finding your lost dog at the pound. He couldn't help but remember. To remember the clumsy free-willed doctor, a middle-aged mother who was needed here. They very desperately needed her. Mark was seventeen, Mary was seventeen, and the day was May 24, 1985.

◆◆◆

"GOOD EVENING MARY, EVENING Mark." The doctor shook both outstretched hands. "How's Aaron?"

Mark quickly responded while shaking. "Oh he's good."

"Really? Anything new?"

Mary interrupted in a delicate, tiny voice. "He got his first girlfriend."

"I thought the day would never come! It's about time he got those sticks out of his caboose." The couple laughed. Mark gazed up from his splitting sides.

"Yeah well, she's a keeper. They're very happy." He smiled, and Mary jumped from her shy spell.

"She keeps his anger down as well!"

"He gave me the heebie-jeebies. That boy needed a chill pill." She smiled, and her rosy cheeks popped out from under her bright blue eyes. She was their mother, and they wouldn't deny it. They all sat down.

"Wow," Mark added in. "You need to take a chill pill on your usage of idioms." Everyone in the room burst out with hysterical laughter.

"Oh, but that's my schtick," said the young and pudgy Dr. Kennedy while grinning and winking in Mark's direction.

"Are you ready, Mary?"

The couple grabbed each other's hands simultaneously, frightened in different ways.

"Is it bad, Kennedy?" Mary said.

"I confess, we should have brought you in sooner." The nurse's face was blank.

Mary's lips began to shiver. *I wasn't ever going to leave without my death note.* She thought. *Just like my mother, and my mother before her.*

"It's hereditary."

He came in close and whispered in her ear. Her lip calmed and her heart slowed. Kennedy looked at Mary as her eyes glared and darkened.

"Mary, don't make the same mistake your mother did." A rage came from Mary's eyes—her tongue was going to defend her deceased mother. Kennedy caught the powerful rage in her eyes, but it subsided. *She is right. If I make the same mistake, I'll die,* Mary thought.

"Your mother and grandmother died from colon cancer at very young ages. And since it's passed down by generation, you are at high risk even at seventeen. So with your consent, and your father's consent—"

"He's on another business trip."

"I figured." Kennedy paused for a second, not to dramatize the moment but to glance at Mark. He knew what she was going to ask, and he continued to rub Mary's hand. Kennedy continued her speech. "Consent for annual colonoscopy tests."

"But I just had one done!" Mary yelped and wiggled nervously while pulling her clothes down, like worms had just crawled up her skirt.

"Mary, Mary, look at me." She quickly looked up and squeezed Mark's hand, and he squeezed it back. Mary understood but continued to stare into his eyes. *Okay, Mary, I'll ask her to leave,* Mark thought.

"Can you please leave us for a second to talk things over?" Mark asked, smiling calmly at Kennedy with his controlled voice. She nodded and left the room. He then drew attention to Mary, who was in a silent panic, gazing at Mark's lap. Her dark hair covered that beautiful face in a very gentle, fragile way.

She's an angel, Mark thought. *God lost an angel.*

"Mary, it's okay, nothing's happened yet. How do you know what life brings?" She never looked up, afraid that even a single glance at Mark, like the space shuttle *Challenger,* would burst with emotion. "How can you see the entire picture? We both still exist, our hearts still exist, and they'll continue to do so. That's all that matters." Mark held her hand up; her position stayed. "See this? My hand's warm, and so is yours." He placed his second hand over theirs, and Mary quickly looked up. Their eyes greeted each other, hers glistened with fright, but because of his, the fright ran numb, she saw his strength, and she gained some from it. "We give off CRAZY amounts of heat. More now 'cause you're panicking, which makes me panic, and then I'm forced to hold our hands in the air like a couple of lunatics." Mary grinned, then followed it with a loud giggle, and placed her second hand over theirs. Mark felt its touch. "I guess I'm a lunatic, too." She sniffled up a few tears, but her eyes told him what to do, it told him she needed his words, his love.

"My point is that if we can still warm each other's hands, even slightly, we don't have to worry, because we still have each other. I always look into your eyes and quietly say in silence, 'I'm home.' You know why? Because you're the beauty I need and the friend I crave. I look up to God sometimes and thank him for this angel. So don't you DARE cry for a fate that's not yours." Mark let out a lone tear, and Mary's fragile eyes couldn't handle the pressure. She began to cry. This would be the only time Mary ever saw tears on Mark's face.

"So from now on, if you're ever upset, or shaking like you were, hold my hand, feel the heat blazing from my heart. We are both alive! Never have an inch of doubt! God is with us." He kissed their hands.

"And if I'm not there, call me. It doesn't matter where I am! I will travel back to you. I will travel back to you! Your hand is worth more than every dime I've ever made and second I've spent. Because holding hands is a reminder to remind you that I'm still alive and you're still alive, so there's hope no matter what happens in life. Loving and caring unconditionally. You're my Hand Mitten, cause you keep them warm, you cradle and fit in mine, and I fit in yours." Mark's voice cracked from the tears running down his face. "And…and you'll always be mine, eternally. You'll never be alone! We will take that stupid test together, every year, the same operation table. Until we realize that you're your father's daughter, with your mother's warm smile."

She smiled and finally spoke from under her tears. "Hopefully not. I don't want my mother kissing my boyfriend." They both gently laughed.

"There is it, you look better that way. Keep your gorgeous smile." They hugged for minutes.

Kennedy walked in at one point with a paper and a pen but unfortunately caught them in the middle. So, Kennedy did what she'd do in any scenario—quickly run out in fear of ruining the moment but casually slip on the doorstep. Ironically, the couple never noticed her tumble, her strangely silent somersault away. Kennedy stood up soon after and calmly wiped off the fall. When she came back with the documents the second time, she handed them to Mary and pointed to where she needed her father to sign. Mark picked a few forms as well, though he waited until he was eighteen and held the test costs on his own to save the expense from his parents.

The next test was scheduled eleven months from then, and they went in together, hungry, as the test asked for no food within twenty-four hours. When they walked in, they held each other's hands, and when given anesthesia, the doctors had to separate their grasp. Every test was the same. The doctors separated them. The doctors always, no matter what, separated them.

Shades of Blue on the Yellow Canvas

MARK RAN THROUGH A PET scan and an EEG before he finally left the hospital. They studied every reading, and Kenny called in Aaron. Tom listened for a while, talked to them, but never truly got a voice in their conversation. Mark stood outside, soaking in the rays from the sun, wearing a Metallica T-shirt and a plaid pair of shorts, which Aaron had picked up from the house. There was a pale brown medical wrap around his arm from the IV and a neck brace, which he threw off when no one saw. He didn't speak much but was still in thought, still wondering why and how everything happened, both in the past and the night before. He was anxious to return to his wife but disturbed by another thought, the thought of that boy, his cancer, his life. He could already see his wife, seeing her run into his arms outside of the hospital gate, crying out of fright that he might have died from this terrible collision.

She loves me, I am loved, that's all that matters. I need her. She needs me. I can't ever leave her. If I do then my life would be over, everything I've done would be pointless, the promise would be broken. With that broken, there would arise a broken man. There are too many broken fools out in the world. I have to fill the spots. I must be on top. The power of wisdom is good, but the power of knowledge is great.

Mark stood there in silence. Minutes passed. His words were none, but thoughts were many. One thought was of his wife, a very joyful memory recalled whenever in stress. It was a habit to fade toward it.

They were young, at the beginning of their high school relationship. Mary's mother was out of town with her husband, and Mary had the responsibility of keeping the house safe, feeding the pets, watering the plants, and everything else. But this time invited Mark over as well.

He remembered every moment on that day, the heat from the July sun, the type of flowers he brought, the way Mary did her hair, her beautiful smile and vibrant cocoa brown eyes.

◆◆◆

"MARK, I'M SO GLAD you're here!" Mary jumped into his arms, leaving her toes lightly grazing the ground. Mark caught her with one hand, holding flowers in the other, and kissed her head while he dropped his bag.

"Missed you," Mark said.

"How was JROTC?"

"Terrible."

"Why?"

"Because you weren't there." Mark looked down to see her gazing up. They sealed the moment with a kiss. Mary showed him around the house. Every bit of furniture or decoration was perfectly placed, and there wasn't a trace of dust on the floor. The living room had a lone white couch and two armchairs, symmetrical in a way that seemed almost unreal. She explained how her parents would sometimes sit there and talk for hours when they were both home at the same time, since her mother had a day job as a secretary at the city bank and her father as an international entrepreneur. Except now her mother had stopped working per Mary's father's request, so these moments occurred more frequently.

Her father sold the popular Plant Pants, a special type of paper wrapped around any houseplant to supposedly give them better growing conditions. Printed out in the look of denim jeans, with cute little pockets and a zipper in the middle, it was a very good idea. Mary told Mark it was a scam, how people would believe anything if you told them like it was the truth. He never forgot that phrase and always thought of the possibility whenever he talked with Aaron or any classmates. But whenever her father was home, he'd be present physically, but mentally unavailable, since the gaps in his life were now spent also fighting for a degree in medicine, a new obsession.

Everyone knew it was impossible. The concept of a degree was time, which he never had. Except Mary seemed to love the idea, supporting him but not minding his absence.

"Dr. Kenny," Mary said while laughing. "It sounds so weird. I can never see him as someone who would be in a position with so much stress," she gleefully admitted.

She showed Mark the kitchen. Everything was neatly placed in a special spot, with almost no trace of anyone ever occupying it. She told him almost no family meals were made, just heated in the microwave. But sometimes she'd drive over to the corner store and come home with bags and bags of groceries. Then she'd cook something wonderful to eat while her parents were out, like a batch of muffins or enchiladas.

Lastly, Mary showed him her room. It was on the second floor. You'd run up the white wooden stairs and make an immediate right into a brightly colored room filled with paintings on the walls, ceilings, and floors, with paintbrushes tossed around canvases of paintings that all carried different colors splattered uniquely, creating beautiful images of sunsets, people, or abstract patterns. She began to talk while pacing around the room.

"My entire life, they tried bottling me up, keeping me neat and clean like them. Always showed me how to make my bed, fold my clothes, organize my closet, and the benefit of alphabetizing darn near everything. When I was little, my parents limited me to one poster, and it couldn't be bigger than a six-by-eleven-inch size—their words, not mine. So I chose a painting by Wassily Kandinsky, called *Composition Eight.* Its random, spontaneous lines amazed me that someone had an idea to draw such...such—chaos!" Mary passionately wondered. "There wasn't a reason for each individual line and shape, there wasn't an explanation, it was just...there. And in the end, people loved it. They were drawn to the chaos and the patternless disarray like a whale to a school of krill, drawn to the artwork because of their lack of control. So I begged my parents for art lessons in first grade, and in third grade they finally allowed me, believing after a week or so I'd let it go. A year passed, and I finally got a drawing on the fridge. My parents had to buy a magnet from the store." She chuckled. "When that happened, everything changed—they let me paint all my walls white and take out the carpet to replace it with plaster. I've drawn and painted over the walls for years and years, never being satisfied with what I drew, which scares me."

Mark looked up from admiring the work. "Why is that?"

She quietly stared at him. "Because I might actually be their daughter."

Mark continued to look around until a question fell through his lips. "What inspires you to draw?"

"My emotions," she said without struggle. "How I feel at the moment. When I'm upset it helps me cope, but when I'm happy it helps me celebrate." Mark looked around until he found a photo of a sick, bald woman, with a lone tear streamed down her face. The only colors used were different shades of blue. "Maybe it's not good to look at all of my art." She laughed nervously and took it away from his possession.

Mark picked up another painting. It was a portrait of two young swans in the middle of a tight forest, kissing on a lake, while a sunset full of bright orange and pink rays reflected off the water from the sky, with many different animals from the dense forest never noticing either the swans or the sunset.

"When did you draw this one?"

Mary walked over and looked up at him.

"When I met you."

◆◆◆

MARK CONTINUED TO WAIT while that memory buzzed in his ears. Emotions rising. Now these were sour memories from a distant past. Tom snuck over and sat with Mark while he tapped his shoes and felt that ring through those large fingers, an item he normally fiddled with when under stress.

"Man, they won't stop talking," Tom said while lying back on the bench. "They're going to roll themselves to their graves if they continue worrying like that."

Mark never looked over, and this time there was no pride from the thought of Tom. He was too absorbed and responded quietly, as if his response were shameful.

"I wonder how Tyler's doing."

"Tyler?" Tom asked calmly.

"Yeah!" Mark looks over with distraught. "It's all my fault, Tom. If he dies, I killed him."

"Shut your mouth, Mark, he's not dead," Tom corrected while rolling his eyes. "Well, not yet. Go talk to him. Mary's fine, she's an independent woman and can manage herself for five measly minutes. Also, trust me, she would want you to check up on Tyler, and worrying about your wife doesn't make her any better." Tom patted Mark on his shoulder, then shot his arms to the sky. "Don't think, just go!" Mark finally ran back into the hospital. He didn't think just like Tom said, but Mark ran too fast, and the ring that he fiddled with slipped through his fingers onto the bench.

"Mark! Your doughnut!" Tom yelled with hysterical laughs of joy. "I didn't mean she wanted to be alone forever, you goof!"

He felt pride again.

Mark ran to the elevator, where a few were gathered, and went for the button, both were pressed. *I can't wait,* he thought. So he ran to the stairs and flung the door open with emotional exaggeration. The door yelled out a loud squeak, all eyes were on him, but he didn't care about their thoughts. Mark ran up six floors, beat the elevator by a few pointless seconds, and bumped into two doctors and a floor nurse before he spotted the room. Memories flashed through his eyes, but he ignored them and slowly walked toward the single door. He was out of breath, but there was no time to take notice; Mark shouldn't think at all. There was a security screen that locked the door from the small waiting room and a camera. *Maybe they won't let me in because of how I look. I must look pleasant if they'll ever allow me inside,* Mark thought. *These fragile, sick children are too precious. Too precious.* But he heard a noise—it was the locks from the door, unlatching from both vertical ends. Mark thought he'd never hear that noise again.

The door swung open. When the room was visible, he scanned every feature over in the first three seconds. The room, with white walls, the patterned ground of red-and-blue two-by-two-foot tiles, hurt. The nurse's scrubs were covered with fun, exciting patterns. The smell of bleach, the cold temperature running through the air. The playroom filled with toys sterilized thousands of times to keep them sanitary, the chalk drawings on the mirrors of SpongeBob, TMNT, and other childhood role models. Alarms and lights from the isolated neighboring apartments roared for the nurse's aide by a button pushed by a patient from inside. For whenever in pain.

"It's a jailhouse," Mark whispered, and a tear ran down his cheek. Then he finally saw the nurse who promptly let him inside. An older lady with blue-green eyes opened the door, and she grinned.

"Mark! I can't believe you're here!" The old woman did what she could to reach him but wasn't fast or fit in anyway. *Who is she?* he thought. *She must be a nurse I once knew, she must be!* The nurse opened her arms. Mark accepted the hug and dug his head into her shoulder. The only other woman he'd ever hug, but he never remembered any nurses being so old and fragile. Her thin white hair and old eyes. The white-haired woman's job was clearly to be the front desk clerk for the department, a position with far less action and skill. This was a perfect spot for an old woman whose time in the medical world had expired. There wasn't any doubt that she was someone from his past, someone he couldn't remember, although her face was candy to his past-driven eyes. He also saw how afterward his face was covered in tears—Why was this? He thought of how disappointing this repetitiveness of wiping off the water from his eyes was, and quickly wiped them off like they were a disease, maybe so. The woman acted as if his tears were never present, as if she were blind. The white-haired lady was far from this.

"Why have you come to visit now? Wow, Mark, you haven't aged at all! And I must have shrunk, because you seem much taller! Is your shoe size still a size fifteen? I bet you still lift, don't you?"

Mark was shocked and confused. The woman continued to speak and speak as if she didn't expect answers. She knew Mark as well as he knew himself and looked him up and down multiple times while smiling through her rattle can of a voice, with an unnatural abundant amount of energy that didn't seem to ever give. Although her speaking gave him peace, Mark didn't care that he didn't know who she was.

All he knew was that she had aided him and his wife somewhere in the past. This gave him peace.

"I actually came to see Tyler Castillo," Mark stated with a light grin, which he fought because of the thought of Tyler. The woman with thin white hair lost her smile as quickly as she found it and stepped a foot back with one hand on her heart, tears in her eyes. Mark was also hit with shame, though hoarding it in his throat, still attempting to seem motivated. The response from the frail white-haired lady was far less talkative than her last, as all she did was point a finger to a younger nurse, and when Mark turned she quickly walked off not to be found.

"Excuse me, miss?"

"Yes sir, do you need help?" The young nurse turned around, not knowing of anything that was said before. He saw her face, the brown hair mixed with the young features and short height. A familiar face on a stranger. *Ignore it Mark, ignore it*, he thought.

"Yes, ma'am. I'm looking for Tyler Castillo's room." Mark found that she frowned as well. Tyler seemed to be a subject that wasn't to be spoken of.

"How do you know him?"

Mark scratched his head and nervously smiled.

"I'm a family friend, ma'am."

The woman wished to find the older nurse for guidance, but she was gone. Fresh from college, young with knowledge and rules, the small and fit woman was lost as to what action to perform in this situation. The small woman looked up at Mark and smiled anxiously.

"He's in ICU, sir. He can't accept visitors," the brunette lied.

"When will he be out?"

"We don't know, maybe I can get his parents to—"

"No. No, ma'am, that's okay," Mark stated frantically, and with Tyler's name as a sensitive subject in the air, the air grew thick with glares. "I'll just...go."

Mark walked through the bolted door and the blank expressions into the tiny waiting room next to the elevators and overlooking the town, thinking of the mistakes he'd made. This time the first one was Tom.

Tom, I'm so sorry. If only I could protect you better, you'd still be alive, Mark thought. He sat in a chair and covered his face with those huge hands, peace gone and joy used up. He began to weep again. Minutes later, the frail white-haired nurse walked toward the waiting room. She sat in the chair to the left of him and didn't speak. He thought of his decision, if this boy was worth the effort, the time. Mary was worth his time, she always was. Tom was worth his time; he was like a son. *Why is this child important?*

Then the woman began to speak in her dry, ancient voice.

"You know, throughout my entire pediatric oncologist career, our patients either came in strong, with ignorance of what's truly happened, or scared, with knowledge of the truth. But when they left, the ones who knew nothing in the beginning knew everything and lost that strength they had. However, whoever came with no strength and knew everything just had anger in the end. Now the question is, which one are you?" The nurse looked up with her fragile eyes.

"My wife thought she knew everything when she got sick, but she didn't understand at all. That's why she has strength, and that's where she's weak."

"How is that a weakness?"

"Because she's oblivious!" he cried while shaking his fist at the ground. He whispered, "She doesn't know."

"Ignorance isn't always a weakness." The old woman touched Mark's shoulder. He lashed it off.

"How? Tell me how!"

"When knowledge is the enemy."

"When is knowledge the enemy?"

"When the truth becomes too much to bear, ignorance is strength and knowledge is the enemy. Even if it's fake." The woman closed her eyes, as if she began to hold in emotions of her own. She was the only one who didn't freeze when Mark spoke of Mary, although the woman began to half ignore Mark's existence, as if she were attempting to purge him out of her mind. Then he realized that she wasn't attempting to convince him but continuing to convince herself of something far deeper.

"I will walk you over and wait outside. Don't you dare mess this up, and I mean it, you bugger."

He couldn't speak. Mark was struck with understanding of who the nurse was and fell in shock. A person only found in memories until today, *I found her. I can't believe it.* Mark stood up, and a dull pain from the wreck shot up his back, but he ignored it and walked around. The old nurse, washed up from the unavoidable curses of time. Those years lost, the years that felt like minutes, seconds, maybe time had never passed. Some feel like it was yesterday, maybe yesterday happened twenty-four years ago, anything was possible, even for them. Even for Mary's family doctor, an eyewitness to Mark's marriage, from the beginning to what seemed like the end.

"Kennedy?"

She reacted to the name—a tear fell from her face, and a smile unfolded. She looked up from under her shameful hands, and the mothering face showed once again, a face forgotten by everyone but Mark. It was only yesterday.

"Hello, Mark."

The Telemarketer

WHEN MARY'S MOTHER DIED, the outside gossip circle froze. An unexpected phenomenon occurred. A woman with meningitis passed, and on the same day was confirmed with no trace, but instead colon cancer. The funeral was held in a wealthy, green-lawn cemetery, with a short sermon but a large attendance. Neighbors, relatives, and friends all gathered to mourn around the lifeless body in an oak casket. The sun was covered, and the old pastor with his white ceremonial gown spoke with ease, another funeral in his eyes. The noises consisted of sniffling and crying, but Mary stood in the back of the memorial with Mark, gently holding his hand. Unlike the others, Mary didn't weep, cry, or even mourn while the pastor asked for anyone to say a few words on behalf of her dead mother. She didn't shake when her all-black-attired aunt was taken off the podium by Mary's round, bald uncle as she burst with tears for her younger sister. Her gaze wasn't affected when a young, close friend began to speak about how much her mother changed the world with her beautiful smile and admirable personality. When her mother had passed three days earlier, Mark drove over to Mary's house in a rush and arrived to find Mary speechless, seeming to have a mind occupied with absolutely nothing, as if her mentality decided to abort from the body, leaving the remaining parts to only comply with basic functions and tasks that would continue her natural lifestyle from before with the least amount of effort. She was sitting in a white bench outside their front door when he came, with a blank expression and a straight, awkward posture. She gave him a light hug and tucked her hand into his robotically. The next day, her father sent a formal letter to Mark. He told him that Mary would "enjoy your presence at the funeral, on Wednesday at 3:00 p.m." So two days later, Mark came in with a worn coal-black suit and dirt-brown sneakers from his father's closet. All Mary did was hug his waist gently and fragilely hold his hand, again without anything special in movement or emotion. Aaron told Mark he wouldn't miss it for the world, sounding as sincere and supportive as he could, but he never came. Mark continued to watch the main road into the cemetery crowded with engraved stones. When her father stepped onto the podium, she spoke for the first time in three days. Her voice was not soft, but controlled and clearheaded.

"She knew."

Mark quickly turned his head toward Mary. She never looked away from her father's formal speech, watching him cry for the first time in her life, even before his speech.

"What did she know?"

"She knew about the cancer, the risk." Her voice was angry, clenching his hand harder than before. Mark knew what she wanted him to ask, so he did.

"Why didn't she do anything?"

"Because she was a coward. She was afraid of the treatment."

"I'm sure that wasn't the case, Mary."

"She told me herself!" Mary yelled under her breath. There was a period where they only watched the speech as Mr. Kenny continued to sob into the skinny microphone, projecting it through tiny square church speakers. However, every emotional word was comprehendible, from both a combination of Mr. Kenny's adequate speaking skills and the simple idea that sorrow understands sorrow. Then Mary spoke again.

"Our entire family covered for her, even the doctor." She squeezed his hand. "I've never felt so terrible in my life." Mark went down on two knees and pushed her into a tight hug. She began to cry aggressively. Angry tears burned on his chest like battery acid.

He murmured softly, "I'm sorry honey," and closed his eyes. Mark wanted to cry, but didn't, and in fact did not until seven years later, tears that landed on Mary's shoulder while they both sat on the carpet, the same day they met Christian. "I got you, shh, I got you, I'm not going anywhere. You're safe now." She shed bitter tears with loud whimpers. Many looked over and assumed she was mourning like the others. In a way, Mary was. Some stared and whispered into each other's ears; others ignored her and the noises she made, being thankful they were not the daughter to the polished oak casket.

"If only Aaron came," Mark whispered and lightly chuckled. "He'd cheer us up. "

"That's a joke. All he does is make me feel like a tool," she snickered. Mark laughed again, knowing beforehand what she would say.

"Yeah, it was a joke, hun."

"He means well, and when I'm not around, he's nice, but he just needs to accept me." She let go and found herself staring into his eyes. Later that day, Mark would barge into Aaron's trailer; he would almost seem to be waiting for him to arrive.

"He will, and when he does, we'll celebrate!" Mark hugged her again, and she began to cry, although softer. Words didn't have to be said—she missed her mom.

◆◆◆

KENNEDY WALKED MARK TOWARD Tyler's room, through the patterned hallways and the smell of bleach, but when he arrived, there was a cart full of gloves and aprons. Kennedy told him to gown up, so he did, very used to the procedure. Before Mary was quarantined, this was what Mark did. When Mark was finished, he had on a pair of large dark purple gloves, a traffic-cone-yellow apron, and a plastic mask wrapped around his head. He knocked on the single door and grabbed the cold metal handle. There were rules to the door: it couldn't be open for too long or the room would begin to screech. Every room was equipped with their own air-conditioning units to keep the patients away from others who could pose a threat. Many didn't have immune systems, so this system was critical, and no one was able to visit—this is all Mark was told as Kennedy repeatedly glanced to each end of the hallway. Mark somehow knew that once he entered the room, she would leave with an air of ignorance. Kennedy would pretend that nothing of the abnormal happened on the sixth floor, and if asked about the event would curse her own mother's grave before risking herself.

"You have five minutes, don't touch him." Kennedy rushed with a harsh whisper. "He has neutropenia, and if he isn't up for talking, don't blabber off. Leave him alone! He also might be asleep. Tyler just got out of a surgery. Very lucky, but that doesn't mean he's okay. You understand the basics, right, Mark?"

He turned to his right. "Yes."

"Then go on!" She motioned him.

"Wait. Kennedy."

"Yes?"

"Why was Tyler driving to the hospital? What did he need?"

She whipped her face toward his, then turned away just as brisk. She tapped her foot like a hummingbird, crossed her arms, and let out a long sigh.

"Morphine. He needed morphine but ran out and couldn't wait. So he called us to admit himself. Now please, go inside before I change my mind." Her words rushed out like a fountain as she led him again toward the door.

He opened it with caution as his heart slammed against his skin. Kennedy folded her arms again with haste, tapping her foot and feeling a force of dread. She knew Mark wasn't the same, though she didn't know how or why. Yet forces she knew too well pushed her against her own will. Kennedy gave him what he wanted for the chance of finding peace with her own mind. Mark was the root to her haunting guilt, and seeing him again with a request gave her hope that the past could be forgotten.

"Hello? Tyler?" He peeked inside the room.

Everything was familiar. Across was a thick, semi-opaque sliding glass door covering the bathroom. On the right, farthest away, was a mini whiteboard bolted to the wall, with Expo markers of three colors on the metal holder below. It had the name of the patient, the caregiver, the date, and a blob of scribbles from a child, some child that has been there before him. In the top middle of the wall on the right was a miniature television, angled low by the anchors from the wall, playing Fox News on mute. Underneath was a miniature plastic chrome fridge. There was a half-eaten plate of fruit, with a green tea and a woman's purse. Closest to the door was a medical supply bin full of syringes, bandages, port-a-cath needles, tubes, and almost everything needed for the nurse locked in their shelves. On the other side was a sink, with a hand-sensitive paper towel and soap dispenser above. There was a dresser against the left wall next to the bed, full of clothes and notebooks. On top was a clock, holding up a row of books by authors from Jim Gaffigan to Ernest Hemingway, and another notebook face down, with a pen on top. Someone brought all of this in one day's time.

On the far side of the bed was a long pole with two brains attached, which were machines that controlled the flow of medications through the IV. Two brains alone were bad news, one on top of the other, pumping antibiotics, IV nutrition, a newly placed blood bag, and saline fluids for hydration, all hanging on the pole with casual existence. Above that was a screen hanging from the wall, monitoring blood pressure, pulse ox, and heart rate by different colored numbers on the screen. The typical heart rate line ran from side to side, with the noise dimmed down to almost a silent whisper. All body activity was monitored. Directly in front of Mark was a thin couch that flattened into a bed; it had a thick royal blue soccer blanket with a pillow and a bag of makeup, all spontaneously thrown into different positions on the couch. Above was a window, overlooking the gigantic plum-purple Arizona mountains. Between the bathroom and the couch was another bag that seemed to have just recently arrived. It was brown, with two leather straps and a razor sticking out of the side pocket.

Tyler saw the man peeking from the door and began to speak.

"Are you a Jehovah's Witness?"

"Um, no?"

"Telemarketer?"

"No?"

"Then come in, friend! Just drop the pizza off on the side of the bed."

Mark walked in. Tyler was drugged without doubt—every motion was very slow and clumsy, as if he were made of licorice.

"Sorry, buddy, I don't have a pizza." Mark checked his pocket and found no pizza.

"Good, I didn't order one!" He laughed hysterically and rocked in his plastic bed. Tyler had a neck brace and a cast on the left leg and arm, with bandages in multiple spots, including the head, body, and knees. The skinny body fit into the small twin-size bed. There were many thin blankets from the hospital, but he wore nothing but scrubs. *What have I done?* Mark thought. *What have I done?* He closed the door and slowly walked toward the bed.

"How do you feel?"

"I was in pain, but I got morphine. Then the morphine made me hyper. I'm better, but..." Tyler smiled and looked down.

"What?" Mark asked. Tyler hesitated to speak about himself, almost identical to the way the nurses reacted before.

"I don't enjoy it, though, any of it."

"What don't you like, the hospital?"

"No, the drugs." Tyler looked up and began to laugh again. Mark was struck back and surprised that he'd share something like that with a stranger, and so quickly. But he also felt guilty of his judgment on Tyler, guilty that he assumed the exact opposite.

"Why not?"

"It's been a while since I've felt normal. To walk and feel no pain in your feet, to laugh and feel no blisters in your mouth, to think without drugs fogging your thoughts. Those are the three big ones. I wish I could walk, and I wish I could think, but hey, at least I can laugh." Tyler let out a loud laugh. "So I'm blessed, even if it's a fake drugged laugh, I'm blessed by God." Tyler fell into another laugh, cradled his head from a headache, yawned, and laughed again because of his yawn. Mark's eyes fell in anger.

"But you're, you're bedridden, drugged, sick, and hospitalized, how can you laugh?"

Tyler was silent, as Mark, his anger toward God, was shown. Then Tyler laughed again and spoke with ease.

"Because I have God."

"But how do you know God's not the one who gave you cancer and the inability to walk? What if he's letting people drown, starve, and die?" Mark began to race with memories after yelling across the room. He wasn't understanding what Tyler's condition was. Tyler spoke, this time very calm and sober, while enjoying the fact that someone was yelling at him.

"If God is the enemy, why are we alive? What's the point of being the founder of life and death? To just create and destroy, to give life to a chicken and then murder it. A hypocritical God, a God who looks down on the world, on his children and tortures them, no, that's Satan. A God who says he loves but hates the same person at the same time, no, that's Lucifer. And if you're still not certain, then how can death lose its sting? If God is the founder of death, then how can I rise above?" He closed his eyes and lay back down. "Where, O death, is your victory? Where, O death, is your sting? The sting of death is sin, and the power of sin is the law. But thanks be to God! He gives us the victory through our lord Jesus Christ. Therefore, my dear brothers and sisters, stand firm. Let nothing move you. Always give yourselves fully to the work of the lord, because you know that your labor in the lord is not in vain." Tyler opened his eyes. Mark was shocked from the kid's knowledge and whispered, "But why do I suffer?"

"I don't know, friend, I'm only sixteen. Please don't ask me." Tyler smiled gently with weary eyes. "I don't understand your struggle, your life. You said it yourself, don't ask me."

Mark was silent, with wide eyes and a frightened feeling of accusation on his shoulders. The boy knew he was the officer. The officer who slammed in the back of his Camry, accused, cursed, wanting to sue and arrest. As well as the man who put him in surgery, two casts, a fracture, and countless bruises, then later Tyler's death. But through the helpfulness of Mark's quick thinking toward Tyler's interaction, he knew an apology would have been worse. He could have apologized, told Tyler the situation would have changed if he only knew. But Mark didn't, that wasn't valued—pity would murder the joy. When a normal life was wanted, pity was the real fault. The plentiful saw him as a disability, a boy with a disease, to look at and pray you never become. People either avoided contact or craved it. It looks beautiful on your resume. *I helped cancer patients.* Or to gain a few followers, just caption it this: *My best friend.*

A selfish game played by the plentiful, but soon enough they leave. All who are left are those in public, who see the boy as a truth that can destroy *their* happiness, their day. Or just someone to make you feel blessed, glad that you're not him. Thank you, Lord, that I am not *him.*

So why didn't Tyler tell Mark when he was pulled over? Why didn't he take the benefit others believe is the sweetness of cancer? The slip, three meaningful words that slide you through hallways, lines, VIP rooms, and events. His decision explained itself, so Mark smiled instead.

"Tyler, you look like crap."

"Not as bad as you. Wait, that's your face, old man." Tyler laughed. Mark quietly placed two hands over his heart.

"Don't surprise me. You might just give me a heart attack."

"The ER is on the second floor, third door to the right."

"And you would know, did your shedding make anyone slip?"

"At least my hair will grow back. When yours falls out, don't come crying to me."

"It's okay, I'll find your hair and glue it on mine."

"Gross, haven't you heard of a wig?" Tyler laughed.

Mark followed and sat on the bed. He then saw a basket full of random gifts. Many people come through the cancer center and give gifts to the children, usually small knickknacks or cheap presents. The baskets are typically for the younger children, around three to ten, past that age the little things never caught their eyes. Teenagers were usually left out when it came to the general public, but nurses and foundations like Make-A-Wish usually covered for the loss of attention. Unique visitors occasionally walked in and passed out books. Candy was given as well, but most patients usually couldn't eat. In the basket was a deck of cards, a very generic brand sticking out of the side, next to a slinky and a superhero coloring book. The basket must have been dropped off when Tyler was in surgery. He picked it up and began tearing off the clear plastic.

"You want to see a magic trick?"

"Is it good?"

"You tell me."

"I guess I will tell you. Especially if it's bad."

Tyler smiled heroically while Mark shuffled and bent the stiff cards. The boy laughed, placed a hand on his head, then laughed again.

"Do you have a Sharpie?" Mark spun around and snatched an Expo marker, asserting his own question. He then took a card and showed it to Tyler, who gently smiled.

"What card is this?"

"King of Hearts?"

"Yes, now write your initials on the card."

"Steady it on my cast!"

Mark did what he said; when those initials were written, he snatched the card back and showed Tyler another.

"Now what card is this?"

"The King of Spades."

"Good, now I'm going to write my initials with a message." Mark took the marker and wrote his initials in the bottom right of the card, next to the spade. "What should I write?" Mark looked up, smiled and scratched his head.

"I don't know."

"It can be anything!"

"Really?"

"Yeah, whatever you want."

"Sexy beast." Tyler smiled and Mark wrote the message on the card, with the heart monitor occupying the silence. When he finished, he gave Tyler the King of Hearts.

"Okay, now look it over and make sure it's your card." Tyler did what he was told, and confirmed that it was. "Now I'm going to take this card I signed." Mark openly showed the card to Tyler and began to tear the card into little bits, onto the ground. "And I'm going to tear the card up. You better pick that up."

"Are you crazy? I might contaminate the ground." Mark and Tyler both laughed, then they stopped and Mark spoke.

"So everyone enjoys sending letters, either to a girl across town, a close friend, or even your mother. Now the cool thing about magic is that I can also send messages, but without a mailbox." Mark shuffled the cards and spread them over the bed. "Pick a card without looking, and put it with your other card."

"I'm not sure I can trust you."

"It's magic, of course you can't trust me." Mark smiled, and Tyler, while trying to see him through, swiped a card from the deck. He took his time and placed the new card with the other, thinking what this new card might be.

"Now close your eyes and say a magic word." Mark clasped his hands together while Tyler squeezed his eyes shut.

"What's the magic word?"

"Whatever is magic to you." Mark gently smiled while watching Tyler think of a magical word. He thought for three minutes; Mark thought he has fallen asleep, until Tyler finally spoke his magic word. A word that could define and save his life, that could lead to a thousand possibilities, with only this one goal.

"Cured."

"Okay, then say it louder."

"CURED."

"I'm a little old, I can't hear you."

"I SAID I'M CURED!" Tyler screamed aggressively, and Mark's eyes watered, but he held them back. Tyler wouldn't appreciate tears, rain. Kennedy behind the door heard his scream and silently cried, not even a sound. Then she left in a hurry, back to the front desk and away from her shame.

"Check the ground, Tyler," Mark spoke with a firm voice. Tyler opened his eyes and peered under Mark's feet. The bits from the card were gone. He looked up with amazement. Mark gestured him away. "Don't look at me, you're the one who said it." Mark boldly stared at Tyler and smiled. "Now check your blankets, Tyler."

Tyler reached under the sheets and felt the two cards. He slung them in front of his eyes and found Mark's card intact, with the words "sexy beast" gone. The message flew onto the other card, his card, with a few extra words. It said:

TC, you are a Sexy Beast! From your favorite old man, MW.

"Wha—How did this happen? I must have gotten too much morphine." Tyler looked over the cards and the ground again. Mark watched him struggle to comprehend the miraculous trick and plainly looked under the bed. That was where he'd kicked the card bits. Mark quietly laughed and stared back at Tyler.

This shocked me, children, because he hadn't been happy like this in a long time, and I mean a *long* time. That's one depressed man! But as I've explained, he didn't always have this old, tough personality. Mark was once gentle, kind, romantic, and godly. But he hit the road one day and died. Of course not physically, but you understand. His kindness died, that's what I mean. When Mark lived his life in kindness, around the time the second colonoscopy test rolled by, Mark and Mary celebrated. He was nineteen, and she was eighteen. They were both still so young with the future in sight. Oh, and of course it was negative. I got carried away, sorry about that, how clumsy of me.

Anyways, she was home alone, and heard the doorbell ring. Sitting upright outside her door was a bouquet of flowers, a huge bouquet, with a note. It read:

Put on something pretty. If you have trouble, just know that with you in it, it's perfect! Meet me at the park in an hour, you know where I am.

Love,

Your Hand Mitten

◆◆◆

MARY USED THE ENTIRE hour that day painting her face with makeup, fighting for perfection in eyeliner, mascara, liquid foundation, blush, lipstick, and loose powder, juggling to rush through the door and see Mark with her normal routine complete. She always took obsessive amounts of time just to impress him, even though he'd proven to Mary that looks were not everything to him. Mark loved who she was, her natural appearance. The park was a golf course; its terrain was filled with hills, slopes, and an occasional lone golfer. Naturally, it was empty, since the old and outdated course had only two holes, cheaply produced grass, and accidental cactus obstacles. Golfers were now attracted to the much newer and modern courses with lakes, turf, and trees. When she arrived, Mark wasn't hard to spot; the light bouncing off the ground from the sunset made him seem like a light at night. Mark watched her slowly make her way up in a large red dress.

"I thought I told you to wear whatever you'd like," Mark laughed and swatted a fly from his face.

"I thought you'd come down here and help me." Mary looked up and smiled. She watched him take his time down the hill, raving on about how she can make gourmet meals but can't do this simple task. But while Mark babbled, Mary glanced down, and purposely snagged her dress on a short cactus near her feet. "Mark, my dress is caught! Mark, this is a very nice dress!" She panicked. Mark trotted over with a sense of care in his steps, like a quail to its partner.

"It's okay, I got it." He calmly ran down the hill and knelt on one knee to untangle the dresses threads from the ground. Mary smiled, lifted a leg in the air, and balanced while watching Mark pick out the last few needles from the dress. When the cactus was fully removed, Mary pushed him down the steep hill, thrusting with her legs. Mark yelped and gripped the grass before rolling down the hill again.

"Mary!" He yelled while Mary cried in laughter.

"Oops, my bad. My foot just slipped."

"Mary!"

"Sorry, I can't hear you, the air is too thin up here."

Mark called her name a third time. She froze. Something was wrong.

"Mark? Honey? Are you okay?"

"I fell on a cholla, it's everywhere." Mark moaned and rolled over. A cholla is a cactus with an obvious tree-like base that grows fairly tall. It drops little spiky six-inch limbs on the ground, and when you're caught, the cholla hooks in the skin, making removal very difficult. The typical way is to take a fork, let the teeth go in between the area it penetrated, and yank it out. Then you run your scars through water, hoping it doesn't later burn from the bacteria on the edge of the thorns, depending how old the limb was. Mary ran over in a small panic.

"I'm sorry, I'm really sorry. I thought it would be fun, I'm so clumsy, it's my fault."

Mark rolled over on top of the wound but never screamed. He smiled, frowned and screamed again.

"It's on my leg, *agh*! There's a lot." He looked up and found himself in a hug with Mary.

"I'm sorry."

"Mary, my leg." He patted her back while moving the wound. She ran over and searched for the cholla, but there was none.

"Hun, where's the cholla?" Mary looked back and found him smiling deviously.

"There is none." He lifted his leg and kicked her off the hill. She lost her balance and grabbed Mark's shoe. He took hold of the grass, but for the second time, it ripped and left them rolling down the hill, flopping over each other. This time no one stopped, they both continued to roll off, until the incline disappeared, and they were on flat ground. Mary pinned Mark to the ground. Her dress was stained by the grass, and hair thrown out of control, with a leaf tangled inside.

"So much for your dress."

"So much for the cholla. I thought you were dying!"

"I had things under control." Mark smirked while his eyes wandered to the side, but they found their way back to her.

"I'm pretty sure I have you pinned to the ground. I could do whatever I'd like right now, and you can't do anything." She smiled, because it was a lie. He looked around, at her thin arms, small body. Then toward those beefy biceps, long outstretched legs a foot past hers, the weight difference, and looked back into Mary's eyes.

"Yep, nothing I can do."

She leaned in and kissed Mark, who took her fingers into his hands. "I like your nails. It reminds me of your art."

Mary giggled and let him look them over. They had palm trees bending in different directions for every individual nail. There were sunsets as well, with yellow and orange colors reflecting off the sandy beach below, as well as little white dots that were without a doubt coconuts, with almost unnoticeable coconut holes, punctured by pink bendy straws.

"Thank you! It took me days to draw in the little details."

"But it's missing something." Mark frowned.

"What is it?" Mary threw her other hand in eyesight and looked very closely at the details

Mark reached deep in his front pocket and without trouble, pulled out a ring and slipped it on her finger. The diamond wasn't large, and the band was thin, although on the side there was an engraving that said: *Forever.*

Mary's eyes looked away from the nails, saw the ring, and began to cry. She spoke in a whisper. "Mark. It's beautiful."

"Well? Is it a yes? Life is going to take us, but wherever it does, I want to go with you."

Mary spoke under his arm. "Just please promise me one thing."

"Anything!" Mark yelled enthusiastically and watched her rise and stare in his eyes.

"Let's adopt, no child deserves what I—"

"Yes baby, yes. We'll adopt." Mark felt her kiss on his smile and began to tear up. "We'll be okay. I promise with everything I have. We'll make it out all right."

"Mark, it's okay to cry, I'm here, I'm here, baby." Mary fell back into a hug, and Mark lightly tugged the back of her head. In one way or another, Mary wanted him to cry.

"Why cry? The world is so great."

"Just don't bottle up." Mary pushed up with her arms. "I'm here for you."

Mark snickered and pushed her messy brown hair behind an ear. "You're beautiful."

They continued to talk, flirt, and plan a future while lying together on that golf course. That day they told everyone of the big news. Family and friends gathered from thousands of miles away to the wedding six short months later, and when Mark swooped Mary off her feet for a kiss, the crowd cheered. It was an event where even God clapped and blessed their wedding without a doubt that their hearts were completely made for each other; many called it the perfect wedding, because they were the perfect couple.

◆◆◆

THE DAY WAS SLOWLY dying, and in the distance came another storm brewing through the mountains in the east. In the distance, black clouds with streaks of rain poured down onto the range, another quiet night of rain approaching, without even the howls from wolves at the moon. The hospital still sat under the glaring sun, vaporizing the past storm's residue, but not for long. Soon the sun would set, the houses would close, and the storm would begin again with rage. On the second floor, in a vacant room, Aaron and Kenny argued while Mark finally made the decision to run up the stairs toward Tyler and to later perform a magic trick. The heat of the argument was escalating to a climax. Kenny paced in a circle, shouting down to Aaron who sat on a wooden stool listening to every word. Tom walked back in and groaned lightly. They were still arguing, and he wasn't in the mood for their bickering over simple solutions, so Tom walked out and left it for Mark.

"You told me he was under control, you told me he wouldn't have another episode!" Kenny yelled. "Then he assaults my entire staff and turns my hospital room into a battleground! That's not civil, that's not justice."

Aaron closed his eyes and slowly nodded with grief. "I know."

"Then also covering the fact that his blood pressure is skyrocketing from his last visit. Have you made sure he's taking all medications?"

"Yes."

Kenny's voice shifted from a scream to an outdoor yell while wiping the sweat off his face. "Aaron, I'm sorry, but I can't let him stay on the force this time, I can't cover for him, even if he's a community resource officer. He's become a danger. You can't control him."

Aaron stood up for the first time and whispered, "But Kenny, this is all he has. It was my fault. I let him chase that call."

"What if the next child dies? Is it still okay?" Kenny's voice rose again, and Aaron fell back down into the seat.

"No."

"Also take in account that both of you are now being exposed for committing international crimes that could throw you both in prison for life. Have you thought of that? Do your emotions change for Mark now?"

Kenny walked to a clean metal counter, leaned over with his palms far apart, and stared at a wall with his back toward Aaron. The room was quiet for minutes. Aaron watched him fold a napkin that was on the counter into a perfect square and take a huge breath that filled the blank, clean room with noise. He then spoke in a quiet voice. "Mark has serious issues. He needs to see someone even if he refuses. This needs to be done. It's better if I arrange this before a third party does."

Aaron stood up again. "But Kenny, what about the risk?"

Kenny shifted his body around and yelled back, "The risk? There's already too much risk. This is something we have to do, no matter how much it'll hurt him! He's forgotten who I am, is periodically inattentive by conscious dreams of the past, and can't take care of himself without steady watch. He's getting worse. You understand?"

Aaron sat down and whispered, "Yes Kenny, I understand."

"Make sure he goes to the psychiatrist I prescribed, who has every right to diagnose him with *any* mental disability or gain access to any medication. He's a good friend of mine. Please don't argue with this decision," Kenny said calmly. "And don't think I'm a bad guy, feel blessed I was on shift when it happened, that Mark and I are not close enough for him to be transported to another doctor. Mary is a big part in his life, I would agree with anything he'd diagnose Mark with and any method he would use that he deems necessary. This is the only way we can help him and always was. It is good to start now than to never at all."

Aaron jumped up a final time to speak, his heart pounding with nerves. "I can talk to Tyler's parents and straighten things out—"

"NO!" Kenny yelled. Aaron flinched like a spooked horse. Kenny closed his eyes with a slight pinch to his nose and began softly. "No, Aaron. Please don't interfere anymore. You will only make it worse. There are times in life when you cannot make the circumstances any better than they are, you can only prevent them from becoming worse. If you speak to Tyler's parents a day after the accident, nothing will be resolved. There will only be uncontrollable emotion and irrational demands."

Kenny walked over and placed a hand on Aaron's shoulder, then he froze with a motionless gaze toward the ground. Kenny groaned under his breath and turned pale, but before Aaron could speak, he began. "Aaron, it'll be okay. We'll all make it through. Just please, if Mark gets exposed, try to act as if you didn't know." Kenny's old, wrinkled face to Aaron wasn't noticed often, but the light from a dim bulb and his burdened features struck it in a way that exposed his age, those deep wrinkles, gray hair, and old brown eyes. Aaron nodded and stood up with a sense of dread, walked to the vacant room's door, then stopped. Aaron grabbed the frame of the doorway to his right and rested his head with closed eyes and anguish.

"Don't get excited, Kenny," Aaron said while he tapped his head on the frame, as if he were trying to ignore the sounds around him. "Mark hasn't changed."

Aaron didn't head toward Mark but to the cafeteria and ate. He ate like a madman, devouring the meatloaf and Indian-style rice, with a bread roll and an eight-ounce carton of milk. There were crumbs on his lips and pasta sauce on a faded Beatles shirt, of the four stepping across Abbey Road. Frozen in time with their hypnotizing and internationally recognizable pattern. Aaron didn't worry about Mark because he ate swiftly, without hesitation, without time to think about the taste of the fluffy bread roll or the unopened soy sauce packet to the side. In the winter of 1982, three months after the stunt girl argument, his father was singing "Hey Jude" while opening the front door to their house. Aaron's eyes were glued to the show *Hill Street Blues*, wondering with slight childhood curiosity what it would be like to be a police officer at Hill Street Station. The control and authority were what he loved the most. He remembered his mom screaming in the kitchen as his father pulled her hair and took her outside, singing "Hey Jude" with ease, pulling his mother's hair as if it were like brushing his teeth. Aaron burned with uncontrollable fury while he watched the outdated box television, and instead of either turning up the volume or running to his tattered mattress on the ground of his room, Aaron turned off the world in Hill Street and Captain Frank Furillo, rotating toward the screams of his mother.

Useless, he thought to himself while in taking a large mouthful of spice-less meatloaf, thinking about how pointless his actions were that followed on that night in 1982. Aaron ran over to his drunken, skinny father of thirty in the cluttered backyard and slapped him across the face. He yelled like a Spartan entering the Hot Gates in the Battle of Thermopylae and banged Bailey Hudson's left cheek like a ceremonial Asian gong, staining an ember-red imprint of an adolescent hand as the effect. *Useless*, Aaron thought again as he remembered his father's cold stare and devilish, intoxicated grin as he rose onto his feet. Then he remembered the arguments he had with Mark about Mary and her beautiful, straight chocolate-brown hair. At the time, Aaron was so in love with her, so compelled to the thought of their future that he remembered those involving daydreams. Their children, barbecues in the summer and fireplaces in the winter. He thought of cruises every fiscal year and how they would run to somewhere in California together and gain wisdom through every risk they took and hardship they faced. Aaron didn't care much for Las Vegas and their career in magic. He cared more for her, and whom she was with.

However, like in 1982, despite everything Aaron did, he was no closer to the goal he desired. In fact, every new attempt he made to alter the events he thought he could control would soon build a tumor of fright in his gut. Aaron slowly began to realize the events he knew would happen *would*, the dominoes that would tumble *did*, and all he ever did was yell at a brick wall in New York City while the wrecking ball demolished a building in Los Angeles. *The Passenger Effect*, Aaron thought, *the damn Passenger Effect still controls me. Even if it seems that I made a difference, it is only an illusion. Mark is still destined for what I know will come. He is still idly drifting to that green door at his house, drifting back to her. Then once he walks in there, he will surely die right before my eyes.* He continued to eat for eight more minutes, gulping down the food like icy water after changing an unexpected flat tire in July. Aaron, the chief of police, convinced the deputy chief that Mark was prepared for the call. He convinced everyone that this was the only chance to distinguish the constant dead ends on the local drug smuggling case, while secretly wishing for Mark to head home with accomplishment, to brighten up the bitterness he felt for his dying wife. His idea backfired, turning into another domino, leading to the end. *The passengers and the drivers,* Aaron began to think once more. *No matter how much I fight, I scrape and kick at the walls of my placement in society. I will always be useless, heading in the direction the driver desires. Unless, unless I somehow convince these drivers to make the difference in the world, to help me accomplish my needs as a third party, I can narrow the gap. Those people who seem to always achieve what they strive for in life, always heading toward their passions, passing through obstacles like a current of electricity through a copper rod. Yet now the distance from hope is lengthening. What was once a condo turned into a house, and what was a house has turned into a ballroom, to the point where even the drivers will become passengers, and soon we will all just sit and watch like powerless trees to a forest fire, like a window to a fast approaching baseball, and we will all bow down to the damn Passenger Effect, preparing for impact.*

Kenny lay on the bed that was neatly made, like a stiff rock onto a cushion. He felt a boulder of grief in his heart, while thinking about what Aaron had stated before exiting. Yes, it was true; Mark had not changed. He was still delusional, in deep grief because of his wife's deadly illness, and would not change unless a miraculous work of God was placed onto the town of Tucson. Kenny had lost hope in Mark's recovery, his weakness bitterly and shamefully resting on his shoulder like the sinking feeling in Aaron, almost identical to the shame that plagued Kennedy. Yet something in Mark returned when he smashed his face into the off-white airbag and the Bearcat was thrown through the window, smashing on the black concrete of

First Avenue. Something must have clicked inside the inefficient parts of his mind and rebooted all its functions for an extension of memory he had so desperately blocked from his mind. *Hope,* Kenny thought, *there's hope again. A spark has fired off in me that I lost so long ago, a spark of hope for us all. Then, maybe, when our final mark on the world is on a gravestone, we can actually die with peace. Yet even though it may not last, he may wake up tomorrow and the connections could be lost, there was a step in the right direction, a step closer to dreams that have died long ago. It is possible to change Mark's fate and save his life. With this hope there are possibilities, there are opportunities.*

Kenny closed his eyes and lay in the plastic bed, feeling his age more than ever. At the age of seventy-two, he was two years from retirement from the hospital and, once a good decade or two passed, planned to die there as well. Yet the newly arisen tension and excitement of the day reminded him of the aches and pains in his body, the arthritis in his left knee, which, on that humid day, made the pain even worse. His periodic migraines were caused by his hypersensitivity to dehydration, and high blood pressure kept him from fast food and hot tubs. He felt more aware of his age more than ever but knew he could still replace an alcoholic's failing kidney like a grandmother sewing together a hole in a blanket. He could widen arteries in the brain to prevent strokes like a fourth-generation plumber removing a ball of hair from a drain. He had saved the lives of thousands; certain he could save one more. *I could change everything,* Kenny thought, *it is not too late.* Kenny reached for his hospital pager in the right pocket of his black satin pants and told his floor nurse that he would be on break for an hour. She immediately agreed, as it was not her place to argue with Dr. Kenny; in fact, no one did. Dr. Kenny was the most experienced doctor in both the trauma center and the emergency room. In the medical world, his hands were magic, his opinions were never questioned, and to observe him in the operating room was like observing

Moses descend from Mount Sinai. While performing surgery, he was as steady as a rock and as calm as a vacant pond.

Yet a call came in thirty minutes later that needed Dr. Kenny urgently: a car slipped from the rain and crashed with another. Men from both sides stormed out, yelling and screaming because of the wreckage but not noticing their own scars. The storm consumed them, made them mad. Their sense of reality was gone. The past was more important than the present, or the future, until an on-the-scene medic yelled them out of their insanity and exposed their eyes to their shredded bodies. Reality hurts; one fainted upon realization, the other laid himself down on a stretcher and asked for help, praying quietly to himself. Mark passed the two men and bumped into the nurse who exposed their scars when he ran out in blind fury from the sixth floor. The man who fainted woke up without knowledge of the bloodshed, only the accident, but the one who asked for help remembered both.

After thirty-five minutes of Aaron sinking in sadness and a secret meeting with Tyler's father, which was a failure, he walked back to find Mark had taken his police car. But before that, Mark sat on a chair next to Tyler, talking, joking, and laughing. They talked for almost thirty minutes. Kennedy came in after the magic trick to take Mark, checking the hallways like before to see if anyone had taken notice, but when she saw Tyler smiling, it was more important to preserve that joy. Kennedy checked the blood infusion and left. The danger of Mark didn't matter; being distraught while unimaginably ill was more dangerous. At the end of their talk, Tyler lost his strength and began to slowly fade from their conversation. His body also began to hurt from the laughter. Mark hadn't seen his mouth sores until that moment. They were sores cancer patients got from the chemotherapy, which began in the throat, and if severe—which they always were—they would travel through your entire GI tract, following down toward your bottom. Which made pooping an excruciating experience. Talking was almost as bad; every word was a burning, blistered feeling in the back of the throat. Although not as bad as drinking or eating, most patients quit eating because of the pain and loss of taste, which led to nutrition from a disposable bag. At that point, everything tasted like dirt, since taste buds are reproducing cells killed from chemotherapy along with red blood cells, white blood cells, platelets, hair cells, and skin cells (but not nail cells, if those are a thing). On the other hand, there's no acne, since zits require skin cell reproduction. Go tell a cancer patient that they're lucky they're not you because they don't get acne, quick.

Sorry, I'm rambling on too much, just forget everything I said. Anyway, Mark found out in that moment that he wasn't benefiting Tyler or helping him feel better. It was quite the opposite. Tyler did everything for Mark. Every word he said was a burning pain, a reminder of mortality. His yell for a cure was equivalent to a scorching fire burning and bleeding in his throat, a devilish spirit wanting him to mute his words, wanting him to never be heard again. That's what cancer is—a demonic spirit, yet superior to the other demons that may be lurking in your soul, an incomparable difference. Mark, realizing the pain he had caused, pushed off the mattress while lightly smiling, adjusted his gown and gloves, and gave a short but sweet farewell. Tyler mumbled a response from the bed, tumbled on the pillow, and delicately fell asleep. Mark watched from afar for minutes, the sunken eyes covered by black bags and pale, deeply fair skin around the face. Eyebrows were wearing thin, and all the hair on his head was gone… and the weight. His thin arms lay still under light, white blankets. Everything was mocking him. The casts were small and white, like the scrubs, fitting as a robe. The stitches were white and deep, around the entire face, whispering to Mark. The conversation was not only physically but also mentally draining in Tyler's condition. The amount of antibiotics, narcotics, and injuries was tiring; to spend that amount of time communicating and interacting was quite a feat. The drugs dulled the pain but also the mind and drive to communicate; most patients blew off visitors for rest.

Mark scanned the furniture and felt dim-witted. There were no oral medications, so Tyler accessed everything through IV. *Murderer!* the IV pole yelled. *Murderer!* Mark covered his ears and closed his eyes.

"No, please no." Mark ran for the cold, thick door. The voices were surrounding and closing in. His thoughts crowded and took control. *While Tyler spoke to Mark in the rain the night before, his throat was already coated with blisters*, the voices cried. *Murderer!* He reached for the door, but the door opened by itself before he ever touched the knob. It was Tyler's mother. The door swung from the opposite direction. He stood a yard away but felt closer. When their eyes met, the voices fell silent, the crazy ran out, and her gentle smile made mystery flood through the air. When they met, the clouds outside began to sprinkle, wiping off the dew from trees and wetting cement spots once dry by the sunlight, which was almost gone. It wasn't long until darkness spread from mountain to mountain, animals hid in fear, people gathered around dusty board games, and the sky cried, with rage shortly behind. He was being watched by Tyler's mother, the one who gave birth, nurtured, and raised him, with a sense of certainty like Mark's own mother, Isabell Wegman. The one who spent sixteen years sharpening the boy only to watch him whittle away in the white plastic mattress and thin hospital sheets. She was staring into Mark's eyes. Mark, the middle-aged man whose car's tread slid as he braked, hydroplaning down into the back of Tyler's Camry from the dirt-brown slush of gathered rain water. Mark, the man who had made rash judgments and accusations of her son and would soon walk out with only minor whiplash and a sprained arm from the grace of a God he didn't even believe in. But as her emerald-green eyes gazed bitterly into his own, she smiled. The motherly grin was weak, but it was there. Mark would have told her about the deep guilt he would feel for the rest of his life. He would have pulled out one of the few loose blank checks in his wallet and written $2,000, telling her that there would be more for the safety of her son. He would have even bought Tyler a refurbished car from the Auto Mall. The guilt was haunting Mark, another demon forming to soon join the legion in his worn soul. Yet the earlier epiphany was a reminder of haunting memories all separate on their own, in the years where things began to fall apart, melt, and bend like a gingerbread house under a furnace. Their sweet life slowly turning to mush, liquefying. Soon he couldn't even see the woman staring into his eyes, a foot away and with dreadful curiosity for his presence in her child's hospital room. He could only smell the bleach in the room, the aftertaste of injected saline in his mouth, and the colorful walls of the children's hospital rooms getting closer, closer.

Love Filled Lies

MARK WAS TWENTY-TWO. MARY was twenty-one—three years of marriage had gone by in a flash. During this spent time, Mark joined the Marine Corps. He learned respect, teamwork, morals, family values, discipline, and pain. Mary never approved of his enrollment ("What if you get hurt?"), but ever since the introduction to the Marines in high school, Mark had wanted to join. She rolled her eyes the first few times he walked in with his camouflage and Velcro badges, but as the months passed, she began to find him quite adorable in his suit. The cold bus to his training ground and the harsh treatment during the first few weeks made him cry, but he felt wanted like never before. He didn't feel like a part of civilization, but a part of the Marines, and learned the motto, "For God, Corps, and Country." After twelve weeks of kissing the mud in the rain, fighting the tears, and learning brotherhood, Mark finally joined a unified platoon and moved his wife to a military base on the coast of California. They lived on the base for years, attending church services as a couple, getting ice cream afterward, and watching cars roll by. Because of his new arrival to the base, they lived near an artillery practice range, every morning, waking up at 5:30 a.m. by the fire from the heavy arms until 9:00 a.m. rolled around the corner. Almost every person was from out of state, deployed in California for a short time. Mark continued to work up branches while Mary learned the basic rules of living on government land. Commissaries—government grocery stores on the military base— were cheaper than the regular stores. Mary loved it. She ran in on Monday mornings and bought groceries by the cartful, steaming up stromboli, baking pecan pies, mac-and-cheese-stuffed potatoes, buttery Texas bread, and other countless dishes. The little kitchen would always be filled with complex, pleasant scents of baked goods from the yard-wide off-white oven, or boiled and fried meals from the charcoal-black cooktops, spotted with permanent stains the color of brown bears or the hairs of a coconut. Mark, although exhausted with dry sweat and blisters on his shoulders and hands, would trot over to their house with excitement to see his wife and the new creation she would craft in the kitchen.

Mary also noticed the differences in police enforcement between the town of Tucson and the California base. For instance, the police were less lenient with the five-mile gap over the speed limit, which most practiced in the seemingly empty roads in Arizona. Yet at the same time, neighboring families welcomed the Wegmans with open arms and gave them a warm sense of security. Mark continued to rank higher while at the base, jumping from private first class to lance corporal, and eight months later, with twelve months of training in total, a corporal. The sheer skill learned early in the Junior Reserve Officers' Training Corps (JROTC) at high school promoted him fast and swiftly. His bulked, strong, tall, youthful body also took a heavy role in the Marines; most had very heavy, lean muscle structures, but nothing compared to Mark. He was like his father Henry in construction, an icon. Mark was quick thinking, muscular, broad, and tall. He grew to be six foot seven, like his father before him, and developed fantastic marksmanship, excelling beyond the others of equal rank. However, with his constant kindness and certainty, like the main and suspender cables to the Golden Gate Bridge, he wasn't openly accepted as their rank's leader—but it was common knowledge that their main support came from him.

After a total of two years, Mark became a sergeant. With countless weeks of training on the ground, he became a well-known leader on the base, catching the attention from captains, colonels, and even a general on one warm Thursday afternoon during a drill on infiltrating a terrorist base, using team spirit and team flow as the two key areas of focus. He knew how to lead small squads into horrific war, how to perform simple on-hand medical tactics, and how to carry out a mission with the squad clean and stainless. The promotion wasn't on accident. Mark was on the top of the list and became an excellent leader. His understanding of politics, tactics, artillery, and battlefront made teachers proud, and many—in humility—saluted him upon graduation. They knew that Mark was born for greatness, that he would be one of the future leaders for the Marines. That month, Mark, instead of being serviced in the Active Federal Service for the primary zone, became enrolled in the secondary zone. A promotion program where commanders chose highly qualified people to have the chance in expediting promotions.

Mark taught his team loyalty, discipline, and brotherhood and warned them of the dangers of war. Although Mark has never truly been in a war, his experience in the classroom, reenactments, and lessons on the base were more than the others had. His favorite comrade, if that's what you call it, was Tom Freeman. His name was old-fashioned. After the Civil War, the millions of freed African Americans were given the last name Freeman. Which might seem now like a simple last name, but to the many who were newly freed, it meant the world, and American citizenship. To this day, Tom never talked about his ancestors or the origin of the last name but did explain his family tree all joining the military, fighting major wars in the late twentieth century, beginning with their freedom by the Civil War to the day Tom spoke about it in the 1990s.

Tom's father, John, was in the Vietnam War from 1969 to the last retreat in 1973. He was only five foot four, yet broad, swift in movement, and when they were chased, he ran back to the choppers like he was on fire. His friends called him Jo and sometimes JoJo when they were drunk in their tents, while smoking a few military-produced cigarettes and laughing like hysterical hyenas. John never told stories; many of those friends who had called him JoJo either ended up in pieces from an unexpected mine or could not run fast enough from the bullets or their country's own napalm attacks. Then after he returned, unlike the return of World War II veterans where parades were arranged around every city and town (God- and country-loving heroes), there was no celebration or honor for returning from Vietnam. The war was disgusting. He landed to find a crowd spitting on them and hauling insults about their morality and human decency. He was threatened, rejected from his family, and ultimately left bottling up the war with cigarettes, scotch, and women. Chaos was what John became, and as a result, Tom was born.

The man who willingly signed up for war because of his father's legacy was a fool. Tom's grandfather served in the Korean War, walked the entire country, and pushed the communists back until he reached the Chinese border. Ron Freeman was considered a hero and in fact received the Medal of Honor for jumping onto an RG-42 hand grenade, leaving fragments of the metal shell scattered in his chest and calves. Ron was five foot six, moral, compassionate, and patient to all. He carried a Bible in his bag that had been given to him from his own father when he was young; it was all tattered up with yellow pages and weak, cheap binding, carrying a potent smell of dust and old ink wherever taken. Ron was known for his storytelling and quirky personality, something John was always told even decades after his father's death, and was always called "Ron's little man" even while entering his late forties, as if he were still four years old and desperate for his father's return.

When his father's aged friends began to recite compelling stories of Ron, they also always seemed to carry an old sparkle in their aged eyes. Yet the thing John was always amazed by in his father was how, even though he was black, there was very little racism from the military, the locals, and even his own American comrades. One reason would be because they were all facing the same monster, sharing the same nightmares of death in the following days as they continued to travel north. But the main cause was because he was so pleasantly kind and gentle, and John could only imagine Ron like so, filling up with a mixture of pride, misery, and unworthiness ever since he was four. Therefore, while John grew up, the pain from being fatherless made boxing a relief, a way to empty the rage kept inside, to throw the years of pain and tears toward the other man in the ring. During his boxing career, John was very light and always made it into the championship. An interview with Tom's father was done after a tight boxing match in the sixties, with twelve rounds of fighting and sweat mixed with blood, where he told them, "I blame the man for my father's death and fight like he's a cold-blooded murderer. That's how I win."

But one man always destroyed him, which forced him to never win a single championship. His name was Joe Brown, champion of the light belt, lightweight fights, since 1956. He was undefeated, and John never stood a chance, his face smashing against the ground before he could even comprehend that the bell had rung and the fight had begun.

"In the dark boxers is Joe Brown, and in the white boxers is John Freeman," said the announcer.

Ding, ding!

This is all me, John thought. *He murdered my father and will not make me look like a fool!* He picked up those hands, Joe the same, and with one strike, John fell. His nose split in two like it did the year before, rebroken and splattered across his face, sounding like a child crunching on a lollipop. He fell as swiftly as he had the year before, stiff as a rock and helpless as a drowning fly.

About a week later, John was chosen for the draft, his eyes slightly blocked from his thick gray-white nose cast while smoking a Camel cigarette, reacting in a mysterious way. His eyes began to widen and a smile crept to each cheek, as If he had won an all-expenses-paid trip to New Zealand on a radio raffle. Except this was a trip to the thick jungles of Vietnam, and he knew he would probably die. He thought about this while the smile widened even more and his hands gripped the envelope even tighter. The year was 1969, an already unpopular war, yet John, twenty-one years old, saw the shipment to war as an opportunity to make his deceased father proud, to not feel like a generation of failure to the military name of the Freemans, to be worthy enough to be a Freeman. He drove to a drive-in theater and bought a pack of beer that night, celebrating in his vaguely nicer Tucson apartment, achieved for always winning silver.

But Tom himself was only eighteen when joining the Marines, a tight curly-haired half-African American boy. He loved baseball, the feeling of catching, tossing, slowly striking a man out, with the tension running down the spine, the panic in their eyes. He was small compared to Mark but fast and strong, with aspirations to achieve greatness in the military and surpass his father. His father was the man who abused him, gifted in boxing from an era long ago, yet instead of a crowd, now only Tom and the stained brown carpet knew John's present talent. Tom hated his father and had dreams about fighting him, like Aaron, except he imagined catching his father in the act, with some hidden tape recorder or by calling one of his friends to watch and testify. Yet at the age of nine, before he could execute the idea into words, CPS came and saw the stained brown carpet, his bruised face, and John leading the tour, the one who made the call. John was also the birth-giver to analytical questions of Tom's wonder as a child, toward his own self-worth, while on the bottom bunk in a community foster home and with a broken arm. He fell into a pit of worthlessness.

Mark closely knew everyone in his five-man group, their strengths, weaknesses, struggles in life, and reasons to fight. But Tom was special, taken under Mark's wing, and he taught Tom to notice every detail toward the operations of war and noticeable signs of danger.

One night, a little over a year after Mark's promotion the previous August, Tom, Mark, and Mary came together for a dinner. It was almost autumn. The sun had left for the Pacific and the three were feasting on spaghetti and spiced meatballs. Mark had known Tom for almost two years. Tom was nineteen now.

"Mary?" Mark said. "Tom? Did you know this is the last time we'll be together while you're a private?"

"Yes, and did you know its ten thirty-seven?" Mary said while yawning dramatically.

"No, this is big," Mark said, turning to Tom. "Out of everyone in our squadron, you have shown the most growth, and I'm proud."

Tom smiled under a cold cheek and tipped his head, wondering if his achievements were in part because of his close relationship with Mark.

"Thanks, but it's nothing really, sir. Following your orders and rules is the secret."

Mark and Mary looked at each other in confusion. *What do you think's wrong?* Mary said through her look.

I'm not sure, should I ask? Mark asked by an expression.

Ask just to be safe.

Mark turned to Tom and smiled.

"Tom, is everything okay?"

Tom didn't answer on call and the room fell silent. Mary saw the sadness in Tom's eyes and caught the sense of fear. A scared boy not living with any guidance for almost a decade and now facing fears of the future.

"Mark," Mary calmly said. "I'll be in the art room painting."
She stood up and kissed Mark on the head. When she left, he asked
Tom again.

"Is everything okay? I'm here, Tom," Mark said in a whispered,
parenting tone. Tom looked up and smiled very widely.

"I can't be any better, Mark. I just have moments."

"Moments of what?"

"Of pity," slurred out Tom, denying his own words. Mark became
concerned. He never heard or could imagine Tom say words like
those. He had never shown any weakness for the two years Mark had
known him. He was never silent but never frightened, accomplishing
the harsh training with ease and with the movements of a man born
for his hands to cradle an M16 rifle. He was bolted down by assurance
and understanding of the world, or so Mark thought with his vague
understanding of Tom's past. Mark has never seen him cry and, on
this occurrence, felt a feeling of awkwardness, like watching a stranger
cry, but locked his discomfort away.

"Why? You never seem like that," Mark softly spoke.

"Because what if we get deployed?" Tom said while his eyes
watered heavily.

"Why are you afraid? You trained for this," Mark said firmly,
certain. "I trained you in everything I know. If we're deployed, just
listen to what I've taught you and you'll be okay. This is also why you
joined the Marines, right?"

There was a silence while Tom wiped tears off his cheeks, then
another silence of uncertainty. "Y-Yes, sir."

"Tom, tell me why you're afraid." Mark's strong voice rattled the
house. Tom sharply looked over and responded.

"My grandfather died in the Korean War, and my father became
a drunk from Vietnam. I'm afraid I'll become one of those two, but
most of all I fear that I'll become like my father, that I will never be any

better." Tom began to stare down, and Mark gently tapped the table until Tom looked up to find Mark strictly staring down with anger.

"Hey! I'll never let either of those happen. Not on my watch. Never!" Mark's eyes became strained, and his eyebrows arched down into an intense look of fury and love. Confidence radiated off Mark's skin, instantly providing a wind of assurance through the room, his hand clenched into a fist on the oak table. But underneath, his heart was beating like a hummingbird. There was fear; none of them had truly been in a war.

Tom slightly smiled and began to cry comfortably, assured and adopted into safety.

"Thanks, sir."

Mark fell back into his seat and let out a big sigh, which relaxed the room's atmosphere.

"And also, don't call me *sir*. I'm your brother now, corporal," Mark quietly spoke and smiled with a quick wink. Tom winked back, very excitedly. Then, with eyebrows and cheeks rising, Tom yelped out two little words.

"Y-yes, Dad."

Although Mark and Tom were only a few years apart, Mark took the orphan into their house, and although they could be brothers, after that day, Tom never fell short in calling him Dad.

Then Mark rolled his eyes to a shadow he saw in the hall and yelled, "Mary, you can come out of the hallway."

"Everything's okay?" she yelled back, sticking her head out of the darkness.

The Society Boxed in Mirrors

WHEN THE WOMAN CLEARED her throat for attention, Mark's trance broke and he looked up. She had sweats on with a bun, as well as bags in her hands and under her eyes. She had brown, curly hair with little strands poking out of the Arizona Wildcats hat on her head. Her shoes were old sneakers with a little tear on the top, and her makeup was minimum but still very beautiful.

She has money problems, Mark thought seconds after, *and is fighting for the past to become a reality again but hasn't realized yet that normality doesn't exist. She's fighting for nothing. But her face is kind, probably because she doesn't know who I am, staring at me like another cancer sponsor. My actions are very different than that. I've done horrible things to your family. She seems like a wonderful woman, married to a wonderful man, with an outstanding child, but I'm not a good man in any shape or form. I'm the devil, the killer, and the rage your child doesn't need. Kick me out and punch me in the throat. I won't move.*

The woman reached out an arm. Mark closed his eyes tight, waiting for pain to strike and in a way craving a blow to the face. He knew it would be like a loving lamb protecting her child from a hungry, devious wolf. But she spoke in a gentle tone instead.

"Nice to finally meet you, sir," the woman said, obviously struggling to speak in this same gentle voice but dimly pronounced from her exhaustion. Mark shook the hand loosely with a confused expression and a slightly open jaw. There was awkwardness in the air, a stench of forced emotions and tolerance.

"Do you know who I am, ma'am?"

"You're the man who rear-ended my son's Camry, I know exactly who you are!" the mother said in an unexpectedly harsh voice. Her semi-trancelike state almost instantly dissolved, and she yanked her hand back as if touching a stray dog sprayed by a skunk. Mark felt immense shame, shame he prepared for, and fell silent with his mouth slightly open. Then, in a quiet, regretful tone, he responded.

"I'm really sorry, ma'am. I-I talked to your son. He's wonderful! I made matters worse for your family and, and—"

"And what?" the mother sneered while raising her voice again. Mark flinched and raised his voice so it was impossible for her to hear him wrong. Nurses turned around to watch, asking for security or someone to give him the boot and kick him out.

"And I'll pay for everything that I've caused. I'll help with medical bills, the car bills, and I can bring food to help you, Tyler, and your husband!"

The mother rolled her eyes, crossed her arms, looked down, and interrupted quietly with disgust. "Ex-husband. He's in the cafeteria. A very nice man, but you'll never see that side of him."

The mother saw Mark's eyes tear apart from the guilt, which made her again remember the promise to her son, something she wished she could ignore. So the woman bit her lip, and her eyes locked onto his with fire in them that said *please give me any alarm so I can ruin the rest of your miserable life.* They moved into a waiting room just outside the sixth floor's metallic doors, with two walls of windows overlooking the parking lot and city and another that led to the elevator and a pair of saloon-style doors that led downstairs by foot. On the single row of red cotton-stuffed metal-leg chairs in the back right corner against the windows sat both Tyler's mother and Mark, while on the left corner sat a family of nine who were silently crying. Quiet tears of fear. The mother's weeping was easy to find. She was the one who'd had heavy bags, no makeup, and pajamas. Mark couldn't help but notice them; they reminded him of the past. They were poor, in debt, and losing someone younger than them all, he surmised. There was a black purse next to the mother, and tucked inside was formula and a diaper. Tyler's mother never noticed. She heard the cries but never looked over; these noises were heard every day in the sixth floor overlooking the city. Those soft weeps from families never shook her anymore. Sadness was always in the air, in the water, and in the heart, which will never leave unless their child walks out with their life.

The mother bit her lip and spoke.

"When Tyler was diagnosed, I thought he was going to die. I thought his life was over. I sometimes dream of the days before this place, and before the divorce." She paused, then continued a few moments later.

"Why him? I always wondered why Tyler, of all people, would get cancer. He prayed more than all of us, he would be the one who'd go to heaven." She paused again as she chipped her nail polish off her finger. Then, very unexpectedly, the woman chuckled lightly.

"You know how all of this came about? It was about a year ago, when I was selfish. When I didn't think of others. I was losing a man I loved, and Tyler, my sweet boy, all he wanted to do was comfort me. I heard him sit there in pain. I knew he was in pain. But I was so... so absorbed in myself, that all I did was buy him Tylenol and not even take the box out of the grocery bag. Then I'd cry at night, and he'd cradle me and tell me to trust God. Oh, I was angry at God, but I trusted my boy and I prayed—although I was tired of his talk of life being okay, and I was tired of him acting as if the divorce wasn't a big deal. Then one day during school, Tyler collapsed. He wasn't getting enough oxygen and he collapsed." The mother was violently crying with anger. Her voice wasn't loud, but wasn't quiet.

"He had a tumor in his throat and on his head. In his kidneys and his spine. He had it in his legs and wrapped around his heart. It was my fault. Mine! And every night it's in my thoughts. So I pray every night, I pray because he…he told me to pray. I don't care about myself anymore, I don't. If I died right now, I wouldn't care if I went to heaven or to hell. I love Tyler, and because he told me to pray, I will…I" Then the mother suddenly halted her conversation, finding herself wrapped in Mark's arms. She was shocked.

"No more," he pleaded, "no more."

She hugged back, wrapping her hands halfway around Mark. Many mothers weren't afraid; he had a fatherly look of an old police officer with a big heart and a personality filled with love and authority, but no strangers, or even officers besides Aaron, knew what was occurring in Mark's head. But one thing was certain: Mark began to love Tyler, maybe almost as much as he loved Mary. The mother, though, drenched in sadness, still had endless rage for Mark and pushed his huge body off.

"Please don't…don't ever touch me again." The woman turned herself in her chair and tried to forget the connection they'd shared, the two-second embrace, and hoped he would as well. She wasn't ready to forgive Mark and didn't want their embrace to be a sign of forgiveness, only a sign of human decency. Although Mark didn't think of forgiveness, he began to think about Tyler. Tyler was all he could think about.

The sunken eyes and high chills in a warm car during summer. *I killed him*, Mark thought. *No, I murdered him. This sweet boy. Oh, this sweet child. What could be worse?* The mother looked down on the large city of moving cars, mountains, and working-class men and women. It was calm and quiet. No sound vibrated through the windows, while men and women went on with their day. Every single one had problems they bickered about. The sixth floor was a society made up of young and heavily trialed children, the innocent who were shown the darkness of the world they could not yet understand. It was a society boxed in mirrors that showed the world of carelessness, people who did not carry the same weight of gratefulness that the children do there, bickering and craving less important needs like a new car or better grades in college. While looking through the glass and your reflection, boxed in a single floor, you feel ignored, passed by from the appearing and disappearing automobiles on the busy road, letting your boxed society handle your reflection, and your boxed society alone observing through the one-way mirrors. Even when you leave, there's still a part of you that would always stay. A part that you will always see what was boxed up and hidden in plain sight.

The mother spoke in a calm voice while turned in her chair. "I'm not going to sue you, officer. Tyler, after the accident, woke up before surgery smiling and told both his father and I how you treated him like a normal human, not someone who was sick. This is something that means a lot to the boy. Then this morning he told both the doctors and us that he never told you about the cancer and where he was going, giving you suspicion of drug abuse and illegal use. I was so furious, and I... You wouldn't understand." She kept back the anger, which felt like needles in her throat to be so kind to the man who caused it all. "It was foolish of me to tear up. But Tyler is a very sharp boy. He, no matter what, understands my thoughts and feelings." The mother let out a short laugh, yet not with humor but acknowledgement. "Without hesitation, Tyler made me promise not to harm you in any way and named off the ways I could." This time she laughed with gentle humor. "He told me economically, socially, mentally, or physically, and I couldn't break that promise to him. In that moment, Tyler was experiencing drastic intoxication of pain, he was so taken aback from his injuries, you could see the pain in his eyes." She closed her eyes, took a deep breath, and began again. "I arrived last night from work and they were the first words that came from his mouth. Within a heartbeat, I would have gladly declined his plea. His father and I would have ruined you in every way I could." For a moment, she stopped talking to absorb the power of her words while also realizing she'd lied, never being able to decline his pleas, especially when he had been so certain with his words the night before, so convinced. Her lip quivered. "But I'm not going to disappoint Tyler. It's dangerous."

Mark bathed in guilt. Children, he was being crushed again and again and again. He felt blood on his hands and tears on his shoulder, continuously being poured on by what the mother said.

When did everything change? When was I not the man I am now? he thought. *I need Mary. I need Tyler. God, please don't kill them all, please not my Hand Mitten, please not the child.* Although this request was selfish, Mark wished not to feel guilt. The mother looked over and again saw the love he possessed and this constant, silent trickle of tears making his face shine and his clothes wet. It reminded her of the simpler times, when Tyler was a child with simple problems and immediate answers that were solvable. Answers like a kiss on a cut, a time out for mud tracks in the house, a scoop of ice cream for standing up to the class menace, or a bed to sleep in from a nightmare. She was still outraged at Mark but knew what he needed. The woman stood up, tired of his quietness and looks of self-disgust, wiped off her tears and rubbed the dribble off from her nose, to reach forward and squeeze Mark into a warm hug. All the little battles were practice for hugs like this, and she had perfected it. These were the hugs for the nightmares. Mark quickly halted his quiet and shocked tears, finding himself back in reality with tense muscles. But soon he loosened up and accepted the hug. They both knew how it felt to have blood on their hands. This hug gave them both relief. Mark was able to keep the tears in his head, and the woman's tension also left, yet the embrace, this second moment, was not forgiveness, but understanding. But not too long did these comforting conditions last. "My name is Mary."

Mark shuddered to her response and she quickly backed away. He placed a hand to his mouth and froze in overwhelming, desolating fear. "Sorry, say again?"

"I said my name is Sarah. Are you okay?" Sarah questioned. Mark sat forward in his chair and laid both hands on his thighs, with a slight slant of the neck looking toward the ground's tile and the sealed metal door's crack. Then he closed his eyes and tried to control his breathing. He started tapping both thighs with his hands, breathing through his nose and out his mouth, and thinking to himself, *It's Sarah, her name is Sarah, it's Sarah, her name is Sarah.*

"Sorry, I thought you said Mary," Mark stated. "My name's Mark." Mark grabbed his knees in stress with huge, sweaty palms and continued to grab and release, grab and release, feeling the force of memories trying to weaken his control, pulling off finger after finger of his grip on reality. Sarah sat back down and her curiosity struck; she was fascinated. Sarah had found a trigger.

"Who's Mary?"

"She's my wife."

"And she's dead?"

"No, please no. She's alive. She's at home," Mark said, feeling another finger slip off.

"Why are you afraid of her name?"

Mark froze in his spot. Another ten seconds passed just like the meeting with Sarah at Tyler's hospital room door. As a psychiatrist, Sarah could glean exactly what Mark was experiencing. He was getting worse, the Post-Traumatic Stress Disorder was a given, but some unknown psychological problems were there as well. He was slowly losing reality like he was on a progressing dosage of LSD; she could see the advancement from his voice, his features. *This is bigger than I first believed,* Sarah thought while continuing to stare at Mark's absent face. *Much bigger than I believed.*

Finally, Aaron was on his way outside. He'd had a long talk in the cafeteria with Tyler's father, and Aaron told him everything. During the past hour, Tom had run up to the sixth floor, gone through the bolted door, and found Tyler's room, but knew it wasn't right. Freezing at the door, about to enter in with confidence to talk to both Tyler and Mark, Tom turned around. Mark needed time.

The Prayer

MARK WAS HOME WITH Mary when it happened: when Iraq invaded Kuwait. It was a frightening day for everyone. On August 2, 1990, Saddam Hussein, Iraq's dictator, had been threatening Kuwait for some time. The land of Kuwait was at one point part of Iraq and presently controlled 20 percent of the world's oil reserves and a coastline of the Persian Gulf. Kuwait was also bordered by only Iraq and very vulnerable due to its small size. Within hours, downtown Kuwait City was taken over, and forces began to head south toward the Saudi Arabian border. The neighboring nations, Egypt and Saudi Arabia, quickly called on the UN for support. That same day, the United Nations Security Council demanded Iraq's withdrawal from Kuwait. The Pentagon also had plans to aid Saudi Arabia and met with King Fahd of Saudi Arabia to inform him of their plans. Then, in mere minutes of his approval, orders were sent out, which began the largest buildup of American forces since Vietnam. By the final days of September, two hundred thousand Americans were in Saudi Arabia, enough to defend from any Iraqi attack. This defense was known as Operation Desert Shield. The neighboring country was protected, so the spread of Iraq was threatened, but there was more to be done.

On August 6, 1990, the council called for a worldwide ban on trade with the country, and on November 29, the UN agreed to use "all necessary means" of force against Iraq if their men didn't withdraw from Kuwait by January 15. Time passed slowly and steadily as the days continued to blow by, and every new day Kuwait was still occupied, every rising sun closer to the determined deadline that would never be met, was closer to the day of decided warfare. Lockdown was complete. Hussein refused to retreat his forces from Kuwait. Six hundred eighty thousand allied troops, mostly American, gathered in the Middle East to enforce an Iraqi retreat through overwhelming firepower, a representation of the world's combined efforts to demolish a weaker evil. At 4:30 p.m. EST on January 16, 1991, Operation Desert Storm began when fighter planes were launched from US and British aircraft carriers on the Persian Gulf. For six weeks, the battle in air thickened, bombs flying from UN forces toward Iraqi air bases and command centers, while Iraq aimed their air forces toward main cities in Saudi Arabia and Israel. Mark, Tom, and camp after camp of troops stayed alert and ready for a ground attack, many eager, fearful, and excited all at once. They all left after January 15. The day before, Mark and Mary held hands before yet another operation, lying down on thin, white cotton blankets and rubber hospital beds on their sides. Mark asked the colon doctor if he ever had *crappy* days or if someone ever ripped a loud one mid-operation. The doctor smiled while Mary laughed with embarrassment and good humor, knowing he lightened the atmosphere to ease her nerves. He left twenty minutes after waking from the operation, a kiss and a promise from his Hand Mitten, called a taxi, and left weary while his wife rested in the crowded recovery room. He promised that he'd come back from the Middle East, he and Tom both. The kiss was quick, a passionate peck on the lips as if they had the rest of their lives left to spend together, a casual touch as if he were off to another day of training on the base. Yet seconds later Mark returned, realizing his mistake, and kissed her again, this time longer and more passionate, as if it could be the last day on Earth, and then he left. This was the only surgery they didn't celebrate, as it became tradition to invite friends over for a beer and have a party, and some even half expected written invitations to arrive in the mail or a call on their home phone. He packed up a camo backpack and a shoulder carry-on with blankets, books, a deck of cards, a Bible, clothes, peanuts, and a picture of Mary. Yet before Mark left, his eye caught new designs in Mary's art room, still drying from the wet paint used on the canvas the day before. He stood there as if in mid motion, a camo hat on his head and his military jacket half on, curiosity itching his mind as he saw the diverse colors splattered the way they were. He threw his jacket's left sleeve over his left arm and walked in slowly and cautiously, as if every step were more dangerous than the last. *Her artwork is like her diary,* Mark thought to himself as he drew nearer and nearer to the wet canvas, stepping on the dull orange tiles with periodic crusty, splattered colors of paint on the floor. *This was done before we left for the hospital,* Mark thought. *She must have been painting till the second we left.* The painting had a man in the photo, hiding under brown sandbags while bullets flew over his head, and the man was bawling through his red, puffy eyes, mourning over a disfigured figure in the yellow mud, ugly, broken, and dismantled, with limbs out of sockets and organs spilling out. It was tragically and graphically upsetting, like a mad cartoon with its overly dramatic features. But above him were floating spirits dining at a table, laughing, shaking hands, hugging with other phantoms, playing poker, wearing top hats, while all being well dressed, clean cut, and precise in their shape. The man wasn't; his face had sweat dripping from the side, blood from his nose, and a drooped, dramatic, cartoon portrayal of shock. But behind the man was what could be the dead, discombobulated soldier drenched and sinking in the mud, yet not the physical being, but the phantom, giving a transparent hug from behind, with a glistening, shiny smile. It was the focal point of the entire painting. Mark picked up the painting, studied it with much discomfort, the dark, emotional shades and the waxy, living characters in the drawing. Then, from the corner of his eye, he saw another piece of art hidden behind it. It was much more simple but as impactful as the last. It was a light pencil sketch of a messy, graffiti-looking font written on the side of a brick wall. The wall seemed to be a part of an apartment, with people inside, dining and laughing like the ghosts, almost perfectly parallel to the ghosts. The graffiti said:

You're home, never leave my hand again. I never doubted your return.

—Love, your Hand Mitten

In the street there was a drawing of two swans kissing, with another swan close by. The third swan was obviously not related, painted first as a solid black. Although Mark knew who the third swan was. It was Tom. *Mary's right,* Mark thought. *I'm as clueless as you are, sweetheart.*

Mark wasn't stationed with Tom. They led different groups along the Saudi Arabian front. Mark, in the heat of war, was promoted to staff sergeant, and Tom became a sergeant. Then they left. Eight hours passed in the plane, and they landed in a military camp at Saudi Arabia. Mark met his new team of men with very limited with knowledge, only because Mark was a very skilled teacher in the military. Tom, stationed miles away, was in charge of men his own age and thought of Vietnam. The average age in Vietnam was nineteen, which at the time was two years younger than the voting age. Tom thought of alcoholism and an upsetting return to the United States. *Just like your father,* he thought to himself while observing his team with caution. Mark taught his squad basic rules: Listen and never question; Be brave, but never arrogant; Never stop and think before shooting, because the Iraqis won't. Tom was less knowledgeable and less confident but fought his fear and commanded as he was taught. Mark continued to worry about Tom and Mary. Time went on, and on

February 24, a massive offensive ground attack began, which ended Desert Storm's operation in a massive invasion between the Iraqi ground forces and all the major empires in the world. On February 23, Mark prepared his squad in a small tent. They were not close to alone; endless military tents were crowded together, waiting for the raid, preparing themselves. The night was dimming down, and Mark lit up the room with a lantern. He began with their strengths and weaknesses, then fell into complex depth of their formations and what classified as common stupidity, although most of his speech was merely moral support, since you cannot ace a test with studious actions the night before. When reaching the end, a peanut-brown-haired man drenched in sweat ran into the crowded tent with a letter.

"Staff Sergeant Mark Wegman?" the messenger yelled.

"Yes," Mark said powerfully.

"Come outside, sir, I need to talk to you," the messenger nervously commanded while gasping for air. Mark looked around at his team and then up.

"If that is what you wish," he said calmly.

"Yes, very much," the man said as he turned around and walked out. Mark followed.

"What's wrong, good man?" Mark kindly spoke, but the man, still heavily breathing, exclaimed loud and powerfully:

"I was told to find you as fast as I could. This message was delayed for weeks! You need to leave, sir, you need to go home."

Mark's expression turned very grave.

"What's wrong?"

The man looked up at Mark. He was not young but still carried many soft features in his pale white half-Irish face. He handed him the letter, outstretched by an arm's length yet closer than ever before. The days had marched by without his knowledge as a letter floated around from hand to hand, border through border, from one side of the world to the other, with news about a war to come. The news that was destined to fall into his hands, wasting three years of preparation on the night before war and leaving it all behind forever.

"It's your wife."

◆◆◆

THE PLANE TRIP WAS long, his patience melting faster and faster as he tapped his feet on the ground and his fingers on the arm of the coach chair he rode in. Mark felt as if an hour were far off in the distance, and every hour that slowly passed brought over an even more potent thought of Mary's name on a gravestone. He began to think of what the man had told him. How she had only written that her time was limited and she needed her husband. Mark had called her from a long-distance military phone and given her a date upon returning from the Middle East, asking why she never called, why he didn't find out sooner. *But I did,* he heard her say through the phone, *every day I called, every day.* She told him to meet her at the hospital back in Tucson on the sixth floor upon returning.

This plane, he thought, *is taking too long. I need to feel her heart, I need my Hand Mitten. God please let the cancer be mine, let it be me.* He cracked open his Bible and gently swayed from side to side like a tree in the wind.

When reaching the airport, he left his luggage in the claim area, bought a rental car, and sped through the five o'clock rush hour like a madman, passing and cutting off cars like a stream passing through rocks.

This is Satan's work, Mark thought while passing a red Toyota 4Runner laying on the horn, *because Mary is an angel, she's always been an angel, she doesn't deserve this.* He accelerated toward a yellow light, meeting the intersection the moment it turned red. *How could*

she call me day in and day out, yet I was never informed of any calls at
all? Precious time, oh precious time!

He swerved into the first parking lot available, which said,
"Radiation and Surgery Patients Only" in bold black letters on a sign
above the lot, like the eyes of a hawk waiting to shame any dishonest
guests. He then ran over the cracked concrete and entered through
two glass doors, the face of the building. The front desk woman yelled
for him to walk, but Mark did no such thing and ran by as if she were
some sort of spirit or a brick wall. He tried the elevators, but as he
watched the lights on the top drop patiently from the fifth floor to
the fourth, he knew that by the time it arrived he would have died
from the choking tension to see his wife. So Mark ran up the gray
concrete stairs behind an off-white door and beat the elevator by two
seconds. He bumped into a young nurse and doctor, passing through
the swaying doors and hospital hallway lights as his boots echoed
off the light brown tiles of the hospital floor. He then, for the first
time, approached the metal door—the intimidating front entrance
to a hidden society that he would soon see again more than twenty
years later. Mark pressed a red button on the side, under a speaker, a
circular camera, and a note that said, "press button, await front desk."
He waited, breathing a little heavier than usual, in the best shape of
his life. While he waited, the speaker chimed three repeating notes,
from low to high, low to high, and as he awaited the front desk, felt
like lifetimes passed by his eyes, as if he could watch his own hands
whittle away from the effects of time. *Do-do-do, do-do-do, do-do-do*
the speaker said as his hands clenched tighter and tighter, waiting to
see his wife. *Do-do-do, do-do-do, do-do-do.* His boot tapped on the
ground like a rabbit's foot, *please be alive,* he thought, *please be alive.*
Then the door opened, locks on vertical sides snapped coldly, and the
hinges didn't squeak the slightest. Mark ran toward the front desk,
back in motion.

"Mary Wegman, which room is she in?" Mark asked, frantically. The front desk lady wasn't afraid of his size, but was afraid *for* him. Her young hazel eyes watered on call.

"She's in room twenty-seven, Mark. They're expecting you."

Mark pushed faster than ever before, his heart and mind on hold until he could see Mary alive. Nurses watched his frantic sprint. He followed the numbers on the doors. "Fourteen," he said to himself, yet loud enough to rebound off the walls of the hallway. "Twenty-one… twenty-five." Then he stopped at twenty-seven, stepping forward a foot or two more to catch up with his footing. "Twenty-seven," he said with more voice and pushed the door inside. His heart was racing, nerves high on fear. When the door opened, he saw for the first time the TV hanging on the right, with a whiteboard right to the TV, a window directly in front of the door, a foldout couch under the window, a nightstand to the far left, the plastic bed in the middle of the left wall, a towering pump machine pole on the opposite side of the bed, and a full bathroom with a thick sliding bubbled-glass door. Located on the far left corner of the room were the bathroom door and the IV machine. The pair was helpful for the patient, as many painful days and nights awaited them; they'd roll their machine a few feet into the medical bathroom as sometimes it was all the strength they could afford.

Inside the bathroom was a shower, a toilet, and a measuring cup for urine, all replaced, sanitary, and awaiting to fulfill their purpose. On the door was a chart for food and liquid consumption, vacant, neat, and hungering, thirsty for records to be made. The bed was also neatly made, folded, and keen, impatiently waiting for someone's submission to its promise of rest and recovery. Aaron was by the door; he hadn't slept in days and seemed to be even skinnier. Mary's dad was also present. He stood next to the whiteboard and dropped a call when Mark came in. Mark's parents were also there, a couple he hadn't seen since the Christmas before the last. Old age had made them very isolated, with their own social groups and gatherings, living somewhere far more rural and distant than before. He stared at them like a child seeing a teacher outside of their classroom. It was out of place.

Mary wasn't plugged into any of the tubing; there was no IV in her right or left arm, no PICC line or midline. She was by the window in the back and ran over to Mark crying, wearing a very nice blue dress with green-and-yellow flowers scattered around. It was something that wasn't thrown on in the hospital room. She planned her outfit, her makeup, waterproof eyeliner, and foundation, a face that took her hours to prepare. Mark was very familiar with her process. He knew she didn't spend the night there; no one did. He watched her cry in his arm and lifted her up.

"Mary, why haven't they admitted you? Why are you not getting treatment? You have to start as soon as possible and recover as soon as you can. You can't hesitate. Cancer is something you don't ignore."

"I'm sorry, but I thought if I told you the truth, you'd worry too much," Mary said while sobbing louder and louder. Her eyes and face were red, her voice overpowering the room as Aaron looked away and Kenny warily watched with dreadful, regretful eyes.

"Tell me what?" Mark said, slightly shaking her. "What's going on?"

A man in a white coat had walked in seconds before and now closed the door. The door echoed like Mary's cries, Mark turning around in a flash. They locked eyes for a few seconds, watching the doctor's sober expression, and he finally pieced the mystery together.

"Mark," the man said. "Your family didn't gather for your wife, they gathered here for you." Mary began to cry in Mark's arm again, even louder. He pushed her closer to himself, began to rub her scalp and lightly tug her hair, then smiled.

"Colon cancer, doctor?"

The middle-aged Hispanic doctor walked in more to pat Mark on the shoulder. He was taller than Mark by an inch. Not many people are, but he was.

"Yes."

"What stage?"

"Stage Two. You are blessed we caught it early, but because we couldn't reach you as quickly as we'd like, we need to start with another colonoscopy test," the doctor proclaimed while keeping eye contact. Mark kissed Mary's head and smiled again, a graceful smile toward the doctor.

Thank you lord, he thought. *You heard my prayer.*

Breaking Point

MARK!" SARAH YELLED. THE family in the corner continued to stare, whispering to each other. Mark finally snapped back and stood out of the chair. His violent jerk hit a nerve from the accident and made his scream louder than he'd believed he would.

"Mary!" he yelled in shock.

"Mark, what's wrong with you?" Sarah yelled again, asking the first time while he stood absentminded. Mark turned to her, and it hit him. He'd solved a puzzle he never even thought was there. He walked toward Sarah and got on one knee to match her height in the chair. She backed away as if he were about to be thrown into a violent craze, already hypothesizing what he may have.

"A nurse told me your son had no immune system," Mark said, spitting out, atrabilious. "Does he or does he not?"

Sarah stood out of the chair and screamed. "Don't ever look, talk, or breathe my son's way ever again!"

"Woman!" yelled Mark. "This is serious. I haven't seen my wife because her father and my friend told me she was too weak to have visitors. I need to know, so tell me, does he or does he not have an immune system?" His outcry was so loud that most of the family in the corner stood up and watched with caution, and nurses and doctors ran out of the bolted door to see what might blow out of proportion,

Kennedy among them, hiding in the back. Her movements were well executed, as she pretended to be in as much shock as the rest. Tom went up, apologizing to visitors and nurses as he passed through the crowd to Mark and demanded that he walk away from Sarah and follow him back to the bench.

"You are making a scene, Mark," Tom said with partial embarrassment, then whispered in his ear. "You cannot talk to Sarah like that, and do not ask such questions. Think about your job, your friendships, everything you hold dear. You can't do this, Mark." Tom stared at Mark, who ignored him and continued to stare at Sarah. As she glared back into his eyes, watching the crowd gather around like bees around a hive, she finally caved, wanting to conclude the fiasco and any danger Mark's change in tone would also bring.

"He has no immune system," Sarah said sharply, with a look just as dangerous as her voice. "Now get out of my and my child's life."

Mark stared at Sarah with enlightenment. Time paused for him as this newly discovered knowledge circled through the different chambers in his mind. Lightning struck outside the hospital window, a major storm hit, and the trees danced with fear. The rain was violent and chaotic. There were no wind or rain patterns. The animals hid, and Mark ran off furious while Kennedy ran off as if she were to check on a patient and cried in the bathroom from her own shame. Aaron heard the lightning in the process of leaving the cafeteria, and Dr. Kenny was preparing for the arrival of the victims from the car accident in the surgical room. Another bolt of tremendous power flew from the horrid sky, and then Mark began to cry, pushing through a circle of nurses and doctors, constantly ignoring the pain from his own car accident the night before.

"Mark!" yelled Tom, following close to his side. "Don't do it, she's more than immune deficient."

Mark grabbed and threw a woman into the wall. She screamed and split her head open.

"You're right. She's also a bilious lie from Aaron, from Kenny. He thought it would be fun to steal out precious time left for his own cruel enjoyment." He shoved open two seven-foot doors that led down to the fifth floor.

"Mark!" yelled Tom. "Don't run out of here without any thought of how it'll affect others. Whatever you do tonight will forever be imprinted on you and your friends," Tom aggressively said while two very dense security guards from behind came and tackled Mark, but he punched one's jaw out of line and stretched the other's arm out of socket before standing up and launching them away. Mark continued to run on, with a noticeable broken nose. Tom was untouched. Mark would never touch him. Lightning struck again and he continued on.

"What made you so insane, Mark?" whispered Tom. "Why won't you listen to me? I had a rough path same as you. I understand."

Mark turned and yelled, blood running from his nostrils, and as he spoke the passing stream of red sprayed off his lips. "You weren't there, Tom!" He began to cry with anger. "I thought you died. They told me you went missing. Then Mary got sick. And I got sick. You don't know my pain!"

◆◆◆

"Wow," said his first nurse. "You have very nice and pumped veins! It's like picking fruit. I have so many options!"

Mark laughed loudly to muster Mary's attention. "Don't tell Mary, but I use the food in our pantry as weights," Mark said while curling with an empty hand and winking.

"I don't buy that much food," Mary said proudly, still with raw tears in her eyes. Then Mark smirked and pointed to a vein.

"That's true. Everyone owns five bottles of Progresso."

Mary giggled. Then a few minutes later she admitted that there might be a problem, as the entire pantry usually had no space to spare, and the refrigerator (although organized) was overflowing with condiments, cheeses, meats, and sometimes frozen rye bread. But in the hospital, time left like the flow of cooling lava on the coast, slower and slower. Although the days felt frozen in time, time itself never changed. Weeks continued to pass and Mark lost his hair. One day he woke up and shredded strands were scattered on his plastic-coated white pillow, and every time he scratched, or lightly tugged his head, the hair would come out in a frenzy, as if wanting to be released from the poisoned body. His weight fell from 280 to 110, every muscle was absorbed until there was only bones, and his muscular figure achieved from constant military training dissipated to the point that he couldn't even complete a stroll to the restroom without the help of a walker. The hospital placed an absorbent mat under the blankets to the rubber bed he slept on every night, in case an accident ever came about. "You cannot hold in your bowel movements sometimes because a combination of your morphine and chemotherapy has numbed your body's senses to detect when you have to go, and your muscles are also very weak—same goes with your bladder," the nurse told Mark as she slid the mat onto his bed. "So I recommend that you try to go to the restroom every two hours, just in case you have to go."

"Can I get an adult-size diaper?" Mark joked to the nurse, his voice slow and weak, his movements the same.

"No!" blurted Mary. "Because I'm not going to change those diapers. And you'd need adult powder, not baby powder. And frankly, I don't think that exists."

When Mary came into the room, Mark stepped up his game and stood up in the bed, even when he was thrown in constant fits of upchucking, rejecting the food settling in his stomach, or having a fever of 118 degrees running rapid in his head. He would fight to show any energy he had so she wouldn't fear as much as she should have for the severity of his illness. Mary would feed him with a spoon, anything Mark wanted, until sores erupted in his mouth and he could no longer eat or speak. Then she would read him novels, but his mind would wander from the chemicals flooding his thoughts, and they never a finished book.

"I only liked the beginning of the book anyways."

"Oh yeah? What's the title of the book?"

"The...the rumble? Something to do with monkeys," Mark said, half jokingly, half perplexed, while staring in Mary's eyes full of irritation and humor, which said, *I can't believe you don't remember.*

"*The Jungle Book,*" she declared with her arms in the air like a misunderstood teen. Mark scratched his bald head with nervousness.

"Mary, that title is so complex, there's no way I could possibly remember such complexity."

"Yeah, the complexity of complexness is very complex."

"Very complicated."

Now when I say Mark's mind wandered, I mean he would have short-term memory loss, and he wouldn't comprehend ideas. The doctors called him "chemo brain" and laughed when seconds later he asked what his determined nickname was. "The memory loss is a reaction from the chemo," Mark's doctor told Mary with a thin, friendly smile. "These effects will not last once the chemo is out of his system." Some days Mary would bring in a boom box and quietly play albums from Aerosmith, the Beatles, and other classic artists that he enjoyed. Mark, weaker and weaker by the day, would move his fingers up and down to the beat, and Mary would laugh hysterically. His faith in God was unparalleled; Mark was truly a man of hope. However, on one particular late night, some of his hope was lost as a defining moment in is his life occurred, a moment for both Mary and Mark, which occurred on March 11, 1991, at 2:23 a.m. when Mary received a call from the military base in California.

"Okay, Mark, are you hungry?" Mary asked as she barged into their room and reached for the black hospital phone, her nose running with ruby red, puffy eyes. Her words sprayed out her mouth in frantic panic.

"Mary," Mark's weak, sore-covered voice called, "what's wrong?"

"We can order room service, or order some pizza. You thirsty, hun? Any pain?" Her loose green-striped pajamas and brown hair flew from side to side as she rushed around the room and out. She came back with water a few minutes later.

"Here, sweetie, you need to drink water. I know it burns your sores but it is so good for you."

"Mary, I don't want water." He sat up in his bed while she bent the tip of the bendy straw and placed it close to his mouth.

"No, you can't say no, you need to drink so you will get better, you need to get stronger." She began to cry with terror in her eyes. "You need to drink, drink the water."

"No, Mary, I don't want any water!" Mark hollered, with a little break in his voice from his bloody, enflamed throat. She began to jab the straw into his mouth, gripping the foam white cup.

"Please drink!" she hollered as her eyes ran like faucets. "You need to get better!" Mark pushed her body away with his thin arm with great, burning frustration.

"No, I said I don't want any water!"

"But you need it!" Mary screamed as her fingers folded through the delicate cup, water spraying all over the bed and ground, expanding through the crack and into the bathroom. She looked around in horror as the lifesaving water slid farther and farther away. She leaned onto a wall and slid down to her knees, crying in the corner as the foam cup still stuck to her arm. Mark grabbed his walker.

"Go away," she cried under her arm, "please leave me alone."

"What's wrong?" Mark asked. "What happened?"

"No, go back to your bed," her emotional voice said as Mark waddled closer, his legs shaking and her anxiety rising. "Get away!"

"You need to tell me now. I need to know."

"No!"

"What happened?"

"It's Tom!" she yelled, crying even more. "Something happened to Tom."

Mark sat in his bed, tearless, as she whispered to him from the corner, while sitting in a puddle mixed with the hospital water and her own salty tears. Tom was one of the few who died in the coalition against Iraq. They said he was one of the first yet least recognizable bodies. Mark and Mary spoke for a while, and he soon sent her off to buy mashed potatoes at the Walmart in the neighborhood, promising that he would have a few bites and knowing clearly that his stomach wouldn't be able to bear even basic, plain mashed potatoes. When she left him, she cried some more on the road, feeling backed into a corner, unable to flee from the death in the air. Soon after she left, Mary's father came and pushed Mark's walker out to signal his time for a walk. Mark struggled and fought his tight bedridden muscles into a standing position and cradled every step. Mary's father rolled his metal IV pump pole around next to Mark. The tubes connected to his central line in his chest were like a leash. They walked to a nearby window, where they watched a bunch of men in the dark move boxes into a huge green metal recycling container the size of half a semi. Mark's back curled and made him only half a foot taller than Kenny's height of five foot nine. He had black rings and a white bandage on his face.

Mark continued to squint at the outside sun. He hadn't felt the winter breeze since admission and was beginning to adopt a strengthening unease from the isolation, the constriction to the single hospital floor. The same cool temperature covering his bony body, the same scent of bleach and basic walls. The taste of saline in his mouth, saltier every time it was injected to clean his central line. He rushed so fast that there wasn't any time to absorb the surroundings. To feel a chill from the air, the texture from the rough, sharp desert dirt, and the smell of a rainstorm from a creosote's fragrance. But Mark remembered last season, where the wind blew as if spring were present, while it rained as if winter were still an occupant. He wished for a shower without cords that led to his central line. They were always in the way, and the bandages on his central line needed to be pampered so they wouldn't peel off from the moisture. Then he had immense terror against a bacterial infection called C. diff, where only a few days ago the doctors had asked the nurses to pump his stomach with a tube that entered through the nose, since his stomach was layered with the infection, which caused bile and bowel movements to run rapid, soupy clumps of old blood and a sweet smell of the infection running from both ends. The doctors told him that the chances of the infection returning increased every time he received this bowel bug, which made the infection seem all the worse. The frequent beeping in the middle of the night was another hassle that he hated, signaling the end of a bag's cycle into the body from the IV bag, or if his heart rate or blood pressure increased higher than a certain limit. Then, when he didn't get enough rest, hallucinations occurred. One hallucination happened on that same night on March 11, 1991, where at 12:48 a.m., Mark woke up, and the walls closed in, beginning in a whisper and ending in a demonic screech, yelling, "Cancer, cancer!" He then slowly walked into the bathroom, connected to the IV pump, heart monitor, and stomach pump, feeling controlled from something else, something bigger than him, the fingers of satin luring him away from his bed. Mark stopped in the bathroom, which was when Mary woke and saw all the wires stretched from the bedside behind the sliding door.

"Mary," Mark yelled while half awake, "I love you!" He then fell toward the ground and smashed his head on the metal drain. Everything from the machines tugged and fell along with Mark. Mary ran over, found a red string next to the toilet, and pulled it out the wall, triggering a screeching alarm different from the others. There were two of those triggers; the other was connected to the TV remote, connected to the wall. Four nurses rushed in, checked his pulse, picked up the machines, then asked for him to speak and answer simple questions while one nurse shined a light in one eye and another felt his pulse with her thumb jammed into his wrist. He slowly woke up and said quietly, quieter and calmer than anyone else, "I'm alive?"

The nurses checked his central line, and luckily it was undamaged because he had landed on his side, but the nurses changed the needle. They also checked his nose tube, and for brain damage, his doctor sent Mark down to the second floor for a CAT scan. Mary waited with him in his portable plastic bed, sitting on a chair in her nightgown with almost all of her sleep drained away; then she asked why he said what he did. Mark stopped his jokes that she felt no entertainment toward and patted his blankets.

"I thought I died."

Mary hurt deeply, but the back of her hand on her cheek and her exhausted expression were unchanged. She thought so as well; for a second she thought that a little after the two weeks they spent, the war from the gates of Hell ended, that she lost yet another to the afterlife.

After the CAT scan, they were informed that no problems were occurring in his head. He was as normal as before, only sleep-deprived. Then, at 2:15 a.m., Mary got a call from Iraq, and the rest is history. Now Mark and her father sat at the window. He squinted at the thick darkness outside as Mr. Kenny stood there silent, until Mark spoke.

"You know, a while before Operation Desert Storm, Mary, Tom, and I sat around the table." Mark laughed while continuing to speak, feeling pride from Tom's name. "And, and it was a special day. He was about to be a corporal. Man, he worked hard for that title. I watched him fight, I watched him cry, and he always said, 'Maybe tomorrow, Mark, maybe tomorrow.' He said this whenever he failed, whenever he was yelled at. 'Tomorrow will be better, maybe tomorrow.' But now he has no tomorrow." Mark froze to catch his breath from the exhaustion of speaking, his enflamed throat, and continued. "Well, at the table, Tom told me that he was afraid. Afraid that one day he would be sent to war and either die or become a drunk like his old man, that he would never be better." Mark's lip began to roll out and shake. "I told him I'd prevent it, that I would never allow such a thing to occur."

Silence among the men. They continued to stare into the moonless night, at the two men throwing the last stray boxes into the bin while they laughed. One middle-aged short white man was talking about how drunk he'd been the night before, while swaying from side to side, portraying the severity of his drunkenness twenty-four hours ago. The other, a tall, young Hispanic man, fell onto the ground in uncontrollable laughter. Mark and Kenny watched the two men, as if they were inexperienced children who did not yet understand what life could entail, although the Hispanic boy (the youngest of the two) was three years older than Mark. They were so close, the two hospital maintenance men, Mark and Kenny, from the sixth floor to the hospital ground below, yet both their worlds were so far apart.

"Then he called me Dad!" Mark broke down, and Kenny quickly grabbed his light body and gave him a rough, clasped hug. Mark squeezed with his growing heartache, his uncontrollable gasps for breath filling the tragic floor, yet not an unreasonable noise for a place like this. "He called me Dad," Mark cried. "Anything else would have been less painful."

"It's okay, Mark," said Kenny, "he's with his real dad now. He's with God."

He continued to cry for a while in Kenny's arms as Kenny ran his fingers though his son-in-law's hair, watching the two men outside hop into the hospital-branded pickup and leave without any afterthought. Less than two hundred died in the coalition against Iraq. Tom was one of the first to go and the last generation of the Freemans. This was Mark's breaking point.

Umbrella

MARK CONTINUED THROUGH THE floors in the hospital, his rage building more and more as if there were bugs in his hair, and every step they bit harder, stretching his desire to open the cracked-paint green door leading to Mary's bedridden body. Mark pushed through the doors toward the third floor. Tom screamed but Mark didn't listen; he only heard what was wanted, his mind so far gone as he led a trail of dark red blood from his gushing nostrils. He pushed the doors leading to the second floor, and while Tom continued to follow closely behind with his useless screams, Mark froze in place. "Tom," said Mark calmly. "This is where Mary got the phone call. This is where you died."

"I'm right here, Mark," Tom whispered, rushing to his side. "I'm here for you right now, please trust me."

Mark turned around aggressively and had a face of stiff madness, his eyes wide and fists clenched so hard his nails turned white.

"You're dead. Leave me alone." He turned back and came to the first floor's doors, slamming them open with even more force than before. Everything was ground level, with a door at the end of a short hallway, and another significantly longer, more winding corridor to the right, with a bright exit sign above both doors at the end of each hallway, illuminating its faint glow. The two steel elevator doors were to the left, as shiny and metallic as they were twenty years ago, as if time never passed. The rain pelted the concrete walkways behind the door, echoing louder and louder through the walls and ceiling as a million tiny impacts crashed against the building.

But as Mark walked closer to the glowing exit sign, lost in a trance of desire, Aaron strolled toward the other exit sign on the opposite side of the building. He faintly wondered if Mark was inside, if he had covered his face and run in for the safe haven of dry clothes and comfort. If Mark was sitting, waiting for Aaron on another bench in the hospital. In fact, a part of him wished Mark had run inside and awaited his friend's attendance like a kindergartener waiting for their mother, because a growing itch of nervousness crept into his mind as he strolled closer and closer to the exit sign, somehow knowing by his own superstitions that the bench was abandoned, that destiny had taken ahold of Mark's life once again. Then, through the exit door, past the men on stretchers, fifteen seconds before Mark, who blew passed Aaron like a racing dog, and ran through the long, winding hallway toward the operating room.

"Stop, Mark!" yelled Tom. "You need to live in the present! Stop this insane plot of overwhelming rage, before you walk through those final doors outside! I will not follow you into that darkness, into your own self-pity, your madness, your stubborn denial." Tom stared over his shoulder, toward the roof and back to the sixth floor with a sober gaze. Then he whispered, yet more as a reminder to himself than a statement to Mark, "I must stay in the hospital, for now. I must be here tonight."

The two men on red stretchers raced by like lightning. The car accident victims were bleeding profusely, gashes on their torsos ripped out from shards of metal and glass, their eyes bloodshot red from the amount of blood rushing through their noses, and their calves cut as if touched by a food dispenser for a pinch of time. First responders and nurses surrounded them, holding bags of blood over their heads while rushing them over to the operating room. Mark froze, his insanity paused briefly to muse on how one accident could lead to death, how frail life has always been. One man, an older gentleman, prayed like a frantic rabbit. The other, a young twenty-one-year-old college football athlete, fainted on scene, awakening without a single memory as to what had happened to his ragged body. The one who asked for a prayer remembered everything, yet the one who fainted only remembered his damaged car, a pointless care while Death flipped through a *Rolling Stone* magazine, waiting in the lobby for the opportunity of death. Mark felt a spark flare off as the sounds and screams from the accident's aftermath faded into the second story. His feet, for a few seconds, felt like they were in three inches of dry concrete. *Stay,* some faint, inward voice told him, *stay.* Then as fast as it came, the feeling of his anchored feet left. He opened the glass door without a second thought, rushing to the outside storm like a housefly to the glowing bulb of a bug zapper. The storm was blazing with rampant power and fight, rage and death, love and disappointment. Ironwoods whistled through the wind like rabid wolves, dancing with unpredictable, dramatic movements, while the heavy rain created a wall thicker than a fog. The wind blasted the inside with its bite of rain, drenching and mixing Mark's blood on the floor with the drooling water. Tom reached out for Mark with an outstretched hand from the other side of the hallway, only five yards of length. Distress grabbed ahold of his voice, from the knowledge of what Mark's actions would entail, while he stared at the back of his head. Mark stared at the rain, one foot out of the door, below the glowing red exit sign as his nose continued to stream blood.

"Please…Dad," the phantom said.

Mark responded the instant Tom was quiet, loud and without care. His concern for Tom's existence was completely exterminated. In fact, his concern for the two victims as well, along with Kennedy, Kenny, Aaron, and even Tyler, was gone like a simple cupped hand brushing salt off a table. He faced the raging storm, his mind only on the cracked green door, determined to be with his dying wife.

"Your father is a drunk." Mark stepped into the storm toward Aaron's police car, Mary's room, and the rage. Aaron walked out the opposite exit and saw Mark's ring. It was shining in a puddle from the hospital lights that lit a few yards out into the storm, like a yellow phantom laying his cloak in a three-foot perimeter. He knew what Mark had done, where he went, and what he saw. The sixth floor was a trigger, the hospital itself was a trigger, and Aaron knew Mark's visit was unsafe.

"Mark," he whispered. "No. Please no." Aaron shoved the ring far in his denim jeans and ran over, through the hospital, slipping in his drenched shoes on the smooth, winding white tile and screaming toward his car. There was a fifteen-second delay from door to door, like the red stretchers before. The thunder roared, and Mark ripped out part of the car under the key ignition with ease. He then hotwired the police car, turned on the headlights and windshield wipers, and backed the stick out of the parking spot. He fiddled with the radio, police scanner, and middle console, then found a steel black nine-millimeter revolver, loaded to the top of the wide barrel—Aaron's favorite choice of weapon. Without a second thought, he picked up the firearm and placed it in his front right pocket, with an uncontrollable fit of laughter crawling up onto his lips.

"Aaron," he yelled, "I've known all along, I've known all along that you took all my firearms! You didn't trust me, and I played along because sometimes children need candy, sometimes you have to look out for the little man. I loaded my weapon in secret so you can feel like the man in control, the man with power."

Behind the car, Aaron screamed for Mark, screamed for him to stop. Mark heard but hit the ground with the gas petal all the more and sprayed Aaron with rocks and mud, drenching him as he ran toward his fading car. The fear in his eyes expanded, and Aaron screamed curse words into the clouds, kicking the puddles around him like a child. Then Aaron abruptly pulled out his phone and called the station. "This is Chief of Police Aaron Hudson. My car was stolen. Track it down and pick me up now! I'm at the hospital on Broadway, and hurry, lives will be lost." The man on the phone, Wilber Hexton, hastily informed the station of the message through his adult braces. Then he responded.

"Mr. Hudson, there is an officer a mile from your location that was assigned to an accident on the intersection—"

"I don't care, just get him over here!" yelled Aaron, interrupting. He continued to stomp around in anger, screaming into the darkened atmosphere until the police car came a minute later. Aaron made him switch seats, and they turned on the siren, shining just enough to see the rain, and sputtered off the parking lot and into the road like a rocket.

"What're you doing, sir?" said the sixty-year-old police sergeant in the passenger seat.

"I'm catching the man who stole my car!" yelled Aaron angrily. "And next time don't ask and I'll tell you myself. That mouth will get you fired." The old man quickly forced his head down and apologized. But Aaron knew who had stolen his car, knew the second he saw Mark's ring on the bench, a flicker of light like the end of a match caught in his head like Mark's, his fingers slipping from the illusion of control.

◆◆◆

TIME WENT ON, AND joyful times were in sight. Mark's cancer began to subside, and more frequent checkouts were occurring. He was also growing some peach fuzz, and Mary would rub it while he slowly fell asleep in their bed. She also began to paint joyful paintings; some were explosions of just plain, exciting, and plump youth-filled lines or dots mushed together. But more than those were Christian paintings of churches, steeples, children praying, and choirs singing in the name of God. Since Tom had gone missing, she loved God even more. Tom had been an amazing Christian, and Mary continued to say how it didn't matter if Tom was dead or alive—he'd want them to be strong Christians of the Gospel. So their faith grew and extended past many boundaries because of their marriage and strength. She also began to sell her art to scrape up money for bills and food. There wasn't a pantry full of snacks and cuisines anymore, nothing but the necessities.

"I thought the day would never come when I'd be able to see the back of the pantry," chuckled Mark.

"Any more backtalk and you might wake up bald," Mary said, smiling deviously before she walked over and kissed the feather-light layer of hair on the top of his head.

As Mark became closer and closer to remission, he joined the police force. Aaron was an assistant chief and an amazing influence. He snagged Mark a job on the computers, collecting 911 distress calls and sending the officers out. Sometimes he was able to ride with another officer, which was the luxury of a smaller town compared to Los Angeles and Chicago, but only when there was a safe call to attend and watch. He was still very weak and wasn't contributing much but was respected highly on the team. They would hold the door, joke, and sit down at lunch. But the other officers were also terribly afraid. Men saw him as someone who'd been through a tough, complex life, and so they didn't want to complain about their problems or show any negativity. Mark caught this at first glance and began to detest the ones who did, who sometimes feared Mark's theoretical judicious eyes. As Mark grew in strength, he began to rent books at the public library. Broadway was, at the time, a pleasant, clean road with churchgoers, children running in and out of toy stores, young adults riding bikes from their homes to their work, and a variety of coffee shops to choose from. Full of life and inspiration was that road, full of a bright future. Mark would walk over to many coffee shops, but his favorite was the one called Tempus Garrapatas. He wouldn't always buy coffee because the prices were outrageous, but he would sit down and learn about how a psychopath thinks, how drugs are smuggled, how they affect people's appearances and personalities, and how professional drivers could speed down roads through tough, unavoidable obstacles like water in a stream. This was more than six months past diagnosis: August 30, 1991. After Mark partially read the books, and the sun was falling, he was picked up by Aaron and came home to Mary. She was crying in the corner, wearing a white painting apron splattered with a variety of spontaneous colors and sizes. Her hair was in a ponytail, with a few paint marks in there as well, although significantly tinier and gluing some strands of hair together. Mark ran up with his minimal strength and keeled down. He groaned a tad from the pain of bending his knees but didn't yield to think about his stiff, small muscles as he continued to stare at what he believed was the most beautiful person in the world.

"Mary, what's wrong?" Mark asked. Mary continued to cry and let go of a painting she was grasping toward her chest, the fresh paint on the side of the canvas smeared from her fingerprints gripping the painting. Mark reached in front of her and picked the painting up. It was the graffiti one with the three swans in the front, painted for Mark's return.

"I found it scrunched in the back," cried Mary. "I had to finish it. But I—" Mary began to bawl again. Mark slid his hand into hers.

"But you what?" whispered Mark. Mary rested her head on Mark's shoulder, rolling it as a gesture of self-shame, catching her breath to finish her sentence. Although she tried, during irrepressible tears the words were no better than breathless gasps.

"I, I couldn't paint Tom," Mary cried as her face fell back into her knees like she were a guilty child. She was referring to the little swan in the painting, symbolizing Tom and his acceptance into the family, the endless years together as a family. Yet every time she picked up the brush to paint, shade, and complete this final addition, the black swan, she couldn't. The black swan seemed to glare back, to shame the entire painting as a symbol of deep remorse for her lack of saving Tom. The black swan's glare reminded her of why she had originally painted that canvas: for the endless, joyful years to come once the two returned from Kuwait, a dream that would never happen. Completing the painting was deemed pointless, and she knew it, guilt running wild as she stretched her will further and further to complete that final animal, the black swan, knowing that its simple, solid black color now made it the focal point of the painting, and her fingerprints also turning the original symbol into an idea she never dreamed to plan. With the people laughing in the buildings, the wall's graffiti welcoming Mark's return, the two swans kissing, and the incomplete, glaring black swan to the side, the painting was complete. Mark kissed the back of her head.

"Mary, he will come back, you will see him again. I know Tom inside and out, he survived, just please believe me," Mark said, completely unaware of his own shockingly deep and therapeutic denial. But Mary continued to cry, her gasps for air never more than a second until she cried profusely again. Seeing her destroyed, Mark came forward and gently wrapped his arms around her and began singing a song lightly into her left ear. It was a lullaby that fell in the melody of "Twinkle, Twinkle, Little Star." Mary stopped crying when he sang, and listened.

Umbrella, umbrella please don't go, you keep me away from this cold snow, I'd have no protection so please hug me, or I'd run to the old apple tree. Umbrella, umbrella please don't go, you keep me away from this cold snow. The wind is strong, this is true, but you'd hug me, and I'd hug you, so umbrella, umbrella please don't go, you keep me away from this cold snow. The rain is wet, it makes me cry, but with you we'd get by, so umbrella, umbrella please don't go...

Mary whispered the last verse with Mark. "*You keep me away from this cold snow.*" They stared into each other's eyes with equal understanding until Aaron walked in and turned on the light in the room.

"Is everything okay, guys?" exclaimed Aaron with a concerned face, completely unaware of very direct social signs.

"Yes!" said Mary while quickly lifting herself up. "Just talking about life."

Mark tried standing up but was unable to. Mary quickly looked at Mark and reached her hand out with great concern. She struggled as Mark used her supporting hand as leverage off the ground. She could not support his heavy weight all on her own. Aaron ran over and finished the rest, grabbing Mark's second hand, and together they pulled him to his feet. Mark wobbled when he began to stand again, and everyone burst out into belly-aching laughter.

"Well," Aaron said energetically, "the bar is having a happy hour, and—"

"Aaron," Mark plainly remarked, "I'm on eight pills, an antibiotic, and steroids. I can't drink." There was a nice, crisp silence as everyone froze and thought of a solution. Then Aaron spoke again.

"Applebee's is having a happy hour."

They all laughed and disagreed in their own individual ways. But thirty minutes later, Aaron, Mark, and Mary all scrunched over half-off appetizers.

The Last Day of Freedom

MARK CONTINUED TO DRIVE faster and faster. His siren was on, so traffic dispersed in both directions for him to pass freely. Most cars drove only to drive home and watch the storm from a window, as it continued to prove itself as the worst storm of the year. The lightning lit up the sky like fireworks, as the new moon hid in the clouds and as the mountains popped their heads out of the dark after every spark of light drew a path through the air. The rain fell fast and sharp, while the wipers on the automobile wiped the rain off with frantic force, and as the wind periodically rocked the accelerating car. Mark screamed for the police engine to move faster and the people in the road to disperse more swiftly, missing some by an inch. Aaron was three miles behind, speeding as fast as Mark, pushing the car faster than ever before as the wind also shoved his car with hostility, making it slip and slide in every dangerous turn that could be their last. They both passed through Broadway and the coffee shop Tempus Garrapatas. It was their last day of service until the shop closed for good. A legendary coffee organization known for its love to their customers and employees. Mark, through the town and quiet neighborhood, made it to his destination and, without keys, slammed open the door. It was a house bought once he got cancer, out of the military base and into the suburbs. It had two bedrooms and two bathrooms. The second bedroom was for Tom. Mark completely convinced that he would return. But now it was where Mary's bedridden, sick body lay. Before her isolation, nurses told him he needed to be sterile and scrubbed before entering to see her withered body. Yet as her condition worsened, he was told that he could not see her until she began to show great strides in recovery once again. "Her frail immune system finally disappeared," Mary's father told him with a stern look. "You cannot see her anymore; Aaron and I both will not allow it. You would kill Mary by your introduction of germs into her quarantined environment." *We would both die of meningitis,* Mark thought to himself. *No, I would die of meningitis; she would die from my dangerous touch, if I remember their self-absorbed lies correctly. I will die of meningitis, this is true, but if she's going to as well, then my death with her is the most joyful opportunity available. I can die with her. We can end our lives together.*

"I can feel her soft lips on my mouth once again!" Mark yelled with a roaring laugh while he walked toward the room. Every step made him more and more excited than the last as his smile extended wider and wider and his heart rose with gripping desire. He began to walk through the living room, past the two chairs that they once shared, past the painting of the swans on the stream. He never glanced over to his left or right and continued moving forward. He was pulled by an unavoidable force, to renew his past for one last moment with Mary. Lightning struck and lit up the paintings, all surrounding Mark from every angle. The swans under graffiti that said, "You're home, never leave my hand again. I never doubted your return. —Love, your Hand Mitten."

Tom was still not fully painted, just a solid, incomplete black swan. The ghosts dining on a war ground while the deformed cartoon-faced soldier cried for his fallen veteran. The swans at the lake, kissing in the sunset, a painting with different shades of blue, of a mother that had lived a short life. Mark made it to the hallway, where there lay three doors. The first one was on his left, the gateway to his room, a room with clothes thrown everywhere in a chaotic explosion of institutionalized thoughts. There was the bathroom farther down to his left, with a tiny window over the dry shower. To the brutal windstorm was where that room led, a final escape from his thoughts, the last resort that led into what Mark believed were seemingly endless storms. The last door was Mary. He didn't know what the closed door held but imagined a white room filled with a healthy, excited wife awaiting his arrival and warmth, his hand slipping into hers and igniting hibernating butterflies in his stomach to erupt like they used to years ago. Mark passed the first door, slowly making every step as if nothing would disturb the moment, crying with excitement. "My Hand Mitten!" he yelled with exhilaration. The lightning struck again and pictures surrounded Mark, pictures of their wedding, Mark and Tom in their uniforms, Mary painting happily in the sun while she giggled in her white apron, yet Mark was never sure why she was laughing, or when the picture had been taken. He has always been completely clueless as to where the photo came from. Then, finally, there was the painting Mary was working on in the photo. It was only primary colors painted a centimeter thick on the canvas, covering every inch, side, and strand of white. There was no point of the painting, except that it was pleasing to the eye. It was pleasing to see how it was made, and like an orchestra, it was exciting to wonder what the artist had been thinking when crafting their form of art. The complexity of it was more than just a picture—it was a lifestyle. Mark passed the second door without much thought at all, shaking with excitement that continued to build, knowing he could not hold the restlessness any longer. "I'm here!" Mark screamed with shrieks of loony laughter, and reached the doorknob for the third, cracked green door.

"Mark," whispered Aaron. "Don't do this. You'll kill yourself."

Mark turned 180 degrees toward Aaron, who was aiming a nine-millimeter toward Mark, hiding in the shadows. Only the barrel and his body's outline stood out like a phantom, although ghosts don't fear, and Aaron, still alive, was overwhelmed with it. Mark let his head fall forward and chuckled lightly while shaking it back and forth.

"You lied to me, Aaron. You lied about Mary's illness. Now she's on the brink of death and you threaten me with death?" Mark laughed to himself. "His logic is pointless."

"I didn't lie, Mark!"

"YOU LIED BECAUSE YOU LOVED HER!" Mark's impulsive yell accused, pointing his arched finger across the hall. "That's right, Aaron, I heard your whispers after our argument! You were going to strike me across the face. It was a dream of yours ever since we met. But you didn't. *Why*?" Mark cuffed his ear, as if someone would answer. "Because you loved her!"

"That was a long time ago!" Aaron yelled back, yet with slight hesitation. "The only reason I love Mary now is because you love her."

"So now in our final argument, you become modest? It's hilarious that with a little pressure, even the most stubborn change!" Mark snarled with his wild grin and careless attention. "Shoot me, Aaron, we all know you can't," he hissed, acting again as if there were a crowd.

"There's an entire fleet of police officers outside. Where I fail, they'd succeed."

"Then don't fail!" Mark hollered, throwing his arms apart. "Finally grow some balls. We all know Mary will die soon, so there's no point in—"

"Don't put that disease in your head!"

"Let me finish!" Mark screamed, whipping Aaron's revolver out from the elastic waist of his jeans. Aaron flinched and fled a yard back, farther in the darkness and past the first door. A flash of lightning struck with thunder a second behind, and Mark's face was revealed, his broken nose that continued to gush onto his face and clothes, and Aaron's large Metallica T-shirt on Mark's broad body, yet stained very heavily with thick streaks of blood. Aaron had changed into his police uniform while racing through the slowly emptying streets, the slightly tight dark blue clothes fitting perfectly around his body, camouflaging his lean structure.

"Mary will die," Mark confidently listed, smiling like an entertained hyena. "So I'm not afraid of death. I already know you won't shoot. Now give me one reason why you deserve mercy from me. Aaron, you pitiful little man, scraping through life believing you are more than just a background noise, something to fill up space. But you are, you are the most worthless voice on the planet."

"You won't shoot," Aaron snapped with sharp yet glossy confidence. Mark with no second thoughts raised the weapon and shot it in the air. Ceiling chips and fine powder fell in front of Mark's face, some landing on his shoulder and hair with haste, as his eyes continued to glare into Aaron's. Frightening, cold tension surged between the two as Aaron finally understood that Mark would shoot him with a smile and, as the basic blueprints of the perfect man, would not miss. But the crackling bullet in the house's still air was not what Aaron had expected, he dropped his handgun from the tension and screaming in his head with panic as he realized the gigantic mistake that was made. Aaron reached for the weapon once it was dropped, sliding it a yard away from immediate reach. Men around the house jumped from the gunfire, whispers between police officers died off, and they all stared toward the origin of the noise. The first wave of officers ran through the collapsed front door, snapped hinges, and into the living room. The rain pounded loudly on the roof, and a crackle of thunder above shook the house roughly as the hole Mark's first bullet carved began to leak water onto his head, yet Mark still stood in his spot with a motionless, diabolical glare. Aaron quickly fell to his knees and Mark raised the weapon with form and ease.

"I'll blow your hand off if you even graze the grip of that gun!" Mark firmly shouted. Aaron quickly jolted his hands upward toward the white popcorn ceiling. "I've taught five other men how to, what makes you think I won't?" Mark yelled. "Kick it over."

"I don't," Aaron angrily responded, standing and kicking over his weapon to Mark who, while the weapon was still in motion, pushed the weapon even faster down the hallway, until it smashed into the nearby wall. Three police officers ran toward the hallway and saw Aaron with his hands spread out in the air, but ran back because of his continuous, obvious yet subtle wrist flick. Aaron's wrist extended his palm back, then forward again to its original straight position, repeated a dozen times without looking behind in a frantic motion. The leader of the three was the police commissioner, Francis Baker, a thirty-one-year-old college graduate. They ran out the collapsed door and flooded front carpet, announcing that Mark had a gun pointed at Aaron, who didn't seem to want any interference from anyone else. Francis stood at the front door with a few police officers, grazing his black two-inch goatee with a grave, stern face, his mind flooding with ways to prevent Mark's death. Then, while also speaking into a much more modern Bearcat radio, informing the stationed officers around the perimeter, he began to speak to the small circle of officers around him.

"First, we cannot leave Aaron in a hostage position," announced the police commissioner. "This danger will force us to make very serious and precise decisions so as not to trigger any hostile actions. We do not want to give Mark a reason to shoot at Aaron. Mark has been a very nice, gentle man at our station; we all know his kind, yet sometimes repetitive routines." Some officers let out a light chuckle, all holding fond memories of what Baker meant. "But we all know how aggressive and strong he is as well. So you need to be alert when dealing with this issue. Gentlemen, do not let your memories interfere with your job! Whatever he's upset about is worth holding a nine-millimeter in the direction of his undeniably best friend. He is not emotionally stable! Aaron, I know, is trying with as much effort as possible to calm him down. None of us know why he is like this, but he is, and he will not respond like the Mark we all have come to know very well. I heard many of you whispering, but no need. We do not know if it was from the accident. It could be an assortment of different reasons, although the car accident and the possibility of head trauma is the most logical answer. That is our best guess," the commissioner informed them, his eyes bone-dry with difficult force. "Yet we will go in there again, for Aaron's protection. Know that a split second of hesitation could cost you your life. He isn't stopping, and, as some of you know, he was trained for these moments. Although he is a community resource officer, he is also a Gulf War veteran. The feeling of a weapon isn't abnormal to him. Also know that he was the one who shot his weapon and has someone as a hostage, our chief. We have every right to shoot him. But as you know, our goal is to get them both out alive—do not shoot unless you must and do not hesitate your judgment. Since Mark is close to us all, I will also accept anyone who cannot stay, so please speak now if you cannot do everything I asked." Some officers in the circle agreed easily, but a few stirred officers, one from the circle and another from the far right side of the house, asked to leave. Still the rain poured harder, and small droplets of hail began to form with a strange and slight cool summer breeze, pounding the police officers' heads like bullets and thickening the atmosphere even more. Aaron and Mark could hear the hail pounding on the roof and windows, the wind howling, blowing past their bodies from the front door. Their two motionless bodies in a moment of constant, long-awaited tension. Mark and Aaron, two lifelong friends, glaring at each other's eyes as the moment of testing finally came. Mark's face dripped his own blood and the drops of water from the roof, his only movement from periodic cynical grins erupting on his face like a constant tic. Aaron, his head down and eyebrows arched in a furious, stern stare, thought of what, if any, options were available to get his revolver out of Mark's grip. His face was motionless, cautious of the incubated lunacy that has trickled out of Wegman. Then, after a minute of tense thoughts, began the growth of an idea. He could already feel the tormenting pain his body would endure, a shiver traveling up his spine like a hasty millipede and its tickling legs. A simple-minded idea was what he had, which carried the slight potential in saving Mark's life. *The Passenger Effect*, Aaron thought. *I can fight it. I can prevent what he has always been destined to do, the destiny we damned him to. If he walks through those doors, that cracked green door, we, and three more officers, would all certainly die, until my six-round revolver runs out of its dangerous venom.* Aaron's idea was simple, yet the more he thought about it, the faster his heart sank.

His idea was to force Mark into one of his episodes of motionless panic, for the chance of a window to open up, for someone to make a feverish sprint across the hallway for the weapon in Mark's momentarily limp hands. Aaron needed Mark to be in pain, to ignite deep, unbearable regret, knowing that, for Mark, everything worsened with regret. Though Aaron Hudson knew that his decision to escalate the tension could (or would) backfire harshly, he crafted the plan B to leverage Mark into using as much ammunition as possible, to play with the snake and drain its poisonous venom. They both stood with power in their eyes. Aaron's head was slightly tilted downward, while his two eyebrows continued to arch toward the bridge of his nose. Mark's nose finally became more crusted with fresh warm blood, but his eyes and quiet, unemotional actions stood as well-known red flags of a sociopath. Lightning struck and they both saw each other's grave faces.

"Mary was quite something," Aaron gracefully confirmed in the dark, while curling his arms lower and eyebrows straighter. "She painted beautiful paintings."

"Shut up!" yelled Mark aggressively.

"I was dazzled every time."

Mark aimed the nozzle and shot Aaron in the right shoulder. He gasped for air and fell on one knee, then screamed from the pain in a very loud shriek, quickly covering his wound. *Two*, he thought, while beginning to sweat from the pressure. The commissioner and two others rushed in, but Aaron looked back at them and yelled.

"Get out, now!"

The police officers fled two yards back, soaking the keen, white carpet in the dark living room with water, next to the two chairs. Some others outside had to cup their ears and broke out crying from the stress of their once close friend.

"Mark, don't pretend it never happened."

Mark took his third shot, aiming to graze Aaron's left arm lightly. It was perfect, and Aaron began to bleed from his second arm, a chunk of meat scooped out of his flesh. He screamed a second time but quickly continued without covering the second wound.

"The childhood friendship, teenage romance, and years of marriage! She fed you while you were sick!"

"Shut up, shut up, shut up!" Mark quickly cuffed his ears, began to cry, and oppressively screamed. He shot two bullets in the air to block out the noise and fell to the ground. Water streamed from the roof as huge chunks of plaster lightly fell onto and around his body. Aaron fell on both knees and began to feel the loss of blood, noticing himself drenched in a dark red puddle. "That's five." He continued.

"You guys sang together! Now that I think of it, where were you when she got sick? Where were you?"

"I'm here!" Mark aimed the weapon at Aaron's head with the final bullet. "I'm trying! I'm trying to be there, but I so wish for the pain that I can't bear to watch her fight a disease I would gladly take! She is an angel. Mary knows many things that none of you can begin to imagine because of her heart! I can't bear to watch her suffocate me. She suffocates me! Every time I think of her, I know it's my fault— because of my C. diff, she stayed in the hospital. I was afraid to be admitted again so I waited, and she happened to catch it. Don't touch her! Don't take her!" Mark lowered the weapon down between his legs and centered his memory, crying viciously. He was out of reality and into the past, like a time machine. Aaron quickly turned to Francis Baker behind him and yelled.

"Get the gun, commissioner. Now, or he'll shoot us all!" Aaron screamed in pain once more. "With all my might, I will NOT let him through those doors!"

October, November, and December of 1991, while the Soviet Union also began to crumble from within, was when Aaron knew where Mark was.

◆◆◆

MARK WAS FOND OF the downtown police station, its location next to the public library, and the feeling of brotherhood that made paying the bills more playful. Next to both the police station and the library was a DMV, a very bland, white brick building with a constant stream of furious adults and excited teens streaming in and out.

Through these difficult times, Mark and Mary lived very poorly. Medical bills piled high, and the cash left as quickly as it came. His police duties on the computer were surprisingly high, with many long hours spent at the station, mostly because no one cared to be a 911 responder; it was flat-out boring. Mark's salary was about $30,000 a year. It was surprisingly good for that line of work. Then there were Mary's portraits. She made around $35,000 annually. It began as a fun competition. Mark received a paycheck and placed it high on the fridge. Then Mary sold a portrait and placed that check higher on the fridge with a few stepstools. Mark did the math and said he could double her check in a week. She later punched in the numbers and told him she could whack him with a canvas. One snarky comment later and Mary began painting while Mark sat in a chair and patiently waited for Aaron to pick him up. Mark quickly waddled over to the automobile and rolled into the passenger seat. It was difficult for him to step in because of his weak muscles, but—while only having half his body inside—he hollered at Aaron to step on the pedal. He did so with immediate force, shocked by the aggression in Mark's voice, to arrive at work as soon as he could. Mark held on while Aaron sped down the road, speechless, while Mark realized he had no strength to pull his feet out of the outstretched door, not realizing that the top of his bald head was also grazing the driver's door as well as Aaron's lap. His feet were only a few inches out of the car, along with one sandal, the other lost somewhere in his neighborhood's concrete roads. Then Aaron abruptly halted at the stop sign, still speechless from Mark's loud, unexpected screeching voice. For three awkward seconds they stood there listening to "Now That We Found Love" by Heavy D & the Boyz. Both Mark and Aaron felt as if they were smacked with a hard club full of complete and utter embarrassment, blushing wildly through three different shades of red.

"Aaron," Mark wailed. "I am so sorry."

"We're pulling over," Aaron shouted as he accelerated and jammed into the unusually crowded double-lane road. He accelerated to the right and cut off a new 1991 Chevrolet Caprice, not realizing upon action that the car they cut off was in fact a police car. The Caprice instantly flicked on its siren and lights the second Aaron's tires grazed the black concrete of the right lane and, almost as promptly as his last turn, pulled onto the dirt on the side of the road. The police officer walked promptly over, all smiles, to the driver's window as Aaron slowly cranked it down.

"Hey, Aaron, seems you have a human sticking out of the window. I'd like to inform you that's not legal." the officer said, grinning wildly.

"Hey, Stewart!" yelled Mark in a voice of uncertainty.

"Oh, you didn't tell me it was Mark. How're you doin', Mark?"

"Oh, I've had better."

"You know that's not how you sit."

"I know. I was trying to get to work faster, you see. I made a bet with my wife that I can make more money than her because my check on the fridge was better than hers, and she couldn't handle it. Then one snarky comment later she was painting, and I was chilling on Aaron's lap."

"And how did this happen?" Stewart asked, with chirping birds and "Now That We Found Love" filling the short silence, watching Stewart's smile disappear as a thought rose in his head.

"You guys aren't…are you?" Stewart said, his mouth half open.

"Oh gosh, no, that's not what this was!" Mark hollered as he tried again to push himself off Aaron, who fell into a frantic shuffle to turn off the radio, skipping from station to station. "I jumped in, but my arms were too weak to push me up!" Mark continued to confess. "Aaron was going to pull over anyways."

"I was, I swear on my life," Aaron interrupted, waving his hands like a madman, still trying to turn off his sticking radio. "There are no feelings like that, I swear."

"Oh really," Stewart said, barely holding in his laughter. "Then how do you explain Heavy D?"

"Let's not talk about Heavy D!" Mark screamed as Aaron pushed him into a wobbly, upright position.

Stewart began to laugh so hard he bent over in a fit of hilarity, cramping from his borderline diabetic stomach.

One $320 fine later and they were back on the road with Mark, more angry at the radio than anything else, with him arms crossed and light, provoking words appropriate for children's cartoons. "Raga smaga baga," he jabbered like a madman. Later, Mark took his check off the refrigerator, cashed it in, and paid for the ticket, continuously bickering even with the teller. Mark was upset when he did; once he came home, it was pitiful depression. The tired 911 respondent's feet dragged, his lip hung, and he couldn't even place his coat on the hanger. It lay on the square tiles next to the front door.

Mary came out of her office from continuously painting morning to evening; she was in a classic white painting apron with a few wet paintbrushes in its front pocket and wet paint strokes on the front, while older strokes were faded underneath. Her brunette hair was in a tight ponytail, which also bore fresh paint strokes from continuous, dedicated work. But after all the painting, she was still very energetic, both hands clenched tight around her mouth.

"Mark, how was your day?"

"I got a ticket."

"But you work for the police department. Explain how this happened." Mark looked up and saw her smile behind her two clenched hands, shaking in order to contain herself from bursting out into a loud, joyful roar. Mark quietly laughed to himself, stretching his tired face with his left hand, knowing exactly where her amusement arose from.

"Did you record it?"

"All the way until the stop sign."

"I was struggling to get in."

"I met the neighbors. They thought it was funny, too."

"You showed it to our neighbors?" Mark began to laugh slightly bent over like Stewart earlier that day, believing he should cry instead.

"They wouldn't stop watching it, until the battery died on the camcorder."

"That's fantastic. I'm very glad."

"So I went to the store and bought a replacement. The store clerk's favorite part is when Aaron stopped at the stop sign."

In total, Mary had shown the video to thirteen people. Mark was on the ground laughing at the end.

"Well, I guess I win," Mary stated with complete confidence, after helping Mark up with one hand in his and the other on the ledge of a recliner.

"If you win, I'll eat my shorts."

"Then you better find a good cook, because I'm not going to cook for you ever again," Mary half teased while flicking her chin into the sky. She then turned around and, with her arms crossed, walked over to their room.

"That's quite all right. I'm a better cook, anyways," Mark joyfully claimed with half certainty, knowing with confidence that without her, his diet would only consist of Honey Nut Cheerios, milk, Kraft macaroni and cheese, microwaved popcorn cooked in brown paper bags, and burnt eggs.

"Then it won't be any trouble."

"I can cook circles around you."

"I'll make it easy for you Mr. Wegman, and take a well-deserved nap." Her voice echoed from the hallways as she walked farther into the house.

"You don't want dinner?" Mark asked, unaware that his voice cracked and goose bumps rose when he spoke, as he also tried to remember a time when Mary was not there. He could not, while silence began to overrun the house.

"Are you going to wear a hairnet?" Mary asked, which made Mark smile with increasing joy, and he rubbed his newly growing peach hair with one hand. Hair, no matter what length, was hair, and after months without it, the feeling, the texture of it, overwhelmed him with excitement.

"I love you!" Mark yelled happily.

"I love you too, my amazing and handsome husband!"

Later in the night, Mark made eggs for himself and quietly prayed for the meal. Thanking God for his life and God's grace and mercy. Then, after throwing out the eggs for having too many eggshells, all hiding like Waldo, he went to bed. These were the second happiest days of Mark's life, with him and Mary in the face of hope, living humbly in a small, rented dwelling. Yet when he spent time away from Mary, Aaron was around, driving Mark places while also working in the same station, which they both enjoyed a lot because of their lengthy friendship and strong, brother-like respect for one another. Aaron continued to have more and more awkward moments, drifting away from a time in his life where his heart carried billions of opinions, hundreds of keenly prepared rants, and witty, vulgar responses—now, when in the situation, never knowing what to say. It began when Mark got ill, yet skyrocketed once Aaron became a police officer. His confidence and sense of protection increased tremendously, the control freak finally believing he was the captain to his own future.

At the station, it was easy to point out that Mark was loved for his strength and witty comments, yet at the same time balanced on the brink of ruin, hidden deep in his soul like the eggshells that hid so well in his scrambled eggs. March 11, 1991, was the date when Mark began to run through life like a man walking on a tightrope the width of some surgical stitches. He ran without a back heel, without a net to catch him if he fell. Ever since the breaking point, Mark had been balancing on one thing: Mary.

One week later and they both placed their checks on the fridge, surprisingly close in value. Mark earned an amount of $650 by working forty-eight hours—eight hours of soul-crushing overtime, compared to last month's $590. Mary sold a painting, for $600, of a woman praying on her knees on the front steps of a funeral service, families crying with deep, overwhelming grief. Their faces were all different shades of dense, dark blue, in clothes blacker than coal. Yet the woman on the ground carried a shade of blue darker than them all, her hands clenched so painfully hard in the form of prayer that the intersection of her two firmly pressed hands was shooting off silvery red sparks, like two metal plates at an extreme speed, clashing together with welding force. In the coffin was the woman who bowed on her knees. It was obvious that she was deceased, with the stiff, lifeless body she once called home lying dormant in a box of finely chosen, elegantly bright brown wood, and her newly replicated, slightly transparent, dark blue body and wings only inches from the body. The angel smiled with tears streaming through her clenched eye sockets. Her miserable, overly dramatic tears originated from the grief she felt for departing from the only world she knew, leaving the ones who couldn't see her, the ones who grieved with their own different levels of self-fear, the ones who didn't expect such a thing.

Yet the smile, the beaming smile that seemed as if it were ripped off a much different, sweeter portrait, was filled with bright, welcoming colors. There were shades of her eloquent brown skin around her rosy-red, vibrant lip-gloss, and coconut-white teeth. They were colors you could only imagine in a cartoon nature book for toddlers. The bright colors took up only a slither of space on the painting yet represented the flicker of light many feel once death has been knocking for some time. The colorful grin was the acceptance of death, the overpowering joy of her fast-approaching life in the world of clouds. The portrait was called *And Then There Was Light*, as it represented the woman's first epiphany of her departure from Earth-bound pain, loneliness, and the fear of unworthiness in God's judgmental eyes. The first realization that she was going to spend an eternity in constant, never-ending bliss occurred instantaneously, so quick that only her smile could react fast enough. Now many would say that this was one of Mary's weird portraits, because the woman bowed down to two objects at once—there was the cross over the coffin and, well, the coffin. Although many simple-minded observers might have missed this symbolism, the idea was simple. She just wasn't ready to let go.

Mark saw the painting before a very old man purchased it. An old man that had something completely wrong with him, wickedly wrong, yet Mark could not figure out what it was. Mary had soon begun to advertise her art in many newspapers as well as pitch up periodical tents in art fairs with a tiny yet growing list of numbers from art collectors, whom she would call first, once her most recent painting was complete or her tent was up in the fairs. Mary called these people "Wet Paint Enthusiasts," as they always seemed to chase, and sometimes compete, for her artwork, many times still drying, moist on its wooden easel. They always told her that it was the symbolic meanings she slipped into the cracks that made them so lovely, "are what art should be." One seventy-eight-year-old, feather-voiced German woman told her, "it should make you think." Yet she'd been having thoughts that this, this weird old man with such a darkening aroma, never had a single care for the art or the symbolic meanings. That this specific Wet Paint Enthusiast only cared for her. Mary felt that her shudder from his call was just the beginning stage of a cold, just the sun setting in the mountains, pushing her off track from the glare into her eyes. It rang after she lifted the fine-point gel pen from the bottom right corner of the painting, signing her name. He called her from the phone number listed in her newspaper ad and asked to buy her most recent work of art.

"I enjoy my art fresh," the man stated in his very smooth yet very imperiling voice. "It's a habit of mine, an itch that I must scratch for satisfaction."

He then stated that their meeting must be soon, as soon as they can, so an hour later, Mark and Mary both waited for this man to arrive, the paint so unbelievably wet that she had to hold the painting by its inward wooden frame. She held her painting with a tight fist, and Mark was aware, watching the tension in her eyes constantly burn, waiting for the perfect time to burst. She wasn't only concerned with the man; there was always an emotion that was concealed from the outside, something else within Mary.

"Are you alright?" Mark asked with a gentle, troubled smile. Mary continued to stare at the front door, unmoved.

"Yeah, why do you ask?"

"Well the painting you created is beautiful, although it's very concerning. Is something wrong?"

Mary began to stare into his eyes, both knowing that once she explained why, March 11 and the black swan would all seem like the same day. She burst out in uncontrollable, hysterical tears once again.

"What's wrong?" Mark asked as he lightly held her soft cheek with his palm. Mary broke eye contact quickly, pushing the hand away, and began to explain.

"Well I've been watching many talk shows on the television and reading many books. I continue to find out that we aren't Christians."

"What do you mean?"

"We aren't Christians. If we die today, we'd both go to—"

"Why are you talking about death?" Mark asked with a lower, sterner voice. His muscles tightened and heart raced faster as he took a half step back, immediately thrown out of his comfort zone. Yet from Mark's hostile reaction, Mary seemed to double in her own hostility and agitation. He proved Mary's judgment to be correct, as one of her deeper meanings in the silence proved not to be worthless, paranoid thoughts.

"Because we're all going to face it, Mark! One hundred percent of us will die! You can't live life ignoring it," she said, her fists clenched to the sides of her deep-ocean-blue skirt.

"We aren't ignoring it. Every Sunday is dedicated to God!"

"Even Satan can attend church, that proves nothing."

"Then please tell me why we are going to Hell."

"Because we're sinners!"

"Everyone is a sinner. That's why we have Jesus!"

"But you're not saved by a single prayer and a dip in a pool! You must live for God!"

"I do!" Mark yelled, his voice traveling through the walls of the house, into the street and the ears of their neighbors. His face was turning red, furious, yet more afraid than he could imagine, hardly able to conceal his weakness from Mary's eyes.

"Then why do I feel like I have become your idol, your cane? You don't cry, I have only seen you cry once, yet I know what you're doing. You have changed ever since that day. That dreadful day a switch turned on, and I have a sinking feeling that you will not make it to age thirty. What happens when I get cancer, and you are alone? Are you going to lose God? Are you going to lose all your senses of reality? You can't depend on my life. I'm a ticking time bomb, Mark, ready to go off. You cannot expect stability from a bomb, from me." Mary began to break down from her own words, tears gushing from her eyes like those two times before. Mark ran over and covered her body with his own, squeezing with comforting force, as if she were the priceless Smithsonian Hope Diamond. She immediately grabbed him and cried hot tears on his shoulder, seeming to never end. They both loved each other more than themselves, more than any married couple was expected to. They were together not only through vows but also as a necessity that under no circumstances could ever be broken.

"I won't ever let you go," Mark whispered, grasping her a little tighter. He then shed a tear.

From gravity, the tear rolled, trickling down through the peach fuzz on his face, down to his lips, and then to his chin, pausing as the droplet grew in volume, the stream struggling behind, catching up to the collection of water. Then finally, the tear grew too large, hitting Mary's shoulder, innocently. She flinched from the diminutive, warm drop that touched her shirt, and then smiled to find that Mark was truly human, that he could cry, yet her heart grew with fear, afraid that he was, in fact, human. Then the doorbell rang.

It echoed through the dark house, and Mary leaped up, terminating their lengthy embrace. Mark struggled to get on his feet. He crawled to the couch and used it as a cane to hoist himself to a sitting position. He needed Mary, but she was looking through the peephole to find a dark shadow in the shape of a man. When the painter opened the wooden door, it was slow and cautious. The handle was cold and gave

Mary a chill, parallel to the one she'd felt when he called earlier that day. But when she saw the face of the old man, she took a breath of relief. He wore wire glasses with orange circular lenses, a very fluffy coat made of sheepskin, designer shoes, and a very nice, expensive cane made with some mystery wood withered throughout the years and painted gold. He was old, with very thick white hair and a perfect, friendly smile that seemed to shine back.

"Hello, madam. You seem very surprised to see me."

"I'm so sorry, sir, I've never seen you before and didn't know who to expect," Mary said, her eyes beet red from the crying. The old man, though, wasn't filled with any curiosity for her eyes, nor for Mark's weak, slowly approaching body. He already knew.

"Well, don't be surprised anymore, because now you've seen me."

Mary rubbed her eyes one last time, sniffled a little, then strolled farther inside. "Well, I have the painting right here, still wet, though. I don't know how you will transport it without some of it smearing," Mary said, walking toward the canvas, picking it up by the wooden frame as she did before. "Do you want to see it first?" Mary asked with a twirl toward the door, yet she was shocked to find that the old, white-haired man was still at the door, not a single hair out of place. "What's wrong?" Mary asked.

"I'm so sorry, madam, but as you can see, I am very old-fashioned," the old man laughed, tapping his finely polished leather shoes with his cane. "I can't come in unless you invite me."

Mary laughed from his charm.

"Well, come in, sir, you're invited into my house!"

The old man's smile grew wider, two dimples showed from his wrinkled, rosy cheeks, and without a second thought the man took a step inside. He closed his eyes and took a long, deep breath, cherishing the moment, and let it out.

"And...and what is your name?" Mary asked with a stutter. The old man quickly opened his eyes and smiled again, leaning on his cane.

"Why, my name is Christian. Now enlighten this night with your magnificent portrait."

◆◆◆

THE WEEKS PASSED FASTER than they could ever believe. Mary began to practice speed painting and, in the rush of the week, could whip out three paintings in a day! Of course they were breathtaking, so much that her prices continued to stagger higher and higher until the fridge was consumed with checks. Mark's jaw dropped, his shoulders drooped, as he stared at the increasing gap between their overall earnings. His checks, although not close to Mary's, also began to add up. While Mark started to regain strength, his position also became more involved, more demanding. An open position for an officer became available around the end of December, and although his application didn't have the recommended college education, it did have the support of a few persistent coworkers, edging the chief of police (or as they simply called him, Satan's Little Helper, as he was well known for stealing food out of lockers, for commenting on others' appearances, for throwing his lucky black staplers at anyone who either commented on his own sloppy appearance, rolled their eyes, chewed their ice cubes, or slept in their offices, and for constantly sleeping during the day, cradling the same, lucky stapler).

Mark had to perform an oral board first, where five police officers rapidly put him through tough questions about stressful situations as a test to see how he reacted under pressure, to see if his mind was equipped to do the best in any given situation.

"The window rolls down and you see the driver has a weapon that isn't concealed. What do you do?"

"You are alone and stumble upon five men who are smoking marijuana and will be dangerous. What is your first action?"

"There's a suspicious automobile that has a driver with a clear drug issue. What is your first reaction?"

Mark quickly answered like a robot, calm and collective, yet his nerves ran wild. "You pull the suspicious character out of the car and perform a drug test." He shortly found out that his answer was the most agreeable.

Then there was the fitness test in the following day, which Mark passed, children! He passed! But with the lowest score you could possibly pass with. *Then* he had to communicate with the state and obtain certifications. *Then* there was the drug test, background check, and a bunch of other baloney. After all of that, the "Three Rule" took play—where the chief of police chose one person from the top three eligible and well-performing applicants; although in the much smaller station, there were only four who applied. They all stood shoulder to shoulder, stiff as nails, and when Satan's Little Helper shook Mark's hand, he almost toppled over in relief. Mark heavily bragged about how the promotion would cover the fridge in green and couldn't bear the thought of returning home to Mary's common "I win in everything" speech, telling her that he didn't receive the promotion, the two-dollar raise.

Mark was always accompanied by a second officer, since the chief wanted him to recover fully before handling situations alone. Except this time around Mark was *actually able to step out of the vehicle!*

It was true that they began to purchase nicer material with the extra doubloons. With kitchen remodels, a new television, comfortable spring beds, and a fresh layer of paint, their competitiveness definitely began to *pay* off. With Mark's promotion, they were given medical insurance through the police department. So their entire house was painted a nice, light tortilla color and pine. Mark called it light brown and dark green, so of course Mary laughed from his lack of knowledge of the *glorious* invention of the color wheel. Their bedroom door was painted tortilla, and Mary's office was painted pine green, which they both painted merrily, yet always called "Tom's room" if he ever did return like Mark constantly proposed. Mary did complain to Mark that, since it was her day off, she couldn't help him paint the house. He grumbled under his breath while stroking the house with a paintbrush about how everyday was her day off yet was well aware that she still made around five hundred more than he did a month. Around this time, Mark began to feel pains in his lower stomach again.

"You're probably constipated," Mary said in a comedic manner while pushing Raisin Bran his way. But they both had a different topic glued on their mind.

The annual colon test.

"It's okay, they'll clean you out!" Mary yelled from a distant hallway while Mark scarfed down the Raisin Bran.

Then after about three minutes, as Mark was almost done with the hefty size of Raisin Bran, Mary ran toward Mark, screaming.

"Mark Wegman, put down that baby blue bowl, now!" she yelled in her bee-yellow dress with grass-green polka dots, almost seeming to be stroking her hands in the air with her goofy run.

"Why?" Mark whined, pulling his chair out, facing her. "I need to poop as soon as I can. Everything's backed up."

Mary slowed down and put both hands on his shoulders, three inches taller than him in the chair, staring into his eyes. "Honey, if you don't poop it out by tomorrow morning, it'll come out on the table." Mark took a second to think, then made a gagging noise with his mouth.

"Oh, God bless America, the anesthesia!" Mark wailed, spitting out his half mouthful of Raisin Bran back into the bowl, rubbing his tongue with the spoon before Mary slapped him on the back of the head.

"Mark, how is rubbing your tongue going to help?" Mary demanded. Mark felt the back of his head before bursting out into laughter.

"To get the flavor out," he wailed as Mary began to join him in laughter.

The next morning, while the sun began to wake, Mary was in one bed and Mark in the other, similar to every one of these flimsy medical tests. While her thoughts trembled her body, Mark grabbed her hand and smiled, beginning to rub her thumb with his own. Her body quit trembling from fear of any pain or of what the test might reveal afterward. She smiled back and lost her view of him. The injection of anesthetics separated even the most compelling lovers. She dreamed of some garden in the sky, where grapes were never used to create wine and everything was white. There was a stream, where milk flew, and the leaves on trees had a fine taste of sweet, fresh honey. She plucked one off and ate it, filled with its sweet pleasure. Peaceful. Very peaceful. It was faint, like a dream should be, and seemed like a world only children could hypothesize, yet it was okay because the dream was blissful, a fantasy. Then it faded very slowly. Mary reached for one last honey leaf, but it was too late. She woke up on a white bed, with a pain in her rump that slowly grew into a very painful feeling, worse than she usually believed it was. Mary hummed a little, and a nurse kindly asked if there was any pain. Mary nodded, and more morphine came in through her IV. The pain slowly faded, and Mary quickly began to remember why she was there: the colonoscopy test, and Mark. Mark, her lover, her Hand Mitten who probably took a dump on the table. She giggled to herself while facing a curtain to her left and knew he was on the other side of her. He always was. So with a painful shift in her body (*Why is it so painful?*), she rolled herself to see Mark, to tease him, and to apologize about slapping him on the head, all high and loopy on morphine. Although, there was only a lone nurse and another curtain. Panic. Thoughts coursed through. He was always by her side after every procedure, yet this time was different. Thoughts coursed through.

She jerked up as quick as she could, breathing harder than before.

"Nurse, where's my husband?" Mary slurred horribly. Pain shot up from her butt. *Why so much pain?* she thought again, her focus skewed from the drugs.

"Mrs. Wegman, lie down!" the nurse said kindly but urgently. "There was a perforation in your operation."

"Mark! Mark!" Mary called in a weak scream, her mind too loopy to register what the nurse said.

"Some of your tissue tore during the operation, please stay down. He's in another room. Rest and we will escort you over later."

"He was holding my hand!" Mary yelled louder as she pushed herself further, the pain increased. *Why the pain?* she thought again as she began to fall asleep. *Why the pain?* The nurse watched her fall into an even deeper sleep, her squirming becoming lighter and lighter as her body became numb, and was impressed. The dose of morphine Mary asked for was still continuous, adding to the amount of narcotics in her veins. Yet she almost made the stretch, almost passed through the dose and kept consciousness. Then the nurse shrugged off the slim praise and continued her rounds.

As Mary rushed toward the B-wing on the fifth floor, pain striking with every step, she remembered the doctor's words.

"In Mark's bowel movement on the table, we found C. diff, otherwise known as clostridium difficile colitis. It is in a very severe state since his immune system has strengthened yet is still weak. This is also not his first time with this bacteria, or so I read in his charts, which can also make the infection stronger the next time around. We do not know why he ignored this for so long," the doctor said as he glanced at the nurse, then back to Mary. "His constipation was from the C. diff. there's no doubt, but now he needs help keeping his bowel movements under control," the middle-aged Arabian man said before patting her knee. "Get some rest, kid. Take care of yourself, too."

Mary ran quickly and became lost. Her focus was off and was in sheer panic, searching for a nurse who knew the ground. Then Mary smiled with over-ecstatic glee, seeing Kennedy, her old pediatric nurse, across the hall. The familiar face flooded her with joy as she felt an overwhelming sensation that made her feel as if she were in luck. Kennedy seemed new and was making some small talk to some local nurses, who at that point only smiled and nodded, as Kennedy's version of small talk never seemed to end. Mary didn't understand her move from pediatrics to nursing. She didn't know about Kennedy's two DUIs that kicked her out of the pediatric field, which made Kennedy let out a stress-releasing sigh, also aware that Mary did not know.

"Kennedy!" she yelled in a mixture of panic and joy. Kennedy jumped a few feet from her name, looked behind her and made a half smile from the sight of Mary. Half ashamed yet half grateful it was only her.

"Hello dear," Kennedy yelped, scratching her head. "H-how can I help you?"

"I must find the B-wing—"

"Oh! I was just there myself," Kennedy lied, trying to not seem new. "Take a right, and it's the third door!" Mary gave thanks and half skipped over to the third door on the right, half in pain, half in glee. The other nurses exchanged looks and whispers with one another and turned to Kennedy in concern.

"Isn't...the B-wing to the left of us?" said a small, twenty-four-year-old blond nurse, pointing to the opposite door with one of her glossy violet nails. Kennedy ignored her statement, hoping the other nurses did as well, and continued gloating about her medical career.

Sadly, Mary couldn't hear anything they said after she made the right turn. She passed through the bland, moss-colored doors that all seemed similar. Then she smashed through the third door with excitement, but it wasn't another hallway, it was a patient's room. Her smile fell and died, and she stared shocked at the character on the cheap hospital bed.

It was the old man, with his cane propped on the side of the bed and those beaming orange lenses lying on the cheap, wooden hospital nightstand. He was white and ill in the darkness of the room. He was thin as well, seeming to only be a skeleton of a man she recognized before.

"CLOSE THE DOOR!" demanded Christian, squirming in his bed like an earthworm in feces. Mary quickly retreated her head from the room and shut the door, catching her breath as it raced in her chest.

"Wait. Come back, don't leave me alone," whimpered Christian through the door. Then a nurse named Elisabeth quickly ran up to Mary in surprise, beginning her shift with five charts in one hand and a double espresso in the other.

"Excuse me, ma'am, are you lost?" asked the concerned nurse.

"Yeah, do you know where the B-Wing is?" Mary said with a recovering voice.

"Yes Ma'am, it's—" But the nurse stopped short and ran to a middle-aged man with a terrible receding hairline who seemed to have walked out of his room. Then Christian hollered again, somehow much louder. The walls dulled the sound less and less after every word he spoke.

"Mary, was that you? Please, I'm—I'm scared, don't leave me in the dark!" said the growing sounds of his sorrowful voice. Mary felt awful for the old man. Her heart ached with pity for him, understanding. A foreign feeling rose into her heart, sharing his feelings of fear while her mind continued to widen with fear for Mark's safety. Somehow, his words were almost luring, an overwhelming, powerful force drawing her to his side. The foreign feeling almost seemed to whisper to her, into her inner consciousness with great persuasion, as if all her troubles would be washed away if she cared for Christian, his soul darker than the black voids of space and death. She saw another nurse, opened her mouth, but fell short, and quickly opened the moss-colored door behind her. The old man halted his wails and continued to breathe heavily as if that were his normal rhythm. Christian had a rag on his forehead that seemed to need changing and was slightly bent forward by three pillows. Mary could also see red blisters that covered his entire body. The virus had seemed to spread throughout. Christian looked older, with parted white hair and the rest frail and thin. His figure was thin as well; Christian already seemed deceased. It was hurtful to watch as this new whispering voice grew louder in her mind. Mary's heart broke for him. He seemed to be crying from the pain, coughing, and breathing rapidly.

"Don't, feel bad, for me," Christian stated with a sudden change in voice pattern. "I—I am, an old man, who, who has done some wonders for the world, wonders no one could ever believe. Come closer dear, I—I wish to see your, beau-ti-ful strength," Christian asked, saying the word *beautiful* over and over again, exaggerating the syllables with enticement. Mary walked half of the room's length, her eyes wide with wonder as she stared into his, the whisper in her head becoming a voice, and the voice becoming a dull scream as she got closer, losing control of where she walked while somehow wanting to cry. Then, about a yard away from Christian's deceitful, expanding grin, his teeth rotting and eyes changing in front of her very eyes, an opposing force swept through the room. The first voice, screaming in her head, was cut off like radio connection, and as her knees bent to sprint toward the door, he shot a mist of his saliva all over her face like a reptile, landing in her mouth and eyes. The withered man burst out in relief, breaking out in uncontrollable laughter as she ran, wiping her face as if acid were settling into her skin.

"You may leave," muttered Christian in the middle of his short breaths. He then grinned, more than pleased. "I—I am no longer fearful. Thank, thank you for, inviting me into your house, today a lie became a truth, and a truth became a lie." The heart monitor evened out, as if that moment were planned, circled in his calendar.

Yesterday

THE COMMISSIONER BEHIND AARON wasn't quick enough. Mark, falling out of his trance, stood up quickly and punched the officer's elbow, overextending his joint and breaking his arm. The commissioner squealed and dropped his weapon. Then Mark wrapped his arm around his neck, ran toward the faded pine-colored door, and broke it open with his thick, bulky shoulder, getting nipped by a bullet from a young police officer in the back, who seemed to have had some redness in his eyes from tears. Mark quickly shut the broken door and found a chair to wedge it in place.

"MARK, NOOO!" Aaron yelled. "LEAVE RIGHT NOW!"

Police officers began to swarm outside the room while Aaron continued to scream, crawling over to the door as blood continued to pour out like a cracked metal pipe.

It was dark. The air was stale. While aiming his weapon, Mark took off the police officer's belt and placed it around his own waist, while the man squealed in pain and fear from Mark's behavior. "You'll live, Francis," Mark stated while his eyes wandered around in the darkness. Aaron continued to yell while Mark searched for a light switch, calling for Mary.

"Mary," yelled Mark, "Mary, it's me. I missed you so much!" He continued to feel the walls. "I have so many questions, Mary. Have you been painting? Have you been cooking?" Mark flicked one switch but nothing happened. Aaron still screamed in the background, banging on the bottom of the door as urine began to fill his pants. "I've been cooking. Every meal, in fact. You'd be proud!"

The SWAT team from the neighboring town arrived, and Aaron saw them swarm the building by the open door, with cold, emotionless faces replacing the others.

"Tom said he spoke to you. He's a card isn't he? I know, I know, he's not me, so it's not the same. But we won't be separated any longer." Mark saw the dangling light switch above Mary's bed and smiled. "Because your Hand Mitten's here!" He flicked the light on and looked toward the bed. It was empty, dusty, and crowded with office supplies, papers, and old boxes full of paintings. Aaron began to cry profusely by the sight of the light through the door's crack. The rain fell to a light drizzle, and the lightning lost its thunder.

"Wh-what is all of this?" Mark whispered anxiously. "Wh-where's Mary?"

"She's not here," said a calm voice behind Mark. He quickly turned around, forgetting about the commissioner in the corner, who was still shrieking in immense pain.

"Tom," said Mark, in shock. "How'd you get in here? You must get out, it's dangerous!"

"I promise, Mark, I am in no danger," Tom stated. "You must turn yourself in. Walk out with your hands up. It's the best you can do."

"Where's Mary?" Mark quietly yelped back.

Tom stepped closer with concern on his face. "They never told you, and I never dared for a perfectly good reason." Aaron's yells were still continuous on the other side of the wall, but they faded as he began to lose consciousness. The commissioner was beginning to freak out by the sight of Mark speaking to himself, speaking to the wall.

"Tell me what?" Mark asked in a concerned voice.

"Mark, how old are you?" asked Tom naturally.

"I—I'm twenty-three."

"Why do you believe you are beginning to gray?"

"It's the stress," Mark declared softly.

"Then why did Nurse Kennedy seem *so* much older than the last time you saw her two weeks ago?" Tom took another step closer. Mark began to breathe heavily.

"I…I don't know."

"And that's why they never told you," Tom stated firmly. He began to pace. "Why do you believe Dr. Kenny knows your name? Why, no matter what you do, won't Aaron let you excel at the station?"

Mark's eyes began to water, his heart raced. "Why?"

"Because you're forty-five, Mark. You can't remember past Mary's illness no matter what they've tried. You've been told at least a *dozen times the same exact thing over and over again* but you can't remember! Then, whenever you do, it always ends with you trying harm yourself!" Tom yelled.

"That can't be true! It can't!" Mark cried while he fell to the ground and shut his eyes. "I'm twenty-three, Mary's in her bedroom right now sleeping, she's waiting for her nurse to give her pain killers."

Tom exhaled loudly. "Mark, not this again. You can't live in the past! Please do this for me, I can't stay here long." The SWAT team began to ask Mark to step outside, reminding him of their defense.

"Don't leave me!" Mark yelled.

"Then remember, Mark. Remember what happened and accept it."

Aaron was finally rushed off by a stretcher. He was pale white, reaching for the door at the end of the hallway, fading away as the distance lengthened. Mark began to think very hard.

"U-ummmm, I remember Mary. She was ill—"

"Think past that!" Tom commanded passionately. The SWAT team began to set up snipers around the block.

"I-I remember being angry. Very angry. Drinking, I remember a funeral!"

"Some memories deceive," Tom stated calmly. Mark lifted his head with an idea, his eyes lit up with color.

"Is she in heaven?" he asked urgently.

"Mark, if you shoot yourself, you won't go to heaven."

"It's worth a try!" he yelled as he lifted the gun, his hand shaking as the barrel leaned against his temple. Tom never let Wegman out of his sight, his first dead stare into his eyes.

"I'm disappointed."

Mark was then hit with a lamp from Francis Baker, his left arm gripping the lamp for dear life, knocking a blow to Mark's temple so hard he was out cold before hitting the ground. The dust on the tiles rushed into the air, swirling around his body. Twenty years of dust began to cover his limbs, burrowing into his hair and streaming into his open mouth, the dead air more potent than ever. Tom disappeared. He was instantly miles away at the hospital, on the sixth floor. Even if the commissioner didn't strike Mark, the sixth bullet was a dud, and even if the events escalated, the snipers would have missed major organs, arteries, and anywhere that could have been even relatively lethal. He was, in fact, no more in danger than a toddler cradled by their mother, watched closely by her protective eye.

Mark heard the voice again in between consciousness and his constantly recurring dreams of the past, the same voice he heard after the car accident repeated. "If we don't get blood soon, we'll lose him, faster!"

◆◆◆

MARY'S FAITH IN GOD grew more and more as she lay in her bed. Her fears of death began to fade away. She began to ramble off about how thankful she was for life, and living as much as she did. She never burst out in outrageous spurts of anger anymore, and only in immense pain did she not smile. Mark usually sat in a chair next to her with a mask, gloves, and a full body suit to tell her about his day. While in return, she told him about God, his grace, and its principles, like a small child returning from school. In these days, death seemed to be in every corner of the house. Any day, Mary would pass; everyone expected it.

"G-God wants his people to—walk to, him," Mary stated weakly between her heavy breaths, on her hot and blistery face, "and seek, him. God wants—you. To let go of the stool, you've been…holding on to, an—and reach for him."

Mark ignored what she stated and continued to ask her to save her strength. But she'd always say the same thing.

"Mark, instead of prayers. Praise, an—and be glad, that, that suffering's over. I—I trust God, he'll take me, me home."

"No, Mary, don't ever say that," cried Mark, "you should never say things like that. You will live." While in Mary's presence, Mark still fought to keep his eyes from running, to show his human weaknesses, yet every day made it harder and harder to do so.

"M-Mark, for th-the first t-time in my life, I-I've never felt m… more alive."

Mark stormed out in anger, leaving Mary alone. Then he burst into angry tears outside of her room, anger toward God as he pounded on the wall, screaming into the shirt he wore while biting on his sleeve with great force. This was the third time he'd visited her, and every time ended with him on the side of the wall, screaming into the air.

He soon began to ignore her day-to-day words, believing she was hallucinating. The drugs were forcing her to say so many wild thoughts. Mark wouldn't speak anymore, watching Mary either sleep or praise God. In either situation, he had nothing to say. That day was unfortunately the day where his first solo shift at the station took place. He sat in the car motionless, wrecked, and tired. His rage was continuing to build toward God. He sat there, starring at a lone, stained brick wall about a mile away, made to hold a large, steel garbage can.

Mark ignored any calls that came through, while focusing on that lone brick wall. Possibilities. He then placed his police car in first gear.

"You take away my hair," he quietly stated. Second gear. "You take away my boy." His voice became louder. Third gear. His engine revved back down and escalated again. "You take away my wife!" Fourth gear. The wall was getting closer and closer. He could see the indents in the red wall, the stains and the flaws. The imperfections and the impurities. It was right there. It was glaring Mark in the eye. Then a few yards before the collision, Mark pushed on the brake. The car swerved around to the side and smashed in the wall on the passenger's door. If there were a passenger, they would have died, smashing their crown into the passenger door, and the imploded door would have also wedged their arm in place, like a sandwich. Mark pounded on the airbag with rage and anger, spraying unpleasant words toward the sky while crying profusely.

Aaron was eating dinner with Mark that night. He was hanging out with Wegman more often, in order to offer company during the difficult time. Aaron made eggs, toast, and hash browns. They were nothing close to what Mary made—his meal was potatoes from a frozen bag, overcooked eggs, and the toast wasn't buttered. They sat across from each other and Aaron watched Mark drench his food in hot sauce. "That's a lot of hot sauce," Aaron calmly said with folded hands. Mark didn't look up.

"I don't know why, but I'm just craving a lot of hot stuff lately. Is it a crime?"

Aaron rubbed his eyes. "Well the thing about hot sauce is that it is sometimes used as a pain reliever... How did you crash your car?" Aaron asked firmly.

"I—I told you, man, a dog jumped in front of my car and I swerved to the side. Chill out." Mark looked back down and slurped up those soupy, red eggs like sweet-and-savory ice cream.

"Mark, you're not yourself!" yelled Aaron. "You've been acting very strange—"

"Well maybe it's because you gave me breakfast at seven o'clock in the afternoon! Now my entire schedule is messed up!" He threw his fork at his plate. Some hot sauce sprayed over the table like blood.

"Mark, don't make it a joke. You're very smart and you understand what I'm talking about."

Mark and Aaron didn't speak for the rest of the meal. People at the station whispered around him. But eventually, everyone came around and told Mark that his wife was in their families' prayers. He ignored every kind gesture and acted as if they never spoke. He found relaxation through his job, the authority he carried, along with his badge and gun. Heroin addicts were always waiting for their next high, never as satisfied as they were with the first. Mark was the same way. It all began when the police force came into direct contact with a band of illegal immigrants, caught transporting twenty-five pounds of heroin to a major distributor in Tucson. They almost got away with it, as the transporters were a couple hours from the border, and had their envelope of cash within arm's length before being caught in the desert. A standoff began between cops behind their vehicles, and the transporter's and the distributor's teams behind theirs, all well armed. A police chase with the two vehicles ran them out of the desert and closer into the city before road spikes forced them to find cover behind their own cars and begin a full-on shootout. After one of the two transporters was shot in his ribs and right lung, the bullets stopped flying. After ten minutes of silence, waiting for any reaction at all from the opposing side, Mark randomly stood up from his crouched position and walked through a modern representation of *No Man's Land*. Although every cop shot harsh, sharp whispers while grabbing onto his legs and motioning disapproving hand gestures, he continued to press forward toward the other side. Yet when he walked out of cover, no one fired; his movements so quiet that the other sides were never tempted to look, the risks of checking far higher than not, also believing that no police officer was mad enough to walk over uncovered. Mark then proceeded to walk behind their cars and shoot them all in their legs, all unexpected and too slow to react. One screamed curse words in Spanish, never expecting anyone to pop their head so far past safety, and, as another raised his weapon, Mark shot the man's hand off as naturally as swatting a fly. There was not a single fatality, and, because of what many believed was genuine bravery, Mark was broadcast across the entire country, asking him whom he owed his courage to. He pointed to a random person across the street and yelled, "That man! He gave me the courage!" They all ran over to him, and the college student was very confused. The head and president of the local chess team strolled by on his bicycle after a match in the community center and was frightened when seven to eight news reporters rushed to his side, demanding to know when he and Mark first met.

After this first encounter, his chase for the same high began, living close to death every second he could. The rush was what he enjoyed: smashing someone's head into the hood of their car, the sound of cuffs snapping tightly around their wrists, the feeling of chasing someone on foot, searching a house, and, especially when he was threatened, laughing with complete madness as if the seventeen-year-old juvenile had just told the most hilarious remark in the tens of thousands of years humans have been around. Mark would cry so hard from laughter, banging his fist on the boy's car, denting it even more than when he slammed the boy onto the hood. "Please," Mark said, unable to contain himself, "please do it."

He would work without stop, trying to escape the thought of Mary's increasing severity, her worsening condition. But the heavy work took a toll on his body, as he still was recovering from the cancer. Some late nights as he left for home, the darkened streets would remind his body of how exhausted it was, and he would fall in and out of consciousness, more intoxicated than anyone else under the influence. The sound of a car's horn would wake him abruptly, turning his car back into the middle of his lane only for the process to happen again a few minutes later. There were also moments when work was slow, and Mark was forced to sit there in the police car with nothing to do but reflect. He would stare outside with sorrow, or attempt to blurt out music on the radio to keep his mind from settling. "Sweet Caroline!" Mark yelled as the music blasted through the speakers, and, as he banged his hands on the police car's dash, "Good time's never felt so good!"

Soon Mark began to run home during work to check on Mary and see if she was any stronger than before. He'd sometimes spend the night in that lumpy old chair next to her sofa, wishing to be sick like her. Time passed slowly. He dreamed of lying in bed with the same rash, same pains, to not sit and watch her suffer. But some nights he slept alone in the queen-size mattress they'd had since marriage, acting restless as he tried to forget Mary, her entire existence, for the night. He didn't want to forget her forever but only for the night so he could sleep and think. Except, as little time passed, escape never occurred, because again, all he could do was think about Mary's suffering.

Kennedy did visit Mary once. They talked for a short burst of time. Kennedy—along with so many others—brought a present accompanied with some get-well balloons. Kennedy brought a small, blank sketchbook and some candy but quickly knew it wasn't the right present, since she was unable to ingest or draw. Only Mary and Kennedy knew what she did, and this never changed. Mary's father, Mr. Kenny, also visited many times over. He was as strong as Mark when it came to seeing his little girl. He couldn't control the agony that followed. He started throwing vases, knocking down lamps and dressers, stabbing his walls with a knife, destroying his once keen, perfectly arranged house. He emptied out the pantry, threw his bed down the stairs, and shattered his box television on those cotton white tiles. Then he cried. Control out of his reach for the second time in his life, he couldn't stop what he knew would come. After three weeks of Mary continuing to thin and whiten, Mark began to drink almost every night at Applebee's. He would give the bartender Aaron's number, so once it was closing time, Aaron would race over with his coat over a Metallica nightshirt with worry and anger in his eyes. Mark was at that bar so frequently that the bartender posted Aaron's number on the wall. "Look over here," the bartender said while pointing to the wall and casually swooshing the cocktail shaker with ease, "next we're going to put your name on one of these benches. 'Reserved for Mark Wegman'!"

Mark would then wake up and work out with the hangover. It was painful, and Mark never accomplished any gain in muscle mass. Aaron knew that he did it because it blocked out the pain of Mary, the migraines from the alcohol. The self-inflicted pain made sure of that. Aaron told Mark's oncology doctors about what he did, like one sibling tattling on another. The nurse practitioner yelled at him, listing all the extra dangers caused by the mixture of alcohol and medications for his early remission stages with cancer. She explained how his ferritin levels were too high, how there was iron in his kidneys from the extreme amount of blood transfusions during treatment, and how the amount of chemotherapy and radiation he'd received already made his liver vulnerable enough. "If you continued to drink," the nurse told him, her eyes like the eyes of a concerned yet angered mother, "your liver would most certainly shut down." Therefore, Mark stopped taking his medications. He discarded everything but Mary's alphabetized prescriptions, neatly organized in a corner of the medicine cabinet. Her narcotics went through the IVs. Pills had been used for the first few days of her sickness, but Mark kept them in case she ever needed them, hoping that soon, she could take them again.

Aaron asked for assistance at the police station as well. They were able to give Mark rehab at the Rester Recovery Facility and Institution.

It had two campuses on its twenty-acre property. The one on the left was a rehab facility, and the one on the right was an insane asylum. The neighboring building was motivation for the rehab patients to recover. It was sometimes that extra push they needed—anything to help those poor souls.

Mark began to panic because of their offer, as Satan's Little Helper also told him to take a few days off with his wife while he went to therapy, a genuine smile on his face as he patted Mark's shoulder and shook his hand. He quit his drinking completely and automatically, knowing that if he didn't, the chief of police would extend his leave, lawsuits on his mind, as his alcoholism would be too risky for the station. But Mark did not go to the recovery facility—at the end of it all, no one except Aaron seemed to care. Aaron, on the other hand, had his own growing addiction as well. He became obsessed with Mark, watching him with a cold glare from across the station, replacing his kitchen knives with plastic and transporting Mark's personal rifles and hand guns to his own house. He then called a psychologist from Phoenix, offering the stubborn, self-absorbed man $2,000 to drive down and evaluate Mark in secret.

"He has Post-Traumatic Stress Disorder," the sixty-eight-year-old man said as he pulled out a Camel cigarette, the flame in his lighter starting with a very forceful flick.

"How severe is it?" Aaron worried.

"Very severe. You said he's a police officer?" He stroked his trimmed facial hair.

"Yes, we are both at the same station."

"Suspend him. Ask whoever's in charge to give him a position that cannot place him in any danger, something off the field."

Aaron stood up in his chair, aggravated as both his hands tugged at his long, straight hair. "He won't shoot himself, sir—"

"It's not just about him," the psychiatrist added severely. "It's also about others on the scene, civilians around the scene, police officers supporting the scene. There are triggers for this disorder, and you won't know what they are until it happens! And it happens just like that." He snapped his fingers. "Only an absolute moron would allow him to stay in the police station. You get him out of that. Make the right choice. But for goodness sake, why should I care?" the man said as he blew some black smoke into the air. Aaron's head fell in shame; he, like many times over, had nothing to say to his comment, no reason to argue.

"Was it the cancer that caused it?" Aaron asked shyly. The psychiatrist asked Aaron for silence, and they listened intently behind the walls into Mary's room. One of those noises was a slight sound of weeping, loud enough to make your ears shiver, for your stomach to drop as you listened to those sobs, those that come from the deepest part of your throat, and while inhaling, the struggle to breathe can be heard past your ears, more painful than anything you could imagine. It was Mark's deep voice inside that room while Mary slept: his quiet yet masculine sobs.

"It's because of her."

Later, Aaron convinced the chief of police to temporarily make him a community resource officer, which he seemed to easily agree to. "That man's going to run my station to the ground," the chief of police grumbled to Aaron as he clipped his lengthy fingernails on his desk, "but I do wish him and his wife the best." The chief then let out an unexpected, unnatural smile. It was quick, no more than half a second, yet this was enough for Aaron to be thrown back, shocked to find the chief so understanding. But there were two separate reasons behind his flashed grin: one was because he was going to retire soon, and although Aaron was young, he planned on passing down the torch to him, knowing that he would treat the position with more respect than anyone else. He had also been told by his doctor that his blood pressure was through the roof and had been prescribed anger management classes over at the community center.

Then, once Aaron left the station, he drove over to Mark's house, well aware that he was not there. In fact, while Aaron trotted on the bear-brown tiles with his skinny legs toward the front door, Mark was walking to the chief's office, calling on his Bearcat to drive back to the station and sit down with the old man. Mark was at home when he was called, only on the second day of leave to be with his wife. Aaron knocked on the front door and waited, hearing the click of shoes inside, Mary's home nurse skipping toward the door. Kenny paid for the home care plan, still very wealthy from his Pants Plants idea even after so many years. She opened the door: a tall, dirty blond nurse, a little broader than normal with a square jaw and an overwhelming addiction to exercise and weight training, yet with a beautiful, rare case of heterochromia iridum, having two different colored eyes. One was a dark blue, the other more of a turquoise. They had spoken to each other at least a dozen times since Aaron had been there during numerous occasions, yet no special bond between them was ever made, as both their positions in the house were different, and there was no attraction between the two.

"I need you to tell Mark he can't see Mary anymore," Aaron demanded after she opened the door, his voice slightly cracking, knowing how suspicious his request was. "Tell him that her immune system is too weak. It is very important that you do so as soon as you can." The nurse's mouth was so wide open that a small dove could have flown in. The nurse responded with a kind of sharpness in her voice that indirectly told him how ridiculous he sounded.

"Why in the world would I tell him that?"

"The psychologist told me that if he doesn't, Mark will kill himself!" Aaron lied, his voice louder and louder the more he spoke. "You need to tell him when he gets home. I'm begging you."

The nurse was blown away. "I—I need to hear Mr. Kenny say it. Or it will never happen!" She stormed off, irritated and disturbed, and shut the door so hard Mary woke from a drug-induced sleep, beginning to moan again from the pain. Aaron didn't waste a second to visit Mr. Kenny at the hospital, speeding sometimes over twenty-five miles per hour and running into the building eight minutes after the nursed had slammed Mark's front door in his face, like a disease-infested rat. He was only a few years short of his doctorate degree. Mr. Kenny was more productive than ever before because of his daughter's condition. He ignored the situation by being overly busy with work and education. Aaron ran through the newly inserted hospital door that let in vibrant light through the windows, the same window Mark would escape through two decades later. Aaron called Kenny on his giant phone. He rushed down when Aaron panicked, claiming that there was an urgent update on Mark and his daughter.

"He'll kill himself?" Kenny questioned with high suspicion, his voice slightly agitated.

"Yes, and the nurse won't stop him from seeing her unless you give your consent," Aaron quickly claimed, wiping stress sweat off his forehead. Kenny shot him a look, his hands on his hips, an unwelcoming sign.

"There is no way the psychologist told you and not the nurse. She said no because you're an idiot."

"He wanted to suspend Mark," Aaron hesitated, dissolving his insufficient, short-lived lies. "This job is everything he has! I can see it in him, how much the difference in atmosphere changes a man. At his house, he is constantly reminded that Mary will not live. It's his only distraction left. We need to help him keep this job for as long as we can. Kenny, you have to trust me."

Kenny, so remarkably furious that his legs were shaking, stomped toward Aaron and slapped him across the face. Aaron retreated a few yards back, staring at Kenny as if he were a ghost, shocked beyond belief from Kenny's hostile reaction.

"Not my boy! Don't screw with my boy. If you touch him, I will make sure you're out of this town!"

"You don't think I care for him, too? Think about it, Kenny. If we suspend him from work, he will stay at home more and see Mary more. Mark nearly barfs in her sight! When you get off your shift, go see Mark for yourself, step in my shoes, and watch your precious son-in-law's eyes. Listen to his voice and tell me, with complete honestly, that he could last even a week without his escape!" Aaron screamed, his heart racing as memories of his half-forgotten father began to flood in once again, awakened from the burning sensation in his left cheek, bruising like an apple and heating up like a torch.

"Then get him a job that requires no weapons—"

"We both know if that were on his mind, he'd find one!" Aaron yelled, echoing through the room as the front desk man at the end of the windy hallway began to walk over, twenty-eight seconds away. Kenny's eyes were red with so much anger, his skin seemed to glow with it as he bit his lower lip with tremendous force, yet he was speechless. Kenny didn't say a word as he turned from Aaron. He didn't slap him a second time or tell him that he was an idiot. In some mysterious way, Aaron filled with excitement, as he knew that he had convinced Kenny. Aaron, under the simple illusion that he finally had control, let out a simple half smile. It wasn't enough though—he needed more from Kenny than his acceptance. He needed much more. Aaron yelled at Kenny, his demand so unexpected, so obnoxious. But somehow, they both felt it. They both felt as if this were a foreseen event, destined to be said.

"I need you to also convince him he's not allowed to see Mary anymore."

Kenny stopped next to a painting on the wall of peaceful scenery, with flowers as gentle as the sun's rays and meadows full of endless sunflowers, blowing in the delicate wind, frozen in time. He pounded the wall, his knuckles creating a grapefruit-sized crater in the plaster and knocking the painting off. The glass shattering, scattering across the ground with a desirable force to do so. He later bought the hospital a new painting of a gentle storm in the sea, rocking waves back and forth on a suffering ship, on an endless voyage toward nothing but the same, dark blue unavoidable wave ahead.

"You want me to use my marketing skills to lie to my son," Kenny's calm, collective voice stated. "You'd much rather have me do this than yourself, because you feel that I am the voice of reason, that my demands are far more impactful than yours. Is that right?"

"Yes," Aaron replied as Kenny continued to pound the same spot on the wall until his fist did go through. Then he snapped around, locking eyes with Aaron.

"What will happen if he learns that it's a lie? What will happen if she dies and we are to blame for her husband's absence? Have you thought even a little about the danger in your ignorant scheme? We both know she will, and I don't want this blood on my hands, that Mark wasn't there to be with her when she passed." Then Kenny began to walk off, his feet hammering on the ground, as he was seconds away from a breakdown. It was the first time he had spoken about the fast-approaching death of his little girl; before that, they were all only just thoughts. "I was there for my wife!" Kenny yelled, while the front desk man, five seconds away, began to jog over as he spotted the shattered painting and the hole in the wall of the freshly remodeled floor. "If I had missed that moment with my wife, I would have never forgiven myself. I'm not damning Mark into a life of regret."

"Hey!" the man from the front desk yelled, both hands pressed hard against his temples, fingers deep in his hair. "You need to pay for all this. The new painting and the hole in wall."

Kenny passed the man without a glance. "I will pay for it," he told the man, quietly, his words not going past the distance between their ears. "Go back to your front desk with me, I will write out a check for the labor cost, a new painting, and the supplies to fix it. Tell your boss that Mr. Kenny is sorry—if he has a problem, he will speak with me."

When Kenny began to move again, through the windy hallway, toward the front desk, Aaron's voice echoed through the halls one last time.

"You know very well that if he watched his wife die, they'd share the same funeral." He then ran through the new door, the new exit, toward the parking garage.

The following day, Kenny had the Saturday off to visit Mary. He walked in to find Mark completely exposed, without the gown, gloves, and mask, crying at her bedside. He wasn't afraid of the sickness, its contagious origins. Mark remembered Kenny standing there, watching him cry with a distraught look on his face. Kenny left the flowers he'd brought on Mary's end table and left. She was looking worse, her stomach completely concave, as her torso seemed to only be made up of her ribs, popping out like a curved xylophone. The nurse told him that she just recently got pneumonia, as well as terrible bedsores from not moving for such a long time. "You should start thinking about goodbyes," the nurse told Kenny, her expression overly saddened as both her slightly brawny hands were on his shoulders, "although I believe there is nothing else we can do but wait and pray." The rest of the day Kenny spoke with Aaron at the coffee shop named Tempus Garrapatas, the expensive joint where many college students studied but never purchased anything more than a black coffee. They left at around seven o'clock in the evening, both with utter grief in their faces.

"It's for the best," Aaron stated. "He needs our assistance."

"Ask me for wisdom, but I will never contribute anything more than this. I don't want to be involved with any more lying or scheming. Our actions are not honorable. They are cruel and sickening. But I feel that we do not have many choices," Kenny stated firmly. Aaron was upset, originally planning to ask for Kenny's assistance whenever he knew he lost control, but he accepted his request and whispered his bitter, dry response.

"So be it."

That night, Aaron ordered Chinese food and scarfed down over two thousand calories of lo mien, knowing what this emotional roller coaster would entail, knowing when Mary died, he would have to control him all on his own. That was the last day Mark remembered seeing Mary. She was weak and almost breathless. But still she was small, beautiful, and adorable. He adored her, loved her because of the soul she had, and squeezed her motionless hand until Kenny walked through Mary's door.

"Mark," his harsh tone demanded, "I need to speak with you."

There were, of course, shinier diamonds in the world, but nothing was brighter than Mary, nothing was even *close* to the value she had to Mark. In fact, she was the only thing left her cared for. She was the last motivator that told him life was worth living. If she recovered without a voice, he could sit with her all day long and would give up all the noises in the world to make her gleeful. If she forgot who he was, just the knowledge of her joy would be enough. If she were to die, then friendly words, friendly voices, memories, and the world would have lost its purpose. Her cooking was magnificent; he could still feel the bits of spaghetti stuck in his teeth, smell the blueberry muffins she usually made every other Friday. He could her the way she hummed, always the same hum, when she cooked. The whisks of her paintbrush could still be heard as she painted, cassette tapes of classical music flowing through the hallways like the soft rays of a warm spring day, kissing his skin all over. He could hear the violins, violas, the snare drum, clarinets, and sometimes, if he listened hard enough, the bass vibrating in the background. Then her laughter: it was the caffeine to his heart; it made him smile and it caused him to blush. Her laughter was why he woke up so much earlier so he could make them coffee, why he kissed her forehead when he brought her the cup with room for cream and sugar. It was why he fought so hard for her. All he wanted in life was her laugh, their happiness as a collective body, their vows to live on until their bodies were old enough to accept Death knocking on their door. Mark remembered receiving his check from the police station. It was a Friday and was about to rain. He walked over to the fridge without glancing away from this paper, this valuable paper. Mark then stopped, grabbed a magnet off the fridge, and examined it. It was a bunny hugging a carrot. His cheeks were rosy red, with a smile that ran across his entire face. Then he placed the check level with his eyes—it was almost on the top, above them all, towering over Mary's and his own. He was now in the lead. After a few weeks into Mary's illness, at the end of her life, he was now seventeen dollars ahead.

Three hours prior, Kenny had told him that he couldn't see Mary anymore, that if only the nurse exposed herself to Mary's delicate, degrading body, she had a much better chance of survival. He told him that recent blood work was proof, as she no longer had any immune system at all. "If you touch her," Kenny yelled at Mark, "she will die! If you breathe on her, she will die. If you are even in the same room as her, she will die. You selfish man—if you see your wife again, you wouldn't see her to make her feel any better than she felt before, you would see her for your own selfish desires." Then he placed a hand on his shoulder as Mark continued to cry in the corner of his house. "You must leave for her own sake. I understand that you are upset, but everything you've done in your life was for her. Now please, please… don't make this about you. If you refuse, she's my daughter and as a father I must protect her."

Mark continued to stare through the checks on the fridge. His eyes were puffed up more than ever before as rain began to fall outside. He burned with hatred, uncontrollable, blind hatred that ran through his entire body, more than ever in his entire life. He was demoted, exiled from his wife's side, and now he had closed the gap between their paychecks.

The next day he would work out in the morning, doing an assortment, a mixture of different muscle groups. He would push himself as much as he could toward this goal to regain the mass he once had before the cancer, yet would always fall short, still in complete agony from what happened the day before. Then he would space out, for hours on end, toward the pristine, pine-green door, contemplating his options for hours, if he should see her again. He would imagine her in the room, regaining strength at tremendous speeds, dancing in the sterile environment with a bright yellow dress, painting while she twirled endlessly in bliss from his absence. He was slowly losing touch with reality, emotions much more unstable than anyone ever imagined. Then, at seven o'clock, as the sun began to descend behind the dark blue mountains, he would leave his house with his police car, and the wild goose chase began. Mark would wait for a simple call on some arrogant minor out past curfew, or, while he directed traffic through a broken light, have the moment escalate completely out of control. He wanted instability and panic to rush into pedestrians' faces, for some mass shooting to be unleashed so he could be heroic, to feed his needy addiction for adrenaline, and to feel the cold kiss of death on his cheek like the tongue of a rotting dog. He wanted the fear Kamikaze pilots felt the moment before, seconds prior to their bodies exploding along with their planes. He wanted to feel the uncontrollable rush of fear of a French man during the French Revolution, hearing the snap of the strings and pulleys releasing the knife at the top of the shaft, his head milliseconds from bouncing off, and his mind being released into the next life. His burning rage was built up, the rage that came with the downfall of his life, the unfortunate events that stole everything he held dear and left him feeling more isolated than ever before. Mark wanted to release the pressure. He wanted to release his worries, doubts, and madness onto someone who deserved the punishment. In fact, that specific day of January 6, 1992, was not the worst day of his life, but the most memorable. As the day after the worst, he reflected, waking up in the morning and realizing the day before was not a nightmare, it was not a twisted, false reality, the roads he took led to the sounds of an accelerating train. His life as he knew it was soon to be desolated by tragedy he could not escape. Yet for over twenty years, Mark repeated that day, waking up in his dysfunctional room full of laundry thrown in patternless disarray. His sheets not even connected to his mattress, lying there limp and winded, as half were on the bed and the half other on the floor. He would believe that his wife was still in that room, not even a full day since his banishment from her side. He would believe that the old, hypocritical chief, who died from a heart attack in 2002 while yelling at his grandson during Thanksgiving, still threw his lucky solid black stapler across tables, slept at his desk more than worked, and had his grim, stern face that he only saw once morph into an uncomfortable smile. He always believed that it was January 6, even in the heat of summer, the falling leaves of autumn, the blooming patches of grass in the spring, because his mind was so absent from the thoughts of the day before. He would pass newspapers that said October 8, 2008, or ignore records of police cases that were filed from dates he only saw in science fiction. It was true. His mind was occupied with overwhelming traumatic thoughts about the day before, yet suspicion should have risen once he began to gray, and the police station's white bricks began to adopt faint black outlines from endless neglect through nature's unforgiving elements. Mark began to thin even more, developing heavy bags, his skin beginning to wrinkle at the joints. As automobiles around him became smoother on the edges, more technological, and the gym completely replaced every workout machine, dumbbell, curling bar, and even the carpet and paint color on the walls, after only ten years, Mark continued to live everyday as if nothing changed, as if it were still 1992, he was twenty-three, and his wife was moments from death, undisturbed from his surroundings.

Why?

The same recurring dream, a dream he saw every night after the summer of 1997 on the second week of July, before awaking from the bridge between the same two days. It was only a glimpse, a grim glimpse of a moment he couldn't recall. His forehead gaping open as blood continued to gush through, a young paramedic screaming for them to hurry, as one of her thumbs plugged the stream of blood on his head. He felt the heat on his toes from an explosion and darkness that followed as the two paramedics, a man, vague in the nature of the dream, and the same woman, shut the two doors to the ambulance, wailing its alarming, desperate siren. When Mark would wake, though, the slim moment of agonizing pain was not what he thought of. In fact, seconds after wakening, he would not even recall the sirens, the nurse, the unknown exploding object outside of his peripheral vision. They were the first memories that left. Yet while in the spirit of his dying self in that unexplainable dream, the mind of that man was filled with some sort of overwhelming peace, contentment with the life before and wishful beliefs of an endless future. He became lucid for only a fraction of a second, aware of what happened up until that summer of 1997, feeling the presence of Mary more than himself. His memory sparked itself to life every time, once the doors shut to the ambulance and his eyes closed from the loss of consciousness, the end of his mind's willingness to document time. Then he would awaken abruptly, a strange feeling pushing his heart forward, begging him to continue as Mary's recovery was only a few steps away. That spark he couldn't explain, as the split second of recalling what truly happened woke him during any form of sleep, wanting to escape the never-ending moment of grief, the day after the worst day of his life repeating like a broken record. That spark exploded with shrieks to escape as Mark's day continued, never reaching the ears of the one who controlled the body, who had the power to suppress the mind. What did the voiceless shrieks from the unknown darkness in the ambulance provide? Hope, a strange, microscopic inward feeling of hope, the remainder of the light before the illness, and the seemingly unreachable bliss after January 6, 1992. Therefore, with this hope, he continued to push on, through the same, never successful ways to cope with his loss, with the same desire to always find a way to be on the brink of death. Maybe to remind himself that death was still there, that he was not lucky, he was only just only, still alive. Yesterday, yesterday pained him. But the day after never seemed to end.

Tomorrow

MARK WOKE UP ON a hospital bed. His arm was covered with heavy, thick bandages from the bullet, his nose was so severely broken that the doctors had no choice but to give it a metal brace, and his head was full of stitches from Baker's *bright* idea. He also felt his back burn in excruciating pain from the car accident a little more than a day ago. Almost no time has passed. Wegman completely forgot about the accident, about Tyler Castillo, his mother Sarah, the hospital and the overpowering rage he couldn't control. Yesterday was the day he last saw Mary, the worst day of his life only an arm's length away. All his limbs—even the wounded arm—were strapped down with thick, leather straps. Mark didn't understand why he was there or how he managed to become so sore, finding new pains every other second as his eyes widened with panic, not able to help but resist his containment to the bed as his demolished body continued to scream back in disagreement. He then saw a figure standing behind a wall of blurred glass, dividing his room with a hallway. The figure was talking on the phone, his voice getting more and more irritated at the other guy on the other line.

"Where is he? No, I am not family, but I am a lifelong friend," the man said with a sharp, demanding tone. "Mention my name and get me in that hospital room... Yes, it's true. I was involved. Please, I want to talk to my friend!"

Mark began to scream as his terror grew, struggling with his restraints even more as the local anesthetics applied to his bullet wound began to wear off, as well as his awareness, sharpening. The man rose like a dog hearing a rabbit in the bushes, and Mark could tell he heard, because this mysterious man made a few last remarks through the phone and shoved it deep in his pocket without a second thought. Then the figure walked in. He was very elderly, with light brown eyes, thin white hair with stray hairs of brown from half a lifetime ago, and deep indented wrinkles on his face, shining off from an open window.

"Do you know who I am?" said the old man, calmly, collected.

"No," Mark stated with confidence. "Where am I? Let me out. I am a police officer, and whatever you want you won't get it!" he yelled. The man's face fell into a very distraught and upset frown.

"What do you think happened last night?"

Mark performed nimble judgments with his surroundings.

He was in immense pain, with a broken nose, head trauma, and a deep tissue wound on his right arm, possibly a nine-millimeter. He was inside a mysteriously clean room, strapped down to a bed, and unable to move at all. The man who stood by had coal-colored bags under his eyes and looked worn out. His clothes were messy, and the phone he was using seemed to hold clear sound, speaking to another man so he could enter someone's hospital room.

I must be the connection to this mysterious man in the hospital room. I must be the bait. Aaron will more than likely come over to my house in the morning to see how I'm doing, since we both have a late-night shift, Mark thought, slightly smiling. *Hopefully when I was jumped there were no bloodstains in the house, and the nurse wasn't awakened. If I am able to escape without any assistance, then that promotion will be mine. I can get out of that useless civilian uniform and put on a badge that means something.* Mark glared up at the man and spit at him.

"You broke into my home while I slept, jumped me to abduct and torture me for information about something you wish to know. I'd like to be the first to say that anything you do won't assist you in any way, you slob!" he yelled. The man seemed very upset from Mark's answer and sat in a chair across the brightly lit, peanut-colored room, then hid his face in his palms, Mark's spit still wet on his forehead and cheeks, soaking deep into his pores. His reaction to Mark's accusation was so subtle, so controlled, as if he'd half expected him to answer in that way. The man was thinking about something while wiping the spit off with his left sleeve, Mark could tell. He sat there in silence while stretching his face, folding his fingers and resting them on his lap; then, once he made up his mind, he stood up and walked over to Mark's bed, with a nervous quickness added to his step.

"I am a friend of Aaron and Mary," the old man calmly stated. "Mark, you did something horrible last night, something that can't be forgiven."

"What have you done to them?" Mark yelled while shaking the bed, burning his arms on the restraints and shoving his shoulders, trying to reach for the man. His lip was quivering while his eyebrows were bent, full of both anger and fear.

"Many people have given up on you, but I want you to understand that I won't." The old man's voice was louder, more passionate.

"What have you done with them?" Mark yelled even louder, scraping the bed with his nails. The man continued.

"I am paying for your stay here. You are in good hands. It was a blessing that you woke up right now because I only had thirty minutes before others would come to question you, and right now it seems there's only ten left." The old man checked his watch very quickly.

Mark continued to look around as he panicked, realizing that he was hooked up to IV fluid, a heart monitor, and a blood pressure pump. Then he saw his wrist. There was a red-and-blue band. It wasn't an abduction, it was an admission. His confusion was spiraling.

The heart monitor began to beep and scream for someone's assistance as his fear grew. The old man quickly turned it off.

"Mark, don't ruin this moment with me. If someone walks in, I won't see you for a long time," he whispered firmly.

"Who are you?" Mark said as his arms began to shake, moments away from peeing his bed.

"If I told you, you wouldn't believe me, Mark."

"Who are you?" he yelled. The man shook his head and rubbed his eyes before answering.

"I'm...I'm your doctor."

"Where am I?" Mark asked, his eyes glistening. He began to understand that the doctor wasn't harmful, through his looks and body language. He seemed to care for Mark.

Kenny thought about the question given to him, where Mark was. Why he was there? Kenny sat in the chair for minutes, thinking. It wasn't a matter of ignorance toward where they were located, but a matter of words used to explain how the road led there. Kenny has been a doctor for twenty years. He was the messenger; he was the one who told the family that their daughter, husband, or brother died. He was used to being blamed for *murdering* their loved on;, he was used to being told they would sue for his inadequate skills; and yet he could still enjoy his tortilla soup and chicken wrap an hour later, sleeping that night with little to no regret. But he knew that whatever he told Mark, he would not recover. The guilt he would feel would linger on until he died, disrupting his sleep as a reminder of the dry blood in his fingernails, what both he and Aaron had created. The shadow of his son that would forever live in Hell, the endless torture Mark faced. Kenny was afraid to speak; he continued to imagine Mark as a random patient to ease the tension teasing his nerves. It wasn't effective. He attempted to psych himself into believing that this event would be wiped clean by the next rising sun from Mark's amnesia, but that only made it worse. Then, after seven minutes, Kenny checked his watch to find that he only had three minutes left to speak with Mark.

He imagined that this news was an act of love, a way to aid his son-in-law; then he stood up fearless by looks, but fearful by heart to speak words of knives.

"Mark, I have three minutes left with you. You are in the Rester Recover Facility and Institution."

Mark took a deep breath, his muscles relaxed with relief as he returned a calm response. "I'm here for rehab?"

Kenny gave off a hard stare. "The institution. Mark, last night you…shot a police officer." Kenny gulped.

"How?" Mark asked with anger. "I was at home the entire night. You have the wrong guy!"

"No Mark. Listen to me, you have amnesia—"

"You scammed me! I am a police officer and I've never committed a crime in my life! I can go into details of what I did yesterday! I first—"

"You first woke up and ran to your wife's green door to cry for hours by her side, wishing that she was making you breakfast and painting, dancing in the sun and showing you her warm smile. You sat in that circular chair for so long, your feet went numb, but you didn't seem to care, Mark. It was how you spent your day off, until about six o'clock your father-in-law walked into the room and told you that, by very recent blood work, Mary's immune system was so low that even a breath on her skin was fatal. His exact words were, 'If you touch her, she will die, Mark. She will…die.'" Kenny began to cry. "'You must leave for her own sake. I understand that you are upset, but everything you've done in your life was for her. Now please, please…don't make this about you. If you refuse, she's my daughter and as a father I must protect her.' Then you sat on your recliner next to Mary's empty one, thinking about her cooking and her health. Then you walked to the mailbox, received a check of two hundred and one dollars from the police station, and Mark, you know what happened after. You've told me before." Kenny placed both of his hands on Mark's bed while his eyes puffed up and tears wet the bed from this old man. Mark was crying, too. He was unable to move while tears streamed down his face. There was one minute left; the nurse was outside. Then Mark received an epiphany, and with a shivering lip, he spoke.

"Wh-what happened to you, Kenny? Why are you so old?"

Kenny starred up into Mark's eyes, his tears instantly turned to joy, and he laughed through astonishment.

"Mark, listen carefully," Kenny said swiftly. "These men in this institution don't personally care about you, but they will assist, so please communicate smoothly. You will also talk with some police officers, because last night you…almost murdered someone. There is talk that you may be charged with a life sentence in the Rester Institution, but there is always early release with good behavior. After the police officers comes the press. They will attempt to cause an outrage out of you. There is a chance that no one from the media will communicate with you today, but there is a crowd outside wanting anything they can possibly grab, and it hasn't shrunk. The news of what you did is nationally known, so they will come. Believe me, it's not like the media coverage that interviewed you when you shot those drug smugglers. They want you to crack. The reporters want to see gossip. They will throw you in a straitjacket and a pillowed room if you react. Ignore them."

Mark's heart monitor went off again, and Kenny quickly muted it. The nurse didn't hear. "Why can't I remember, Kenny?" he asked while pee began to trickle into his sheets.

"There was an accident. You have amnesia. Please trust me and don't be afraid. Your heart rate is at one hundred twenty, and this type of machine won't mute if it passes one hundred sixty beats per minute. I will be thrown out."

"Where's Aaron? Why isn't he here?"

There was a knock on the door. Kenny quickly glanced behind and saw the outline of professional suits. They were the government officials. They opened the door with tremendous posture.

"Aaron is going to jail. He broke a few laws that aren't easily forgiven," Kenny whispered. Mark's heart rate exceeded 160, and the monitor began to screech with a higher pitch. A few nurses ran past the government officials and Kenny in a panic, their pagers creating the same high-pitched noise. Mark began to sweat in terror and yelled one last comment before Kenny was completely gone, another man in a suit leading him out the door and whispering into his ear.

"Take care of Mary!"

After those words, he was surrounded by nurses fighting to lower his heart rate. Kenny's excitement from Mark's epiphany was extinguished. He didn't respond or look back as his eyes fell to the floor, shamed beyond belief. *I will*, he thought, *I will*. Kenny then ran to the bathroom and cried, leaning over the toilet and knowing that everything he'd said was wasted.

Then his phone rang, and Kenny picked it up. He wiped his eyes and cleared his voice, doing a poor job of it. "Hello," Kenny said. "So what's the news?"

The voice on the other line responded, "You're in."

The doctor set forth out of the institution and toward the hospital. He was accompanied by two police officers for protection from the roaring crowd outside that seemed to expand with different news teams across the nation. They all had many questions, and as reporters flooded in front and behind him, a small crowd of rioters that were outside the reporters began to throw half-empty cups, small rocks, and screamed insults. "You an enthusiast for police brutality?" one twenty-four-year-old college student screamed. "You allow the mentally ill to protect our neighborhoods? Our children? You let them carry a gun?" *He didn't carry a gun*, Kenny thought. *We had it controlled*. When he arrived to the hospital, Kenny was again assisted by police officers to pass through another riot of reporters attempting to thrust themselves inside, sneaking for a glimpse of inside, or a word with Kenny. He was escorted to the recovery room for surgery; no one walked in his path, every nurse disgusted by the sight of Kenny, most glaring at him, some whispering into each other's ears, and a few, only a few, having no idea. Another police officer met with him halfway, allowing the other two to walk back and help restrict the crowd. This police officer led him to Aaron, behind a maroon curtain.

"How are you doing, Aaron? I heard the eight-hour procedure went well," Dr. Kenny enthusiastically stated, a weak smile on his face.

Aaron mumbled something in gibberish.

"Mark was great. He remembered who I was, in fact! If we just pray for him and let God handle it, the outcome that was meant to happen will happen."

Aaron muttered another sentence that was too sloppy to understand.

"Your lawyer said that they want to charge you with forty years in prison for harboring Mark on the police force. But there is always an early release with good behavior!"

Again, more murmurs were spoken through the thin man's mouth, his chest, shoulders, and neck wrapped tightly with bandages.

"Did you ask how I was able to visit Mark? Well, I spoke the truth for once. For once I did what was right. It is going to be a very heavy fine because of my knowledge of Mark. I'm also going to probably lose my job, which means I will more than likely become an entrepreneur like before. I'm not certain yet if this publicity will be helpful or harmful, but I'll find out very soon." Kenny was very silent; then he spoke again with a warm yet tattered voice.

"You know why I became a doctor? When my wife found out she had colon cancer, it was the mid-eighties, and a cure was like roping a fly. There was more of a chance to kill it with the rope than to catch it with a loop. So she decided to do nothing at all and tell no one. While she began to grow ill, we all made up a lie that it was meningitis, to cause worry but not the loss of hope. While I watched my wife slowly lose her strength, Mary did as well. She believed that her life was only going to be as long as her mother's and fell into a depressive spiral. I promised my little girl that I would become a doctor and find a cure. That lifted her spirits, and her color came back, so I broke open the books and learned as much as I could about the disease while earning my doctorate and continuing my entrepreneurship. When Mark was diagnosed, I was afraid to lose this perfect son-in-law. I felt like if I failed to help him, I'd also fail my daughter. So my visits were very limited with him, as every spare second was spent staring at those college library books and theories. Then Mary became ill with the first lie I ever made." There was a silence. "I knew almost nothing about meningitis except what is essential for a doctor to understand. Then my lies spiraled out of control. I believed you. I believed that a lie would help my son-in-law just like my wife thought a lie would help her friends. I repeated the exact mistake my wife did. I destroyed the person I wanted to protect. The truth became even worse than if it had been told with honesty. True, Mark was in a deep depression that would have needed professional help and a suspension from the station, but if we let him be, only waited one more week and didn't jump to conclusions, what a world it might have been," Kenny said with wonder. "You know what's ironic? Out of everything in Mark's life, the poverty, the cancer, the death of Tom, the memory of his wife's warmth that was enough to create a depression so strong, insanity was the only out. Insanity was the lucky ticket in our cruel, spiraling lies that brewed a maniac through the course of decades. Maybe Mark knows she's dead but can't ever accept it. Although, if he ever remembers, let us hope he is furious enough to make up a punishment for our mistakes. But I warn that if Mark doesn't fuel up in rage, let us throw on straitjackets and buy rocking chairs to pass the time, because the guilt will drive us mad."

◆◆◆

Every day was the same. Mark was strapped down in the mornings because of the panic attacks and outrages, and he would eat breakfast with restraints in his white room because the doctor knew there was no avoiding them. His first screams were almost always commented on by a neighboring younger woman who was very annoyed by him, who would scream back as if she were the sanest person in the facility.

"Oh, shove a sock in it!" she would yell. Mark would ask her questions immediately, always surprised that there were other human beings present. The woman only answered a few while being very annoyed, since he'd asked the same questions yesterday, and a week ago, and the week before that. She'd look at the time, see that it was a minute before 8:15 a.m., and sigh. "It's almost time for the rooster to crow," the woman yelled with a slight slur. "How's Mary? 'Oh, I just saw Mary the other day and we had a play date with Johnny Rodgers and Bruce Springsteen!'"

She was a regular.

Mark would then be questioned on what he remembered, then left to reflect on the situation for an entire hour, with the news playing on the TV that hung in the corner next to the glass door; it was on mute. The doctor left it on to allow him access to the date, so he *might* admit his insanity sooner than later, so he would be able to sneak in some exercise.

The same old and wrinkled nurse that cleaned his room at 11:00 p.m. asked him the same question before she left.

"Would you like anything to drink, dear?"

Mark responded the exact same way since his admission more than three weeks ago. His nose was light purple, with the swelling almost gone. The bandages for the bullet wound that had scraped his right arm were reduced to only one thin cloth, the stitches on the side of his head were finally out, but he continued to experience mild headaches at night. The only injury that hadn't been improving was the concussion from the car accident with Tyler Castillo, the boy Mark believed was a drug addict exactly a month ago, although he had no memory of the incident.

"Why am I here?" Mark asked the old nurse. "I need to see Mary."

Of course, these reactions were all too common for her, so no emotions were attached to his words. She would smile and walk out thinking about the next few routines that needed her assistance.

The woman next door was named Whitney. She stomped on the ground in the mornings while sucking on her chewed-up, irregularly curled blonde hair, while reading the newspaper comic strips the nurse gave her. Then afterward, she'd stuff her bed with the colorful cartoons, as she had been doing for the past six months. "If only that selfish nurse would give me more than these damn government brainwashing cartoons!" Whitney would scream while stuffing her *secret stash*, watching the door and hoping no one would hear the sounds of the gathered, hoarded comic strips. But this was not news, as the nurse always heard her taunts and, every morning, would offer her the newspaper like she demanded, since the doctors promoted the practice of reading. Yet every time Whitney would turn her head in disgust and say, "I am disgusted that Dr. Mac brainwashed you to give me that newspaper, and I liked you, Nurse Trinity."

Her plan was to burn down the institution with the plastic bed as a diversion, during the rush of lunch. Then she'd pick the lock on the far right door in the wide, dull, white lunchroom, which led to the cafeteria where the lunch ladies were. With the way the air vents ran, and how vast the institution was, the woman believed she could crawl through a vent and reach the front desk behind the cafeteria in under three minutes. There was a police officer always stationed there, but she told another inmate that she would play a board game with him if he created a riot to attract the police officer away from his post.

"Tomorrow, tomorrow's the day!" she would yell unknowingly, every day as dawn cast dim lights across the rooms. "I can feel the freedom!"

During lunch, Mark would ask the nurse who brought the food into his room if he could get up and walk around. Since it was routine, the staff was aware of his thoughts to escape. It was nearly impossible to restrain him after allowing this request, as both times Mark was inches from the automatic front doors, his neighbor drooled with jealousy. So the nurse would ignore his plea, turn her head, and walk out. They couldn't loosen his restraints until it was past three in the afternoon. Once that hour passed, Mark fell under the illusion that the following day had more fortune, and a strategic escape plan was the only solution. The problem was that his mind never saw tomorrow.

A day after the narcotics wore off Aaron from the assault, he was interviewed by a reporter named Brody Johnson for the HFA (Highlights for America). Since he was a part of a national newsroom, Johnson was given first dibs on the story. In that interview, Aaron decided to speak the truth, beginning the day they met. The magic tricks they performed and those childish dreams of performing in Los Vegas. Mark and Mary's relationship, with Aaron's secret passion toward her. Tom's death in the Middle East. Mark's cancer in their town, and his notoriety across the town as an outstanding police officer, a marine, and a survivor of cancer. Then Mary's illness, Mark's insanity, and Aaron's secret to keep his sanity. Then the days past Mark's memory, with Mary well and healthy for five more years. Their normal love until the accident, and Aaron believing that he was an astonishing friend because of Mark's continuous job at the police station. Then Johnson's final question for him was what his final request would be for America. Aaron lost his control.

"I deserve everything I receive for my punishment as everything I did was wrong," Aaron cried on his hospital bed, "but Mark, he's my best friend. This is all I ask for in America, all I ask is to see him one last time. I want to calm him down, I know what he needs."

The interview went viral, and Aaron's words moved many in the homes of the United States. There was a national statement a few days later from the Rester Recovery Facility and Institution's owner plainly stating, with his ghostly white face and acne scars under his grimly white hair, that Mark was too unstable to have any visitors because of his attempts to flee and the outrages in the morning. Then the nation shook with rage; every station continued to interview Aaron to refresh their audience's minds, and they all skyrocketed with views.

Each new interview became a sensation, as families digested them like *People* magazine, hearing about each individual story coming from Aaron's lips. He spoke about his abusive father, how he would walk miles from his house as young as seven years old, full of fear and anger as his classmates used to also call him "Angry Aaron." Then Mark approached him with a handshake and humility, saving his life and showing him that compassion existed.

The interviews didn't yield results. The owner stood firm on his answer, hoping late-night talk shows would laugh about the matter and it would pass through time. Then Aaron told one of the many newscasters about how, at eighteen, Mark willingly signed up for annual colonoscopy tests with his girlfriend, as the cancer for her was hereditary. He described the way Mark looked at her, the gentleness in his gaze, the humanity in his touch, and how they held hands before they went under, staring into each other's eyes with completeness. The news stations then began to bribe the owner. Lucky for the news stations, his crescent smile showed, and the old man asked for the highest bidder, greed being the key to his heart. The HFA felt the anxiety and need to win this story, since it was their video that had begun the excitement. So they won the bidding, this overwhelming trending story with the highest bid of $4 million, giving it away happily and gleefully as if they were writing history and doing a favor for others. The HFA swiftly cut as much as needed out of their normal TV schedule to broadcast this event live without commercial breaks, beginning with Brody Johnson casually stating lines he'd half memorized, while pretending to personally pick up Aaron from the police station. Aaron was given one-liners to respond with, but he didn't care—he was thinking of Mark, not about the media that to him was a pain. Aaron was severely irritated with Johnson as well, his phony smile toward the camera with his shiny, gelled blond hair and a dash of foundation on his face, in a very professional suit.

Brody didn't have any care toward anyone but himself. Behind the camera he snapped at the interns, yelled at the filming crew with a spoiled, and had an impatient need for everyone to bow down to his greatness. He carried a tiny spray bottle that could have been used as a perfume sampler in its life before, full of half lemon and half onion juice as a spray he rubbed on the bottom of his palm. Therefore, when the time came, he could rub his eyes with the residue on his skin and break down in tears behind Aaron if the interaction came to be emotional.

Aaron was also given a suit to match Brody, although it was painful to put on because of his bullet wounds that were healing much slower than normal, even when the size was twice as big and worn more like a cape than a suit. A blood infection after a few days past the incident was found expanding his wounds, turning them yellow as puss flooded out and increased antibiotics ran in. He also had lead poisoning, as one bullet was lodged into his clavicle. Hours were spent to collect all the pieces, as doctors searched diligently to find all the shards of lead and bone, but a few were missed. Except this did not stop the news station as they tried to bribe the hospital to straighten Aaron's arms out so he could fit into the suit, lawyers all the way from New York manipulating and threatening the hospital as they waved around the $4 million document in their faces, yet the hospital did not nudge. Therefore, his clip-on tie hung around his neck very loosely, and the clothes he wore were a size larger so that they didn't interfere with the injuries. Because they couldn't put Aaron into a fitted suit, the station then decided to take the opposite route, overdramatizing his condition with messy hair, baggy khakis, and a tight belt around the waist. His right arm was in a sling from the bullet that shot his shoulder, while his left was still in pain because of the deep graze, but bendable. Therefore, they bent his left into a sleeve and tucked the rest under his sling so it could be seen while they filmed.

His legs were weak from being bedridden for half a month, and the infections made them even weaker as he couldn't walk. Aaron also adopted a fear of high fevers and vomit, afraid that the shivers, dry hacks from an empty stomach while his body continued to vomit, would come again. But the doctors told him that those were over. He had begun therapy in the prison to learn how to walk again, though he wasn't anywhere close to normal. This was his second day in the small-town prison, and once therapy was over, Aaron would be transferred to Arizona's most secure prison. Brody pushed Aaron in a wheelchair while smiling with his sparkling teeth. Aaron couldn't stop thinking about Mark.

When they arrived, two cameras awaited them outside. They stepped out of the cab the HFA had rented for a humble appearance, and a crowd outside cheered. "Thank you, Mr. Driver, I'll meet you back in New York!" Brody stated while handing the driver a twenty-dollar bill. "Keep the change, my friend, I like to give."

"Gee thanks, Mr. Johnson," the actor at the wheel stated, "and oh, Aaron! Tell Mr. Wegman I send good wishes his way!"

Aaron sat in his wheelchair motionless while everyone waited for his line. He stared at the front doors of the institution.

"I—I believe he's a little nervous," Johnson stated quickly and swiftly while the crowd laughed. Then he turned to the camera and spoke with enthusiasm. "Wish us luck!" America's hearts melted as Brody pushed Aaron's wheelchair through the front doors.

It was three o'clock, the only time the owner and doctors agreed and allowed them to visit, double-checking and booting out anyone who didn't sign a waiver. The news crew first entered Mark's room to set up the cameras and lights, blinding his eyes and crowding the room with joyful thirty-year-old men tossing cords and reordering furniture to find a plug in the wall, while completely ignoring the mentally insane patient, panicking from their lights and laughter. Then Aaron and Johnson strolled in, Aaron still staring at the ground. The room was concealed with a metal door and was obviously one of the most secure rooms in the institution, as the Rester staff prepared for everything that may go wrong. Brody grasped the cold handle and pulled the door out with his commercial smile. Aaron finally looked up. Brody pushed Aaron inside. The three cameras in the room all focused on Mark and Aaron's faces. Their eyes connected in a flash. Aaron quickly and weakly stood out of his wheelchair from Mark's sight. Mark was amazed as well; his eyes sparkled for only a second, the nation stood on their feet, and families far and wide began to tear up. They were waiting for excitement from both ends, for uniting these lifelong friends, and it was a fight to do so. Millions of dollars, viral Internet videos, and slight riots led to this moment. But Mark's sparkle turned into tears, obsessive tears, and fell into a fit of despair. Aaron knew this would happen. He wanted to be left alone with Mark, but they wouldn't allow such a request. They needed the cameras. Millions of families began to lose their smiles as they watched.

"So, this is how we die, Aaron. Out of all people, I can't believe they abducted you, too. Then they beat you up and decided to record our deaths, is that right? That's what they wanted? Those nasty terrorists. Those sons of (the language was bleeped out, and the families watching were in shock). Well, I'm glad they did, I wouldn't want to die with anyone else." Mark smiled and sniffed his nose heavily.

Aaron built with rage, and he turned around to Johnson. "I told you that we needed to be alone! Look what you did! Look what you've done! There was a reason why I lied for so many years, to prevent... this! To prevent Mark from living in misery for the rest of his life! This is your fault!"

Aaron tripped and landed on his back, then the cameras turned off. A few nurses quickly came and helped him into the wheelchair while Johnson stood about two yards away, demanding that they cut out the scene of Aaron's rampage. The editors weren't fast enough to completely cut off Mark's despair, but they did cut off Aaron: every single word that came out of his mouth never left the secure walls of that metal room. Live television was HOA's greatest regret of the day and their greatest despair. Then Johnson screamed for a makeup crew to dab off the moisture from his face. Aaron demanded to be sent back to prison, knowing that he wouldn't be left alone with Mark, and therefore anything extra was damaging. Mark was now in a rampage, screaming and crying for them to return Aaron. He was fighting the restraints, and his concussion from the accident began to build up again, shooting through his neck and down the spine like never-ending fireworks trapped in his body. The cleaning lady who always came in at eleven ran in quickly to calm Mark down, while another nurse took out a syringe full of two grams of Ativan. "It's okay, sweetheart," the elderly cleaning lady stated with her calm voice and motherly eyes. Then she began to sing while the nurse pushed the antidepressant into his IV line. It was a song Mark seemed to react to more than any other; his mood always seemed to change once she sang. "Umbrella, umbrella please don't go, you keep me away from this cold snow, I'd have no protection so please hug me, or I'd run to the old apple tree. Umbrella, umbrella please don't go, you keep me away from this cold snow. The wind is strong, this is true, but you'd hug me, and I'd hug you, so umbrella, umbrella please don't go, you keep me away from this cold snow. The rain is wet, it makes me cry, but with you we'd get by, so Umbrella, umbrella please don't go."

Mark whispered the last line with the nurse before falling asleep, "You keep me away from th-this cold…snow." Mark lost consciousness from the drug, and his anxiety was gone. He then began to dream. He dreamed of his wedding day with Mary. The perfect, warm sunshine tickling their skin. Mary, as pretty as she could ever be in that white dress, holding her tiny hands with the feeling of suspense. He couldn't wait to kiss her, it was boiling in his skin, it was making his heart soar! She was everything he wanted, not only in beauty but also in her heart that reflected through her eyes. The vows first, then he placed the ring on her finger. She saw him as someone who didn't exist, a man who couldn't have been real! He was too romantic, his eyes never wandered, and he was moral. Mark never cared what she said and always seemed to have something to say for every issue thrown her way, even if the words were said through an emotional hug. Then he was tough. He was someone who enjoyed protecting the ones he loved, while simultaneously never showing anger. She slipped the ring on his finger.

"I, Mary Kenny, take you, Mark Wegman, to be my husband, to have and to hold from this day forward, for better or for worse, for richer, for poorer, in sickness and in health, to love and to cherish; from this day forward until death do us part." Mary began to cry with slow tears rolling down, while giggling lightly and smiling with tremendous joy. The preacher began to speak, and Mark copied what the priest declared with confidence, with his eyes glimmering in the sun.

"I, Mark Wegman, take you, Mary Wegman—" the two families went wild, clapping and cheering! Mr. Kenny gave him a thumbs-up from the audience, and Aaron, the best man, shook his head while laughing, while the preacher asked for their silence in his old, stern voice.

"Groom, may you please say her last name correctly?"

"Sorry, it—it just slipped," Mark said while Mary laughed hysterically, snorting a little in between giggles, causing more laughter in the crowd. "I, Mark Wegman, take you, Mary Kenny, to be my wife, to have and to hold from this day forward, for better or for worse, for richer, for poorer, in sickness and in health, to love and to cherish; from this day forward until death do us part."

The preacher began to speak again, finally smiling. "You may kiss the bride." Mark reached over, swept her off her feet, and they kissed. She slipped a little, but he caught her behind with one arm, and the crowd cheered with immense enthusiasm. There wasn't a dry pair of eyes at the wedding.

Then Mark woke up in an instant with a cold sweat across his entire body. He was in the same room, with the TV on silent and the sun steadily setting on the day. Mark searched for any sight of Aaron, panicking by the thought of his disappearance, believing that Aaron might have been killed. But what he did find was a white paper tucked away in his left hand; he was gripping it with force, and miraculously, that restraint was loose! Mark teared up from the sight; his heart began to race as he tried to slip his hand out. It was still too constricted for his palm to fit through, even while his fingers were straightened and his palm was crushed. But Mark wouldn't miss this opportunity, he *knew* that Aaron had to have been killed, and they would be insane to let Mark out after what he witnessed. Mark continued to pull and strain his arm tighter and tighter, creating a burn across his wrist. Mark held in his screams that were caused by all his effort placed toward the one arm, knowing that the nurses would hear his hollers from the room beyond those walls. He was halfway out of the cuff. Wegman inhaled and pulled again with all his might, turning red in the face. He knew that if one arm was out, he could untie his entire body and while alone slip out of the room's window with ease, breaking it with his knuckles and squeezing through the tiny hole. One arm was freedom from those terrorists and further away from death.

Then finally, it was free! Mark was speechless, excited beyond belief, kissing his hand and celebrating because of this small token of freedom! Then he went for his other hand, until a small, white piece of paper fell. It was the paper that was stuffed in his fist, squished into a tight, compact ball.

Maybe Aaron's alive, Mark thought. *He must be the one who loosened my restraint and slipped a message into my hand!* Mark quickly reached for the paper and unraveled it with one hand. But it wasn't from Aaron—it was from Tom, written in the color of honey.

Dear Mark,

I know that you will make it through these awful trials. You have changed many lives, ever since childhood. One of those lives was mine. When you adopted me at seventeen, I didn't believe there was a soul on Earth that cherished mine. My birth father made it very clear that his interests weren't toward me when he left when I was ten, and while we were together, he used to work on his boxing form on me. Then you spontaneously walked in one day, and just like that I was eating dinner with you and Mary, every night, feeling like more than just a punching bag. You pointed me toward morals and gave me goals to look forward to. For seven years, I wished to prove my father wrong, to prove that I was a unique soul and not someone to throw on the street. I wanted to be better than him, better than my grandfather, better than every Freeman who ever touched Earth's soil. But once I began to learn of God, I found out that I was unique. So I enlisted at eighteen, and although I still felt like I needed to prove my father wrong, it was also to prove you right! That you chose correctly.

I apologize for my early departure, but the reality is that I never came down to gentle your thoughts. I was originally sent to assist a young boy who was a firm believer and needed an answer to his communities' prayers. It was an honor I was blessed to receive, but God also knew you. He knew about your pains and the repetitive fights to see his daughter, Mary Wegman. So God allowed me—someone I might add very unworthy—to communicate and answer the prayers that were also pointed toward you. So that's why I came down. Please don't mistake me as a death angel, because that's misleading. I'm just some angel that was given a gift to continue in assisting others even after death.

May God rest in your heart,

With all my love,

Tom Wegman

P. S.: I'd also like to add that I succeeded in answering the young boy's family's prayers, which was for God to cure their child, Tyler Castillo. Tyler has the best sense of humor. He makes us all laugh out loud with his snarky comments! And man, can that boy run! Climbing trees and causing laughter from the little ones and Jesus! God is Great, and Tyler has never looked back!

Mark began to panic, screaming and yelling, knocking over the entire bed while still being strapped with three limbs. Two nurses ran in and called for Ativan while attempting to restrain him. Mark saw the nurses and remembered their names, he remembered what day it was, he remembered the lunch from the day before, Mark remembered the questions he'd asked his neighbor for more than three weeks straight, and every occurrence. He remembered the rain that fell last Saturday, he remembered the broccoli-and-cheese soup a week ago. Mark screamed because of everything he was recalling from the past rushing through his mind. Mark remembered the car accident and his hatred toward Tyler. He remembered the call; he remembered the rage.

"NOOOOOOOOOOOOOOO," Mark yelled, "TYLER! YOU CAN'T LEAVE! YOU CAN'T!"

They brought out the Ativan. He saw the needle and began to fight back. Mark remembered the time he was forced on the bed by eight nurses and Dr. Kenny.

"No! Get that away!" Mark yelled as he slowly picked himself up with the metal, a 120-pound bed attached to his back. Then he began to remember the repetitive thoughts at the police station, walking up and feeling the same as yesterday, and Aaron's smiles from Mark's appearance. Everyone thought that he was Aaron's favorite, not knowing that Mark was forgetful and unstable, believing he was a middle-aged man with a daily pattern. They respected him because of his past struggles. Everyone smiled, never second-guessing themselves about his character, which was all fake, so Mark was never pitied. He despised pity.

The nurses were multiplying, and Mark fled to the corner. All they saw was the bottom of his bed, the silvery color, shining dimly off the light bulbs in the room with its wheels and frame. Nurses who'd worked in the institution for more than half their lives snickered and laughed at Mark's retreat. Others were aching from the sorrow he could be feeling, understanding that Mark must have already forgotten where he was. He continued to scream.

"This job is too sad," said a young nurse with her bottom lip out.

"He's just confused." A male caregiver tapped another snickering nurse in the shoulder. "I bet he's in the corner 'cause he forgot how to sleep on a bed."

"Shut up, Zack!" yelled the young nurse. "He didn't ask for this. Do you ever watch the news?"

"Has he watched the news? He's on every channel and we leave his TV on every day!" snickered Zack while others giggled behind. "Oh wait, maybe he forgot how to watch TV, too."

Mark began to remember how he saw the newspaper's dates every morning but stubbornly tossed them aside, believing that it was a gag from Aaron. A way to cheer him up and toss his mind off of the subject of his dying wife, believing for some bizarre reason that if he waited for only one more week, she would return.

Then he remembered the accident.

It wasn't a dream. Her blood. Him carried off the scene quickly before the car burst into flames. The sirens. It was all black. He heard voices. It was a male, speaking before the ambulance doors closed.

"We…we couldn't save them both. There were gas fumes and… gasoline everywhere on both the—" The doors slammed on the ambulance. A female began to speak. She was skinny, blonde, and was in complete panic.

"Go faster! He's bleeding out from his head! If we don't get blood soon we'll lose him. Faster!" Then Mark lost consciousness, darkness surrounded him, and the woman whispered into his ear. "Sir, whatever you have left you have to show it now, fight for your life, if you have any more purpose, fight."

Mary was alive. Alive! There was life after Mark's memories. Five years! Five years of forgotten bliss, and almost two decades of fear toward a sickness that never… Wegman began to rage with fury, and he quickly pushed back with anger, bashing Zack in the head so hard that he was pushed toward the front wall, banging the same spot in the metal wall.

"We had a life! We had a life after Mary's death! She lived!" Mark screamed as a nurse ran over and forced in the Ativan. Mark swung his hand, which slightly loosened her footing because for the first time, an attack that wasn't precise. "Aaron, that bastard!" The Ativan was slowly affecting his speech, but Mark continued to triumph over its effects for a few seconds, fighting for a rampage through the nurses.

"Mary was alive and no one told me! No one told me!" he yelled while letting the bed fall and hit the ground with him attached. Mark's concussion began to strike his spine because of the collapse toward the ground, a pain he could now remember.

"Aaron, Kenny, what did you do? What have you done?" Mark began to cry, although the antidepressant and tension reliever coursed through his veins. "Did you know? D-Did you know?" Mark pointed at the nurses, who were helping to place his bed back on its wheels. Wegman never fell asleep, but continued to weep softly. Mark finally saw Mary die for the first time.

He never knew she departed; it was as though it was yesterday that Mary was by his side. Except yesterday was at the Rester Institution. It was an illusion that Mary was alive. It was as if he were drugged to believe this horrific memory for many years, a torturous event worse than death. Mark finally accepted that she was gone; he finally accepted her death. He could finally revert his memory back to the feeling that burned his stomach and kept his thoughts from believing Mary was alive, the spark that exploded with a desire to escape. The slight thought of her survival dancing in the light, tickling sun—it was from their life after her sickness. That was the root of the insanity in his eye. A memory that wasn't connected to any tragedies, but only joyfulness; it was as if it were Mark's childhood replayed in adulthood. He continued to sob lightly, dwelling in these thoughts, for the first time without furious anger and rage, while outside it rained, except this was the first autumn storm. There was a damp, light drizzle, cold to the touch. There was no thunder, there was no flash bang, there was just an overcast of humid rain with promising spring after the season. His fits of rage had finally concluded, as a man with restraints, at an institution, with his memory retrieved. Mark was finally cured from amnesia, although his Post-Traumatic Stress Disorder might stay with him for life. Now, if you asked a police officer off the street who was in high spirits because of the major town drug lords finally being filed into court, he would have confidently stated that Mark was mentally insane. A lunatic, children. Someone who would need assistance every morning to get dressed and someone to help feed him three times a day. A man who couldn't tell from day or night, while being told the answer when asked.

He sobbed for hours for his lost wife, and now as a man with sanity, Mark began to speak.

"Mary," he said, "you've always told me that it was okay to cry. Well here I am…crying. If only you could see."

There was life after death. There was happiness after despair. There was Mary, after her last day, and there was a dull moan.

The nurses ran toward Zack, forgetting everything about his injury once setting up Mark on the bed. He was in shock, with a huge lump on the top of his cap. It almost seemed like a cartoon. He stood up slowly, as flimsy as silly putty. He forgot where he was, and who he was. This memory loss lasted for an entire week, and Zack forever disliked even the slightest thought of Mark, if he could remember.

Yes, children, Mark felt despair when Tyler died. He was still a body on earth with limited flesh and time, if you can remember far enough, past this beautiful bliss and glory—death was a tragedy. But of course, you see the boy everywhere, a child of God and a jokester, as we all are well aware. I've never, in all my years, seen such a genuine and loving child for God and mankind. He saw angels before he was under those trials on Earth, from those dreams of his accomplishments in changing people's souls, because Tyler knew about his sickness before, knew of what Satan wished to do in order to destroy any random child, like he does. Tyler rejoiced in his soon-to-be accomplishments, succeeded from the sickness. He knew his death, and Tom, beloved Tom, blessed him with his company through it all. In total, Tyler saved five souls. This included his bitter and heartbroken mother that soon found God after understanding that Tyler would have wished only for that. His father that suffered from the divorce soon found God after facing tiny trials of drugs and alcohol, ending up in the hospital, and finding a second wife who brought him to love what his son loved. Then there was Mark, a man who found his past in time to build his future, and through the past, his wisdom was increased and his love for God began as healing took place, which became his new passion. Then, without physical connection, Tyler saved Aaron. A man who lived in fear that he would be caught for what severe crimes he had committed, while charging others off the street day by day. Aaron felt obligated to allow Mark a job on the police force, since it was what Mark believed to be his life was every morning, and Aaron was to blame for it all. When the news spread out that Mark's lost knowledge randomly sparked in his brain, Aaron cried with joy and partial relief, then praised God for forty years in prison. The final saved soul was Kenny, who felt the guilt of a thousand sins for slipping one lie into his son-in-law's ear. Kenny felt as if he needed control of this situation, all control, while not being involved at all. He wished to ignore the entire day-to-day conflict Aaron fought while solving the difficult situations that needed his assistance. Truthfully, Kenny felt the blood of Mark's quick hand of lead into Aaron's body and the blame of every mistake that came from Mark. Seeing Mark was like glaring at his imperfections. Kenny couldn't face the guilt he stored up in his body for decades. No punishment was worse than Aaron and Mark's sentences combined, because he knew it was his one choice that had begun the domino effect. Kenny lost it all: his acknowledgment as a doctor, his riches from those checks, and his determination to stay away from soup lines. He found God through poverty, knowing that God's glory never left, and because God's love never left, he felt as if he never needed to please a man again. A year passed and he became an employee at a gas station, then lived eight more peaceful years in an apartment until he left the earth with humbleness and thoughts of God. Kenny faced his guilt because of his poverty-stricken life from Mark's rampage, which came from the epiphany of Tyler's immune deficiency. Tyler saved Kenny, and although Kenny never knew until he joined us as a young man again, he was thankful for his poverty.

Kenny and Mark are easy examples of Satan's quick hand on a man who fights to accomplish what is right but fails because the world is wicked. I am an example of Satan's attempts to weaken others. Kenny married, had a child, and continued to do what was correct and morally right. Then his wife faced a trial and fell into the earth. So Kenny fought to understand how to save his daughter during a time of little understanding. Scars were dormant but healed as his daughter married. They grew for only five years, then Kenny's son-in-law fought obstacles, which made his goal to find a cure even more meaningful, because Kenny loved his son-in-law. Then he obtained his doctorate in time to watch his daughter face what seemed like the end of her earthly life. At this point, Kenny threw away God and didn't return until he repented for his one lie to Mark two decades later as a poor man. Of course, you all know he faced death and now walks through our trees and through our grass with youth forever in his soul.

Now, Mark was born in poverty and fought for social justice as a child. Since his heart was large and understood what his inner personality was, it was never difficult to understand whose advice was right, whose advice was wrong, and who was at a loss of identity. Mark grew up without mental bruises, as the worst childhood memory was a shattered arm. Then he married, adopted a child about four years younger than him, and lived for the Marines while loving his wife and adopted brother that, through time, called him "Dad." Satan, like the lion he is, stumbled upon Mark and gave him cancer. When Mark rejoiced and praised God for Mary's wellbeing, Satan stumbled upon him and his son and took away Mark's brother from earth. Mark fell but recovered, and while his cancer faded away, the community began to love Mark's redemption and strength. Satan, angered at his failed attempts at devouring the Wegmans' confidence, threw his wife in a trial of pain. Mary won as she praised God while Mark lost his mind in agony. This has always been the war between Good and Evil, and even though free will is given to man, the fate of many sometimes lies in the decisions of the powerful; sometimes cancer cannot be cured. Sometimes meningitis cannot be avoided, and sometimes insanity burrows itself into your mind. Aaron called it The Passenger Effect, as he soon found out that at a certain point in situations, no one can stop the inevitable, no one can stop the hatred, no one can separate love. We simply called it spiritual warfare and the stubbornness of man. Satan whispered into Aaron and Kenny's ears to lie, which with their free will and weak hearts, they did. Then, wanting Mary to die without God, Lucifer waited, circling the sheep for years as they grew, while the sheep hugged the shepherd. Then a man drank and smashed into their vehicle. Satan failed as Mary concurred her trials and left earth. He threw a fit since God won again. But he saw Mark and kept him in his one month of hate toward God. The snake loved his craftiness and laughed as Mark cursed at God every morning for a story he partially knew. Although Mark walked into the community, acting as if he were still a Godly man, Satan knew what he said in silence.

This cursing and praising is constant in many lives, with the length of waves depending on the strength of your heart. When Mark found the note from Tom, he began to praise God once again and taught the Gospel for ten years in jail as Satan spit and whined for not getting his way, while circling him again, whispering to weak men and beating them up. Finding sneaky ways to put Mark down, make him feel as if no one cared for the Wegmans' existence.

Now why do I care? Why tell a story about Mark and his struggle through Satan's Earth? What makes me associated to such a story? It's because I'm his Hand Mitten. I was the art in his everyday life. I fed him while Satan whipped harshly. I kissed his lips as God joined us in marriage. We found lovely Tom at a foster home together and loved him like a son. I was always there for Mark, even when my vessel from earth became a nest for worms to grow. I watched him grow, I watched him fight, and I held his hand through it all as a promise for warmth we vowed long ago. Now he is ninety-five years old, and Satan once again beats his chest and screams angrily with another failure. Because Mark did it! My Hand Mitten beat Death's sting! Now with his final earthly breaths, I prepare to descend and take him with me to the bliss of our painless world. Children of God, I am blessed to have my husband join me for eternity. I'm ready to finally tell him everything! To look him in the eyes and feel his attention on mine. I don't miss the earth, but I do miss Mark's smile, his love toward me, and our conversations. Oh! It's time, it's time! I can't wait, I'm so excited! I've waited so long! It's time.

Epilogue

ARK WAS EIGHTY-FIVE, AARON was eighty-four, and they walked through a narrow hallway colored by the bland steel of an old prison. The chains across his wrists were of the same design as forty years ago, except they now seemed more for decoration than restraints. The prison officers were on their lunch break while they followed Aaron through the hallway, eating sandwiches with mayonnaise and avocado. Aaron saw the avocado, forgetting the taste of such a thing, though he knew the taste of mayonnaise very well, the taste of bread, milk, pizza, ham, meatloaf, and sometimes, on every blue moon, a cold Coke or a slushie from the staff room.

They stopped at a bland white desk with spots of black, shown by half a century of wear that can't be wiped off, since it was the color under the white.

A woman behind the desk was drinking a Frappuccino while typing on a keyboard made of light. Aaron was starstruck by the sight, although it would make sense, since the year was now the spring of 2053. She didn't look up to speak, and her attitude was different than that of the children her age when Aaron was last outside. She carried an annoyance of a ten-year-old, with what seemed like little respect for anyone.

"Aaron...Hudson?" the woman said with a bitter sting that fell off her lip. Aaron hesitated from the sound of his name and smiled lightly. "Y-yes ma'am."

"Well, Mr. Exitus..." said the woman as she starred with strain at the paper-thin computer screen. "You are a free man."

The prison officers walked Aaron to another room while he was immensely touched to be called with the prefix of "Mister." The officials spoke casually to each other while this next room with the same chipped white walls came nearer.

"My wife is very nervous," said the tall blond officer with pale white skin and a bent nose.

"She's afraid that the Japanese and Turks will crack their orbiting missiles any day now."

"There's no way war can't be prevented," said the officer on the other side. "The United Nations can't prevent this. The time for negotiations was years ago."

Aaron walked with his head half to the ground, with wonder still flooding through his eyes toward this war. He continued to quickly glance up without being detected, fearing that the prison officers still saw him as an inmate.

When they arrived to this next room, there was a high table in the middle. The blond officer unlocked the handcuffs while the trim bearded one played a game on his phone. Then the blond walked through an old automatic door that immediately recognized his face, coldly beeped, and swung open while they walked. The bearded man continued to play on his phone, knowing Aaron was too fearful of a slipup to even move, and he was right. Aaron stood there speechless with his head half down, keeping his hands in the exact position of where they were cuffed. He couldn't believe what was happening! He was leaving! An event Aaron believed his mortal life wouldn't see. Aaron was now very old and frail, with gray hair, and muscles from youth stripped. He'd lost track of time decades ago, yesterday believing that he still had years of time.

"Agh!" yelled the officer to his game. Aaron hesitated from his reaction but calmed down once he understood that it was toward his phone. The officer was an older man, although every staff member still used phones, so age wasn't the factor.

Aaron wanted to go back to his cell. He knew that this day was Friday, which meant that it was meatloaf day, and time turned it into a meal of luxury. *Take me tomorrow!* He thought. *So at least it can finish on a day of normality.* Aaron was in a crossroads of feelings, wondering if his heart wanted to stay or go. Anxiety came with the thought of leaving the horrific prison, with the idea of his death in his cell still logged in his thoughts. Then there was joy in seeing the outside world and what it had become, although Aaron didn't know what to think of the joyful feeling he carried.

The blond came back with a dusty cardboard box full of belongings. When Aaron looked inside, he was struck with emotions to find so many memories. There was an old Fossil watch that had run out of batteries long ago, a leather wallet with the wear from Aaron's use still visible around the corners, and a smartphone, which the blond gazed at with a glance and knew about its little worth in technology. There were keys to his car that was long ago scrapped, with a keychain of a bunny sticking out of a hat, coincidentally matching the magnet Mark had on his fridge many years ago. The bunny held a carrot with rosy cheeks sticking out from its face. There was a pair of clothes, off-brand denim jeans and a Guns & Roses shirt that was now too ancient to be played and enjoyed by the new generation. Then, finally, there was a pack of very ancient Bazooka Bubble Gum.

The bearded man continued playing while the blond began naming the items very blandly on the table. When naming off Aaron's phone, the bearded man heard and commented gleefully that the software was made around his birthdate.

Aaron quickly grabbed the items like a child grabbing candy and began rummaging through them. Aaron began to remember everything that was in his wallet while surveying the contents and saw it as bitter joy to see the items from his last day of freedom on his first. The money didn't seem to matter, but the items and cards had half a life. Aaron quietly asked to change out of his plain orange clothes and was granted his request mostly because of his age. It took ten minutes for him to change into the dusty, forty-year-old outfit that reeked of dust, and he grinned very gleefully to see himself in clothes that weren't orange. Aaron knew he was stalling to leave. He knew he was afraid to leave. He knew he never expected to leave, and yet here he was. Aaron sat with his clothes on in the staff bathroom until there was a knock on the door by what sounded like the bearded man with black hair.

"The man who's here to pick you up has arrived."

Aaron opened the bathroom's white door very slowly as it squeaked in a light tone from extensive use. He attempted to dust off as much of his clothes as possible, although it would take a washing machine to properly clean the faded look of sitting in a box for four decades.

They walked through another hallway of solid metal, and it led to outside where it was spring, with flowers on trees and bushes and a thin layer of grass that would be soft on bare feet.

Then there it was—the door that led to freedom. It was part of the wall that surrounded the prison and the size of every other door. Metallic like the wall, except perfect, since there was no anger involved with this door, just excitement and fright for what was waiting outside.

Aaron wondered what waited outside. He wondered who would pick up an old man that had no family and how he would kindly thank them. He wondered where he would live outside of the jail and if welfare still existed for an old man like him. The bearded officer walked over to the metallic door, and the door recognized his face, so it opened. The sun was the same as it was on the other side of the prison wall, but what stood there was different. It was another old man, who wore an old Arizona Wildcats cap with a black-and-white suit, which had been purchased long ago. His shoes were Nike sneakers, and it was obvious that this man was very poor when it came to matching. Aaron knew who this man was, and he began to cry, remembering his first life as a liar and a hypocritical police officer. He began to speak, but words didn't leave his lips while they moved, only slight syllables that were close to murmurs. Mark looked up from his long wait of standing at the door and saw his old friend coated with age as well.

"Sorry," spoke Aaron as he looked toward the ground. "Sorry," Aaron spoke again while weeping with pain, but before he could say it a third time, a pair of arms lightly wrapped around his chest. He opened his eyes to find himself in a hug with Mark and was shocked to see that he was forgiven. Then he engaged in the hug and realized that it wasn't forgiveness in the embrace, but a sense of missing his best friend. Aaron was already forgiven long ago.

Mark drove Aaron back to their town, and on the way, they ate at Domino's for lunch. A medium pizza was now twenty dollars—inflation—and people paid through fingerprints or thoughts.

"It's an implant in their brain," said Mark blandly with his aged voice while tapping a spot just above the eardrum. "It also records all vital signs and knows any sickness that you get in your body right when you get it. It is said that with the device, the age of death will go from ninety to a hundred and twenty. If you see close enough, there's a colored ball that sticks out of their head."

"Why didn't anyone at the prison have them?" Aaron asked with quick words.

"Because if someone smashed it hard enough, you could go brain-dead," Mark added with frustration and a shake of his head. Then Aaron joined him in frustration, and they laughed subtly. They were old men; it wasn't a worry for them.

They spoke calmly as they ate greasy food, and Aaron enjoyed the delicious pizza, since the prison's was healthier and staler. Mark spoke of his adventures around the world, preaching his story and acting as an activist for cancer and PTSD patients, then retiring to be a local pastor who began every sermon stating that he was going to preach like it was his final day on earth. This was Satan's final defeat, when his interferences only became annoyances like pesky gnats, which never affected Mark again. He spoke of the community that became his family and his present status of living alone as a bachelor.

"There is a room for you, too!" Mark said with comforting words. "It was your dream, right? The Amazing Aaron and Mark, bachelors in the city."

Aaron smiled with an expression of excitement and joy, and the offer made him blush to be treated with such respect again. "Y-Yes… I'd love that." Aaron humbly stated.

Then everyone in the building froze. It was as if time stood still, women gasped and men shook their heads in anger. Children were too young to understand what was told through their medically inserted brain pieces, although some did because of the repetitive talks their parents had with each other. Then finally one very muscular man spoke out of his plump and well-fit face in shock.

"We are at war." An inflated balloon of excitement had just popped in the room. The staff of Domino's attempted to continue their cooking but couldn't. Many were shaking with fear. Some customers began to walk out, others stood around in shock, not knowing what to do, and a minority of men over seventy waited for their order or continued eating. There was a large population of older men. Eventually, they left as well because the owner knew his staff couldn't continue, and in the town everyone was family. On the ride home, Aaron's curiosity forced him to ask, and Mark explained all the political disputes he'd missed.

"When I left jail in twenty twenty-six, we were in the middle of a Cold War with Russia," said Mark. "They continued to push south into Turkey and west toward Europe. Soon after, the Russian Empire crumbled; for the world around it, it was first come, first serve. The countries that gained the most land were Japan and Turkey, and they became the dominant countries in their regions. Then the two countries became allies after pressure from the United States. For some reason we were afraid that their sudden rise to power was dangerous." Mark then began to wonder about the same topic he was explaining: why the United States, the last mega power of the world, was afraid. "Then we built a nuclear military satellite base four years ago, and a few months ago the Turks and Japanese set up a nuclear satellite as well. Both orbit opposite each other, and people feared that the Japanese-Turk alliance would fire at any second. Now apparently, what their technological implants said, is that we declared war." Aaron didn't panic in the least and watched what seemed to be small drones flying through the sky. He noticed that there were far less people in the city. He noticed that there was almost no homeless population selling newspapers or playing guitars. He noticed technology's growth in buildings and in automobiles, like Mark's 2048 Toyota Camry that ran on something other than gas, something like electricity, and the roads it drove on seemed to hold a glue that made the ride even smoother. Or maybe it was the tires that seemed different, with their shiny and healthy appearance that seemed to him as more eco-friendly than before.

There was now a noticeable majority of Mexican Americans who walked from point A to B, and Broadway seemed crisp, surrounded by technology that crowded these now fairly old buildings. Aaron chuckled under his breath after watching for minutes with wide eyes through the Camry's windows. Aaron laughed because of a thought that warmed the old man's heart. He knew that this was the first time in the twenty-first century that Mark understood more than him. It was the first time Aaron was clueless in his surroundings, and Mark was filled with local and world knowledge—though this thought Aaron held was one that only could be possible through age. In their childhood, it was obvious that Aaron would anger from Mark's rational decisions, although time even alters the most stubborn of people. In the beginning of life, you search to please your heart, and at the end your heart is completely satisfied with what you found. Aaron's heart held no more anger. His heart held no envy. His heart held no rebellion; all that was left was a little wonder, faith, and an old man's love. He thought of Mark and fell in continuous joy from knowing that Mark was smarter than him. Aaron shed off his young thoughts and anger. He was a much different man. Wonder, faith, and love.

Wonder was grown through the metallic cave Aaron was in for forty years. Professing Christianity with the prison's Bible taught him faith, and the thought of Mark's heart during their time of childhood taught him love. Love is an element in your heart that is given to you before your breath of life. Aaron lost and learned again from Mark, and unlike most of the world, Aaron's newfound love stayed even through death.

Now Mark lost excitement. He lost the craving for adrenaline, the craving to become something the world would see as a hero. Although the main qualities his heart craved were still present, it was love toward everyone who breathed, strength toward words that slithered off tongues to only harm, or life obstacles that threw everyone into trials with their hearts. Mark had faith in the Gospel and Jesus Christ because he finally realized what his sick wife's words meant while she lay on her bed in near death. Then finally there was hope. Hope.

His hope came from Mary, now somewhere in the clouds. Mark hoped to one day see her face again and talk to her. He wished to hug her and spend his eternity with the only woman he'd married. Mark was past the thought of the lovely face and figure; those thoughts were for fools, even if young. Her soul was the beauty. Mark wondered what his first words would be to Mary, if they would be gentle, if there would be tears, or what Mary would say. Then he wondered what

Heaven felt like, if there were gusts of light wind, or rain that would cool your body from the sun. Then he thought of God, the Lord's presence, judgment day, and the overlooking of his own life. Toward his religion, this was one of the topics of which Mark was completely certain: he knew that God would make the right decision, if he were worthy for either Heaven or Hell. If his heart craved either love or hate. If his heart craved either life or death.

Aaron walked inside the two-story house and was moved when opening the door that was made without even the slightest touch of man. It had been decades since he'd seen the luxury of carpet and wooden chairs. Of a bed made for comfort and not for necessity. In modern society, the house was fairly plain, with a house payment of only $800 a month and absolutely no technology around. No radio, no television, no drones, no cameras. The stairs were carpeted, and the house smelled dusty. Aaron's wisdom sparked as he asked for a tour of the house. Upstairs consisted of a bleak bathroom and the guest bedroom Aaron would sleep in for ten years until Mark's death. Both mechanical doors were connected to the hallway, and downstairs there was far more room, but not a lot. There was a kitchen with many old pots and pans, a sitting room with ancient furniture from long ago, and the master bedroom, where Mark slept alone. On the walls were photos of Mark and Mary in their youth, paintings that were from Mary, and nothing else. Aaron wondered if the decor was safe for Mark to witness, if the paintings would create a panic attack, if the pictures would create a spiraling visit to the past, although Mark didn't seem like he was in distress. In fact, Mark's appearance made it seem as though his thoughts were solid and his mind was present for every conscious second. Even in their childhood it hadn't been like this—something in Mark made him radiate with confidence and joy. Aaron didn't understand what it could be. How could Mark now glance at pictures and portraits that for decades had slammed him with anxiety and pain of the past? How could such a man as before be such a man like this?

Although dinner didn't help, as Mark cooked cheeseburgers with bacon and fries, Aaron was confused as to why an old man like himself would make such unhealthy dishes.

"I got cancer again," Mark casually expressed.

"Mark," Aaron stated, "are you going to be okay?"

He laughed to Aaron's generous words.

"I've never felt better in my life."

◆◆◆

MARK'S DEATH WAS LONG. He sat on his bed blind and partially deaf. He didn't have any family left besides Aaron, although his days as a pastor brought him a group of about ten young and old friends that he called family. Mark spoke to them softly, lightly, asking one of the young ones by his bedside to tell him of their day. Aaron spoke the least while sitting on a chair in the corner of the room and patiently awaiting his turn to speak. Although both were the only children from their families, a bond like brothers was between them. This day was as casual as any other day; nothing changed except Mark's energy to speak and the nurse's urgency to have his family wrap up goodbyes to the old man's worthless body. So far, Aaron knew this day to be casual, since he was with Mark through all the visiting hours the hospital allowed and sat in the corner to speak as if it were any other day. As if they were still in the small home that he'd come to know in the past decade. Aaron was ninety-four, Mark was ninety-five, and no tests were done to see if the cause of death was cancer or nature. Both were, in fact, slow deaths. Then Mark—with the light pigmentation in his eyes—stared in the opposite corner of the hospital room. He very slowly turned his head and began to cry with a delicately placed smile. Tears wet his skin, and the young boy halted his very nervous sentences about his college and future career. Using frail muscles and bones, Aaron stood up, and everyone easily allowed him to join the front of the crowd and watch his brother's final movements. Then Mark whispered a single word. "Mary." The heart monitor began to slow down, and the room nurse was alerted on her phone, but all she could do was watch.

"Mary," Mark whispered again as he reached for the corner in which no one stood by. "I missed you, Hand Mitten. Mary. I'm ready." The heart monitor was silenced by the nurse and showed Mark's heart rate continuously drop until he was no more. His family cried from the shock of watching a man hallucinate and die in front of their eyes. But during the time of his death, the overcast sheet loosened up and shone inside, with rays from the sun touching the still blood-warm ancient man. The nurse recorded Mark's time of death and covered his face with a blanket, then while mourning over his dead body, the family began to wonder who Mary was. Some believed her to be Jesus's mother; others thought that Mark's mind was too far gone. Aaron knew who Mary was—he knew her very well but never told anyone about Mark and Mary's love, about their struggle and demons. It was the past that wasn't worth more than an old man's story. Aaron stood there with sorrowful acceptance of Mark's death. The true sorrow had passed weeks ago when Mark first lay in that hospital bed. Now Aaron stood with a dreadful feeling in his stomach and smiled with a simple thought toward a now very joyful memory.

"Thank you Mark, for making me the third wheel. I'd do it again in a heartbeat." Then at the end of the day, Aaron walked toward the crisp sun, chewing Bazooka Bubble Gum. All of their lives were the perfect *Composition Eight*.

◆◆◆

"ARE YOU READY, TYLER?"

"Y-yes, Tom! Yes, t-thank you so much!"

"Then push up, one last time."

Acknowledgments

I WOULD LIKE TO first acknowledge Make-A-Wish and Rare Bird Books for making this wish a reality. I have been sharing stories ever since I could form sentences, beginning in the form of "What ifs" in the car seat of my mother's Suburban, to see if possible, specific scenarios had the power to release me from my weekdays filled with coloring in the lines and learning my ABC's. The first story I wrote was in second grade, called "Insac," about a boy (named Insac) and a group of his friends given superpowers from God and the task to end Armageddon caused by the notorious "A Hundred Arms." The villain A Hundred Arms was named this way because his victims, in interviews, would say that when he fights, his speed and stealth were so quick that it was as if he had a hundred arms.

My writing began to escalate in middle school, when I left my eighth grade English teacher the first chapter I wrote of a novel about a postapocalyptic United States. I remember bothering her every day after class, asking if she had read my new work of fiction. I was overwhelmed with anxiety, unnoticeably shaking as I approached her desk, dreaming of being a renowned author by the age of fifteen and yet afraid of the opinions of others. Then, about three weeks later, Mrs. Spanier strolled across the room toward my desk with the notebook and declared, in her noticeable Southern accent, "Austin, good job," then dropped it on my desk. The noise echoed across the silent classroom. I was shocked and slightly embarrassed as all my peers glanced over with half curiosity and half wonder. This didn't mean I could continue writing my story though, as my classmates began to ask if they could read it next. I never saw that notebook again, and one reason was because soon after I was admitted into the hospital.

Writing helped me survive cancer, as I journaled my experience with the chemotherapy and radiation, as well as the rollercoaster of emotions and survival instincts I had at the age of fourteen. I wrote about the dreams I had, about the anger I felt, and the acceptance I had with the idea of death's possible invite into my young, mortal body. I also wrote about love, about God, and about the grand scheme of life. If it wasn't for my escape into those few journals, I would have become a statistic in a medical journal, and what you hold in your hand would have never existed.

Writing was what helped me manage my PTSD, which, at fifteen, made me fear the idea of even having a license, shaken by the thought of being alone with my emotions, to sit in complete silence. I wrote down my pain in the form of a novel for a year and a half, escaping into a world I could control. During this time in my life, writing was my sanity; it kept my head above water as I tried to move on from the pains that almost seemed torturous. My PTSD is still severe, and I have come to the sobering conclusion that the end of treatment doesn't mean the completion of recovery.

In conclusion, both Make-A-Wish and Rare Bird Books not only published my first novel, but have also made my lifelong dream—from my first word to my next breath—a reality. I have to admit that this entire process was emotional, from the moment I signed the contract, to the painful edits I had to write over the past summer, remembering how much of my own anger and despondency I stored inside and exploded onto these pages. They constantly portrayed a sense of patience, acceptance, and kindness that I will never forget. I would like to thank George Friedman, as well, for the inspiration for the futuristic word I create toward the end of my novel.

I would like to also acknowledge Joy Mona, the illustrator for my novel and my good friend for the past two years. Before I even knew if Rare Bird Books would allow her to be my illustrator, she openly volunteered to brainstorm some sketches, wanting to contribute to the cause with no charge for her beautiful work. We sat at the Barnes and Noble café as I began a forty-five minute recitation of my novel's overly complicated plotline, like a lawyer trying to convince Joy why my green door concept was such a special theme in my novel. Then I sipped my coffee, content with what I said when Joy began to spurt out ideas on how to make the symbolism even deeper than my original idea, proving to me that writing and painting are not so far apart. Her recommendations are, in fact, what you see on the front cover (and the inside cover as a full view of the painting), including the light from the cracked door stretching across the painting, the illusion of distance away from Mary's bedroom door, and the face of Mary looking back into the world of Mark, Aaron, and Kenny, one last time. Joy's painting is named *Last Glance*.

Truthfully, it was an impossibility to find someone who could draw something anymore personal and understand my dense, serious themes more than Joy Mona, because we were both in the exclusive, yet unanimously disgusted club called "The Oncology Floor."

Joy's mother's name was Maria Mona and suffered through stage four breast cancer. Just like me, cancer was a tune she had to face while growing up and, from the hell that is cancer, grew her gift, which no one can deny. Joy drew for her mother, looking for a grin on her face, or delight in her eyes, which is why having her artwork is such an honor. Cancer is a double-sided coin; there will always be two separate stories: the story from the diagnosed patient and from the family members who had to witness it. I cannot be more grateful to have both sides of the coin represented in my novel.

◆◆◆

THIS BOOK WAS PUBLISHED *as a wish experience through Make-A-Wish Arizona and Rare Bird Books. Author and wish kid, Austin Thacker, has generously agreed to offer a percentage of proceeds from the sale of the book to go toward granting future wishes in Arizona for children dealing with critical illnesses. For more information on Make-A-Wish Arizona, please visit www.arizona.wish.org.*